DEATH at the CASTELLO

ERICA YEOMAN

Book cover from an original painting by the author

FOR
WENDY ROBERTSON

Thanks to Wendy for her belief, Anne, Margaret, Lorena, Alison for valuable comments on script. To Tom and Catie for computer wizardry.

TUSCANY 2001

PROLOGUE

Not one of us at the castello express surprise when the body is found. We contact the carabinieri, but then gather as usual in the courtyard for pre-dinner drinks. The tension has gone. Callous for me to feel relief. Now we are seven. The auspicious number in Etruscan eyes. Eight had been one too many.

We dine in the flickering candlelight of the converted baptistery, once a Christian building built on Etruscan foundations, and accept this will be an Etruscan Funeral feast. It is fitting.

For those left behind it's a noisy restoring of confidence. And for the victim? Death is but a journey, never a finality; a journey to paradise, to an eternity of eating, dancing and loving. And a banquet is a banquet even if held only for the devil. So we eat wild boar washed down by Chianti 'I Paradiso,' and give no thought for the morning. For the Etruscans believed that the soul grows gradually out of chaos, only to disappear back into chaos,, and I've come to think this is the truth. It is written. It is destiny. There is no such thing as chance. How can it be otherwise, when man is a chimera, an animal living within another, with the blood of birds and the venom of serpents?

ONE

ANNA

Crash, bang, shudder. No. 55 vaporetta churned out into the Grand Canal in Venice, and through the mist she caught a glimpse of San Giorgio Maggiore. It was a smudge of a day, haunting mist blotting out the city: nothing distinct, no familiar landmark until the unmistakeable church; a familiar skyline would be a mirage. The commuters dripped, collars, trouser ends; umbrellas lay against any upright surface like a row of leaning towers of Pisa; a collective nightmare for any preservation society. Only they were not in Pisa.

They sat huddled, introspective as are all groups of workers who face the faceless day with resignation. Heads, hands, feet were flesh, bodies were of newspaper. Anna Miller, always eager to catch a glimpse of the passing city, perched hopefully on the edge of her seat, despite the large rain splashes on the outside and moisture inside which fogged the view. Her fingers itched to rub a spy-hole, but the man's profile by the window blocked her.

Anna found profiles intimidating. A painter of portraits, she was used to eye contact; side-faced, the sitter showed the observer only what might be. She would always start with the eyes and then the rest of the face just followed; heads slightly angled for the nuance of light, then there could be no secrets. The striking Italian in the vaporetta gave nothing away.

Next stop the compartment began to clear, a surge of emptiness as bodies disappeared out into the rain. The man's profile was still there and she was no nearer the window. She thought, I'd like to paint him. He'd be a good subject. He hasn't blinked once. Was that arrogance or just an enviable self-confidence?

She stole another glance at him. Outside, the mist was beginning to clear. What a backcloth Venice provided for the intriguing face beside her. The striking head could be found on any plinth in a dozen of the cities squares. He posed, straight backed, long necked; high forehead, classic nose, firm set lips: only the chin seemed to break the unity of line, a little too pointed. She could not see the colour of his eyes, but then that would be true of any Venetian statue.

Her stop was next. She got up. Her foot slipped on the wet surface and she dropped her umbrella right in the pool of water at his feet. She had always been clumsy.

'You will need that,' said the profile as he stooped to retrieve the sodden object, 'though your poet Robert Browning often found he could not open his umbrella in the narrow *via* and *calle* of Venice.'

Anna didn't even look in his direction, and certainly didn't bother to reply.

There was space enough in the Piazza dell Accademia for the long queue of umbrellas that snaked towards the art gallery: a sinuous line of interlocking scales on a sea monster dripping from the canal. Thunder cracked above and lightening shimmered over the Grand Canal to be lost in the surrounding narrow alleys. What a storm. She was annoyed with the man. Was it so obvious she was a visitor? She liked to think that some of the Italian chic had rubbed

3

off on her during her two months stay. She eyed the queue. At least she had not resorted to the tourist plastic-Mac. How did he know she was English? Well, she had learned that Venetians are nosy parkers and ever had been. Always ready to pry and drop a name in the Doges' denunciation box.

The line slithered across the square. It was orderly and quiet: this art gallery lot as introspective as the morning commuters, gone any blue sky and with it the buzz of expectation. Instead, there was an eerie silence. She shivered and looked skyward and met again those spying eyes. A poster high on the building cowed the scene, muting the waiting crowd; omnipresent, grotesque, ugly; a six-eyed monster with the body of a lion, the head of a goat and the tail of a snake. It had dominated every street corner and billboard in Venice throughout the long hot summer, its eyes following her wherever she went.

Out of the rain at last, without hesitation Anna took the stairs to the second floor of the Accademia Gallery. Ever a creature of habit and why not? she reflected moodily. I'm more readable than that weird creature on the poster. With her, what you saw was what you got: small height and light frame, fairish-brown hair, unremarkable face, no distinguishable features to note in her passport. Nothing very exciting had ever happened to her in her twenty years except her very beginning. That is, until now.

Anna Miller, seen as a promising medical student by her family and now a drop-out.
Her 'road to Damascus moment' had told her she could never be a doctor, yet to throw away that stability, and for what? She still could

4

hardly believe she'd had the nerve to face up to the family dismay, strong and fiercely voiced, against her stubborn rebellion.

Now her success lay in her own hands, relying on her sable brush and what it revealed. Others said they knew, impressed enough at the end of her Art College to award her a summer scholarship to help her find herself. She remembered the buzz she had felt when her fingers closed over the cheque, and the silent promise to the few who were putting their faith in her. Matthew Grant, her tutor, smiled encouragement as he handed her the prize, and somewhere in the audience foster-sister, Caroline, alone of the Miller family there to show her support, clapped loudly.

She went to see Matthew Grant before she left England. Well, she bumped into him in the refectory and shared the same table across the scrubbed wood. In his late twenties, with an open boyish face, square-jawed, untidy stubble, dark, like his thick, unruly hair. As always, approachable but introspective, he smiled as he sat himself down on the vacant seat opposite. He smiled again then turned to his pasta, a large plateful that told it was his main meal of the day. She thought of the full meat and two veg. awaiting her on her return home; Jane her 'now' mother, a good plain cook, had taken for ever to see the virtue of lasagne bolognaise.

'Lucky girl, Anna,' Matthew said, now clearing the last mouthful and at last looking up, 'and not just for the Italian food. There are beautiful things to see in Venice, and the first visit is the best.' His striking brown eyes held her gaze. It was Anna who felt the need to look away, envying him his man-of-the-world experience. 'It's intoxicating; heady stuff. I envy you.' A man of

5

few words, he repeated himself. His enthusiasm lit up his face. 'I love Venice however often I go, but nothing quite comes up to the first time. It's like the first...' he paused, smiled and said, 'Give my love to La Tempesta.'

La Tempesta was her favourite painting in the Accademia and in the entire city. She knew why her tutor had singled it out. Anna took the stairs past the fifteenth century altarpieces, the Bellini Madonnas, the Martagna, the Carravaggio, two steps at a time. She went straight to the small painting, on its white board, on the second floor. She had stood on the same spot dozens of times in the last weeks and the painting was as fresh as at the first viewing. She must remember to contradict Matthew when next they met, and yet he talked only of his own experience. So what did she know? Enough that he too found Giorgione's 'La Tempesta' compelling.

The painting showed a storm, but not the grey, sodden grumbling event she had just escaped. The thunderstorm in the painting was electric. Wild dark clouds, cerulean blue, banked and swirled like a turbulent sea; flashing, throbbing light enveloped the figures caught forever in the Italian landscape. What a landscape! Yet it was the figures that held her attention. It was a mother and child picture, yet in the shadows a man stood watching. A disparate trio caught by chance in the storm?

The picture was a mystery and however often she stared at it her interpretation always differed. Yet even odder was the fact that Matthew Grant had picked it out as his favourite, even though the picture couldn't possibly have the same significance for him as it had for her. Subject, mother and child, two figures merging as one.

6

So loving and so close was the relationship that it did not matter that they were out in a raging storm. The child was safe in his mother's arms. That child had not been abandoned. What made some women give up their child? Anna thought of her own rejection early in life.

Consuming thoughts, and they were counter-productive. She must stop this endless doubt. Why let her angst spoil what should be a truly positive time in her life? She had weathered the disappointment of her family, that she wasn't going to be the first doctor in the family. Next birthday she'd be twenty one. Now, for the future…

She was suddenly aware of someone standing behind her, too close for comfort. She spun round ready to scowl and looked straight into the eyes of Matthew Grant. 'Hell, you made me jump. What on earth are you doing here?'

'I thought I might find you on this very spot.'

'You couldn't possibly have thought that.' She flushed, annoyed with herself. 'I must have conjured you up. I was just thinking about you.'

'Oh really?' He grinned smugly.

'Only because we've discussed this painting and I was questioning how it can appeal to both of us when we are so different?' She was quick with her excuse. Then she added, 'Come to think of it, I'm not a bit surprised to see you. I think, like me, you're a creature of habit.' She was gabbling and she knew it. Only later did she question that her tutor was standing behind her, ready to instruct at the very moment she wanted answers.

'So here you are and just in time to give me your expert

reading of La Tempesta. I find it impossible to read.'

'I'd be very disappointed if you'd reached a glib interpretation.' Matthew Grant was unsmiling. 'Anyway, I'm not here to give you my explanation.'

'Sorry, Mr Grant, I'd forgotten I'm no longer your student.' Anna turned back to the picture.

'So how about calling me Matt? All my friends do.' He stood close to her like the figure beside the Mother and Child.

She said, 'So, Matt, how could you possibly have known I would be here? I could have been anywhere in Venice.' She strove to keep her voice neutral. 'In fact, I might even have moved on.'

'Oh no, I knew you were still around. I glimpsed you on the vaporetta and guessed where you were heading.' Matt's laugh echoed round the gallery. 'Besides, I knew you'd find it impossible to tear yourself away from this city.'

They had the picture to themselves. She indicated the empty room. 'It would seem not everyone else in Venice has our fixation with Giorgione's fantasy.'

Matt nodded, 'I admit I did go to the Bellini Madonna room first, but on consideration I thought you were much more likely to be staring at La Tempesta.' He paused. 'So you don't understand it any more than when you first set eyes on it?'

'Why should I?' she was being ungracious, 'when no one else does. Giorgione liked to be mysterious, didn't he? Anyway, it's obvious this lady is no Madonna.'

'Have you taken to figure painting yet, or is it still portraits?' Matt sat opposite her at a table in Stefano's Trattoria, in the Campo di Stefano beside the church of the same name. It was her favourite eating place in Venice and she wanted Matt Grant to approve her choice. It was good to have a face opposite her that she recognised.

They had crossed the wooden bridge over the Grand Canal, ignoring the exquisite skyline on the way; Anna was determined she wasn't going to let him see that her childlike obsession with the La Tempesta painting also extended to the city he loved. She had trudged across the bridge, head lowered under her umbrella. The fact was she was no painter of city or of landscapes. She had a portfolio of faces to show for her time in the city. This didn't mean she ignored her surroundings; place was important, in Giorgione's painting the deep dark shadows of fifteenth century Italy highlighted the figures.

Yet here today, place had no relevance. They could have been anywhere. They sat inside the trattoria under its billowing plastic roof and sides. When new victims of the storm sought refuge, there was a fresh deluge of water about the seated customers' feet. The waiters were harassed and the crowded tables did not meet the demand. She regretted Matt was seeing the trattoria in such conditions. Under the sun, the square was a city haven, the outside tables providing lunchtime pasta *en plein air*. She stole a glance at her companion, hoping he wasn't regretting bumping in to her and suggesting lunch.

He was engrossed in the menu. She relaxed. It was obvious he fitted in anywhere: uncomplicated face, long hair, casual shirt and trousers, well-manicured hands, his tall, lean frame moulded the chair. He looked as at home in the Venetian trattoria as he had in the student refectory. Matt Grant had no problem with identity.

'I'm still painting portraits. But perhaps I should try profiles.' Matt looked up, raising his eyebrows at her remark, an exaggerated movement but it showed interest. Encouraged, she said, 'Profiles have a certain mystery; you can't see what the sitter is thinking.'

'Yes, but they can be deceptive. Remember the Multifetro portrait by Della Francesca. Everyone recognises the Duke's hooked beak of a nose. How many realise every picture of the Duke is shown in profile?' Matt's voice had risen in his enthusiasm, his knowledge as ready to hand as in his lectures.

'Why was that?' Her curiosity made her lift her head from her plate of gnocchi with pesto sauce.

'Because, the Duke had only one eye, he'd lost the other in battle.' He grinned mischievously.

'Um, well, I don't think that reason could apply to the chap I saw this morning on the vaporetta, but you never know.' She told him about her fellow travelling companion. 'So I can't tell you if he has two eyes or not because I didn't see him full faced. I only wish I had.'

'Could you paint him from memory?'

Anna laughed, 'Oh he wasn't that stunning. And anyway, I prefer to have flesh and blood in front of me. Let me see you side-faced.' The wine was affecting her, making her forget the earlier teacher-pupil relationship. Matt put down his fork and obediently turned his head. She looked at him. Now that he was looking away she felt free to study him. She could no longer see his eyes yet the lurking amusement about his mouth unsettled her.

She squinted at his averted head. He did not have the striking profile of the handsome Italian on the water bus, but the contours of his face were familiar and reassuring. She'd noted the mole on his left cheek.

'If you want me to be your model, you'd better get started.'

'How long are you in Venice, Matt?' At her question he turned full-face. His eyes were friendly and she found herself hoping he would be around for a few more days. She'd begun to miss her friends at home. Any acquaintances she'd made in Venice had been transitory in this city of comings and goings. She knew it was probably time for her to join the exodus, but she was strangely reluctant, as her companion had correctly forecast.

Matt finished his spaghetti alla carbonara. 'I'm only here for a day, unfortunately. I'm come to meet someone– Sorry, I mean beside you, and then I'm off to teach at a summer school.'

'That's a shame. I've been here long enough now to think there might be parts of the city that even you don't know.'

'I'll come back.'

'I think I'll have gone by then.' She did not mean it to be the put–down it sounded but Matt used it to end the lunch.

'Pity. But good luck, Anna, for the rest of your trip. Where do you go next?'

'No idea, but something will turn up. No, I don't mean that. I'm sure there's a place just waiting for me.'

11

Alone, she was free to appreciate her surroundings. The rain had stopped, and she felt the mood change as pale sunshine percolated into the water lanes and the crooked channels became ribbons of light. Her eyes did not seek a far horizon. Venice like her was self-centred, narcissistic in its reflections, no need to look beyond. She retraced her steps to the Accademia Bridge. It arched over the Grand Canal, bringing together the two halves of the city, like a lovers' go-between, so that its balustrade shone. Polished by centuries of leaners.

The Italian from the morning vaporetta stood waiting on the bridge. She would recognise him anywhere; she had seen his profile reflected in every water mirror, rain puddle or canal since their journey in the early morning mist. He did not turn as she leaned her elbows on the rail beside him and gazed to the view of S. Maria Della Salute, the domed church, pink in the late afternoon sun. Jostling palaces on the canal edged and nudged their neighbour for a favoured position and dry feet. Every line, shape and colour was painted on the ripples of the water. An artist's brush was redundant.

'I am glad you have need no longer for your umbrella, one misses so much.'

'I feel the same about dark glasses,' she said as he turned to face her for the first time, his eyes hidden behind tinted glass.

'In Venice one can never be sure what is reality, what is illusion.'

'That's a little impractical.'

'O, we can be practical when the need arises.'

She could not see his eyes but sensed the disdain.

'For instance, a well-known city family had almost died out by the end of the fifteenth century. Only one member remained, and he was in a monastery.' He paused. 'What do you think he did?'

'You tell me.' Anna was not prepared to act as fall guy.

'He got a special dispensation, begat nine boys and three girls, and then returned to his quiet life behind the walls. He was a selfless man I think.'

Anna could not help smiling. 'So everyone was satisfied. That's as it should be. Usually someone gets hurt.'

'But of course, you can smell the sadness of this city. It comes in with the tide. From a palazzo balcony a lover of your Lord Byron threw herself into the Grand Canal.'

'You seem to have made a thorough study of English poets.' They stood in silence watching the water. Then he said, 'La Tempesta. You like the Giorgione painting.' It was a statement, not a question, and she showed her surprise.

'How do you know?' But she knew this man had been watching her through the day, like the eyes of the strange animal on the billboards proclaiming the city's summer exhibition.

'Giorgione, or big George. His real name was Giorgio da Castelfranca Veneto. But the citizens coined the nickname. No one knows why. Was it because he was a great artist, or because he was so successful with women? If you understand my meaning?' Again she was silent. 'My name is Fabio Renaldi.'

'Anna— Anna Miller.'

The water shimmered below them; Venice is terracotta, cream and yellow ochre verticals sitting on horizontals of turquoise,

13

cobalt and grey, with umber shadows deep and reclusive.

She said impulsively, 'I'm beginning to see the city in a new light.'

'Just as you are leaving.'

'How do you know?' She looked at him aghast. 'Oh, I do wish you would take off those dark glasses.' But they remained where they were.

'The city is yours,' Fabio tempted Satan-like as they gazed from the top of the Campanile. Venice lay at their feet, and like a greedy child she wanted to see it all again now that she was about to leave. Even a perfect stranger knew it was time for her to go.

'Tell me where you wish to visit for one last time?'

'Everywhere, anywhere! I am ready to see the city again with new eyes.' Fabio Renaldi bowed and took her hand.

'You can slow down, Anna, there is no great hurry.'

'But there is no time to waste.' She was flustered.

He shook his head. 'The islanders of Torcello were worried as the year eleven hundred drew near. They believed it heralded the end of the world, so they built their cathedral in just a few frantic years. Ten centuries later...'

So they went to the island just to see the proof of this, though she had been there before. On her earlier visit she had sat amongst the reeds, watching the moorhens ripple the pools and the white ibis bask on the willow branches, only the cockerels in their greed stirring the dust. This scene could have been in eleven hundred or the twenty first century. She had sat for a long time, reluctant, almost unable to move and then finally had gone into the church knowing the tourist boat would return in half an hour. She had not painted for two whole days after the visit to Torcello; there was nothing she, Anna Millar, could add that hadn't been done all those centuries before.

Now Anna stood beside the man called Fabio, staring again at the fresco faces within the church, where even the voluble Italian was quiet. No profiles here, the eyes direct, straight-on, for both saints and sinners. In the apse, the Madonna and child was beautiful and very moving.

'When I see these faces, I feel I should give up painting portraits altogether,' she said. 'They're so real, so vibrant. Perhaps I should take up landscapes instead.'

'So you are an artist. Are you famous?' The information was enough for her companion to remove his glasses and it was her turn to be amused.

'So what have I said that's so significant? Do you want your portrait painted? I charge a lot.'

'However much it is I can afford it.' He had an annoying self-satisfied look. 'I am able to be the connoisseur and buy what I like.'

'Too bad that I have just decided to give up painting people.'

'So then you cannot refuse my next suggestion.'

'Try me.'

'I am leaving Venice, going home to Tuscany. Come with

15

me. I can promise you breathtaking landscapes.'

She lied. 'Thank you, but I plan to stay in the city another few days.'

'That is a pity. The well-known English landscape artist Susan Simpson will be there.'

'I've heard of her.' At that name the dark shadows of the cathedral seemed to move as though they were pulling her towards the door. That name again after all these years. She would rather not remember. How young and very foolish she had been then. 'I need the sunshine. It's suddenly cold in here.'

Outside, in the fierce glare of the midday sun, eyes watched their re-appearance; 'What is that grotesque creature? It is quite horrid.' Anna grimaced at the poster on the billboard.

'It is an Etruscan chimera. It is of the past.'

'Well, it's everywhere at the moment and I don't like it. It's taken over the city.' She shuddered. 'I want to go back to the Accademia.'

Half an hour to closing time. Already the staff were returning the last bags, coats, and umbrellas from the numbered slots. They eyed the new arrivals with poorly concealed impatience. Involuntarily, the ticket lady looked at her watch. Anna took the stairs again two at a time, her companion following at a more sedate pace. La Tempesta hung amongst the masterpieces and there before it was Matt Grant. It was as though he had never moved.

The three of them stood in line, like a medieval triptych. A flash of lightening on the painting showed angry clouds above an unknown place, highlighting the flesh of the woman seated under a

16

tree, and in the shadows the man watched.

'*Pentimenti*, the Italians have a word for it.' Fabio broke the silence. '*Pentimenti* are second thoughts. Giorgione changed his mind.' He pointed at the young man some distance from the mother and child. 'When the picture was x-rayed, it showed a different figure painted beneath the man. Originally, it was a naked figure.'

'How strange.' Anna looked at the Arcadian scene, seeing it for the first time. 'So it's even more of an enigma.' She sounded childishly frustrated.

Matt shrugged his shoulders, and turning to Anna, said 'So, Anna, who's your companion?' He held his hand out to the Italian and Fabio laughed.

'Who are you kidding, Grant, suggesting to Anna we haven't met before?' Anna looked from one to the other. Both men were unsmiling.

She said, 'Wow, you make me feel like the chimera goat trapped between the lion and serpent.' She paused. 'Come on, let's get out of here; they're locking up.'

The door banged behind them, leaving them adrift on cobbled islands in the square, trying without success to keep dry feet. Angry, dark clouds scurrying towards the open sea were the last vestige of yet another downpour.

'It will be the same tomorrow,' Fabio predicted, and already Anna knew it would be fact. The Italian had an annoying habit of being right. 'It does not matter. We shall go to the Palazzo Grassi. Be there at midday.' With an exaggerated bow he turned on his heel.

Anna frowned; she'd intended to be the one to stride away.

17

Matt turned in the opposite direction. The independent arrogance of the city was catching.

Rain fell steadily again, though now there was no accompanying thunder. Venice was becoming depressing. Her scholarship to paint in Italy had just one month to go. She must move on. She stood irresolute. She had no intention of going the following morning to meet the pushy Italian, and Matt would certainly not turn up. His face had spoken volumes. But in spite of herself Anna was intrigued, by the weird creature on the poster and the Italian stranger's obvious fascination with it. There was still time that afternoon to go and see for herself the Etruscan chimera. She doubled-back to the Grand Canal.

Fabio and Matt were standing together outside the Palace, talking animatedly. For a brief moment it looked like a cinquecento conspiracy, a dramatic etching in black: Matt in black jeans and top and Fabio in immaculate black trousers and sweatshirt, linked under the Italian's black umbrella. Where, Anna reflected, would she place the highlights in the finished picture? Perhaps it would be in Fabio's burnt Sienna eyes which gave nothing away. Just now they were flashing vividly as he made some forcible comment, and his bronzed hands moved to emphasise the point.

Anna stood perplexed. The two men knew each other very well, that was obvious. So why had Matt pretended not to know Fabio?

'So, Anna, are you following us?' The Italian looked unabashed as he turned and caught sight of her. 'Fair Anna, fair indeed.' He moved to stand beside her, and raised her hand to his lips. 'With hair that colour you are indeed the courtesan.'

Matt scowled. 'Do you know the meaning of that word?'

'I say it to set the scene for Anna,' and Fabio pointed to the ubiquitous chimera banner emblazoned above the palace. 'The Etruscans' girl friends were blonde, their wives dark-haired. Fiat has sponsored an exhibition of all things Etruscan. You will find it fascinating.'

The Palazzo Grassi, square, stolid and sombre, looked uninviting. 'Well, I have absolutely no intention of going inside, that creature is creepy and is putting me right off all things Etruscan.' Anna turned away.

Fabio caught her arm. 'Then you must have this.'

He thrust a small box into her hand. Surprised, Anna lifted the lid and stared with distaste; the bronze facsimile inside had the body of a lion, the head of a goat and a serpent tail. 'It's horrible,' she said with meaning.

'You will change your mind.' The Italian smiled. 'We leave Venice tomorrow. The three of us will go—'

'The three of us?' Matt's voice had risen.

'We go to Tuscany to show Anna the Italian landscape. We go to celebrate the birthday of my mother, Francesca.'

He went off, his umbrella high in the air. 'Of course you're not going with him.' Matt's voice was strident. The two of them had been left standing out in the rain. 'Both of us have got better things to do. And besides, he probably doesn't have a mother, let alone one with a birthday.'

19

Eyes watched Anna as she packed her belongings into her small hold-all. She gazed out at the opposite building. The top corner of the chimera poster had begun to peel from the wall, so that the serpent was hidden; only the lion and goat remained. She turned her back on the diminishing image, and as she did so, her fingers closed around the bronze facsimile given to her by Fabio. The chimera was in her pocket and even closer. Ugh! It was most definitely time to move on. She'd always welcomed a challenge.

TWO

FRANCESCA

Fabio and the girl were to arrive today. Her eyes will look across distance and time; but there will be no glimmer of recognition, no warmth. Yet this one could be different. She would not be like the others.

Francesca was waiting. She had slept fitfully. Early morning and her eyes were tired, seeking only what they wanted to see, never reality. Sunlight intruded, marking the floor in a cutting beam across the dark wood like a finishing line; definitive, not to be crossed. She had opened the shutters for first light. In May dawn is early and impatience assuaged, now almost September she must learn to wait.

A soft breeze floated through the open pane. Hollyhocks from the garden, cream and pink, intense in the eastern light, balanced on the wooden sill ledge, heavy with scent. A petal fell soundless to the floor, a soft shape on the hard surface that made no noise, but a loud crack rang in her ears, and involuntarily she shut out the echo with her hands. Today, memories of the past were loud and still haunting her.

She heard the snapping twigs on that far off day when they had run deep into the silent wood, their trespassing feet violating in giveaway sound.

A new sound usurped the present, bringing her back to reality a car coming up the steep, rocky drive.

'Signora, Signora Francesca.' The call from the courtyard was urgent. She put her head through the open window and waved acknowledgement to the figure at the base of her tower. The indispensable Catarina stood with a foot on the first step, enough to show intent, but she knew better than to enter the sanctuary.

'I'm coming.' Francesca needed no second bidding. By the time Fabio and the girl and their bags were in the courtyard she was ready to greet them. She hugged Fabio to her and as he pulled away she extended a plump, multi ringed hand to his companion. The fragile girl looked diffident, but as Fabio made the necessary introductions, there was a tangible look of relief on her face. She seized Francesca's hand as though she has been waiting for this moment. Then of course it could not be.

'Chiesa a Castello greets you.' The older woman's voice was welcoming and the girl's smile at once friendly.

'Thank you. It looks wonderful. I have to admit, on the journey I did wonder–What–' Her look was unsure.

'I can imagine,' Francesca smiled.

'It was a bad moment when Fabio admitted his mother wasn't alive. He'd made her up so I would agree to come to Tuscany with him.' Her obvious relief came tumbling out with her words.

Francesca looked reprovingly at Fabio, who was smirking, but Anna chose to ignore him. 'He must have known the story of a mother and a birthday was guaranteed to make me want to c-come...' and she was sheepish now at how gullible she'd been. Francesca eyed her guest: the girl's slight frame was tense, making her look taller than she was, her head erect upon a stiff straight neck.

Anna's fingers played with her jacket, the eyes of the zip opening and closing, like a moth caught in a bright light, and the girl's dark eyes flickered in rhythm.

Francesca murmured, 'No, I am not his real mother—well, by birth he is not mine.'

Anna stopped fiddling with her coat. Francesca saw the impact of her words and hastened to cover the moment. 'Well, I may not be his real mother, but I'm as good as that and I do have a birthday soon. I presume my birthday is what brings a dutiful son back, Fabio.'

'But of course, how could I have stayed away when it's such a big one?'

'Oh, is it really?' Anna eyed her hostess, clearly silently questioning her age. Francesca saw the girl's hesitation and wondered how she saw her—an unremarkable middle-aged woman, mousy dark hair with a wisp of grey; a thickening waistline from too much pasta. Yet her skin was good, smooth with few lines, and her legs still as good as any girl, always her best point, with ankles shown-off by her foolishly high-heeled sandals.

And Fabio was enjoying the scene, willing his companion to make a *faux pas*, cat playing with the mouse; but the girl was astute, remaining still, intent on the interaction between Fabio and Francesca; the woman who was not his mother.

Francesca tossed her head and said to Anna, 'No, it isn't my fiftieth birthday, as you might think, but my forty ninth, and everyone is making a lot of fuss about nothing. You could have just sent a card, Fabio.' She glanced at him with affection.

23

Fabio grinned, seizing her hand. 'You know I had to come, through hell and high water, as you English would say. Your forty ninth birthday is highly significant, no?'

'Why is that?' Anna raised her eyebrows.

'Seven times seven is forty nine! Here we are deep in the land of the Etruscans and number seven was their auspicious number. For them the seven year cycle was all important. Every seventh year was a significant stepping stone from one period of life to the next.' Fabio's teasing manner had gone. 'Come, Anna, let me show you something.' He took hold of the girl's hand and led her into the cool interior of the castello.

From the blazing heat and light in the courtyard, in to the dark chill of the ancient building, Fabio needed no torch and Anna followed blinking. The transition into a low-ceilinged room with a far small window was dramatic. He stopped in front of a massive stone fireplace that dominated the space. It was plain and unadorned except for a roughly hewn piece of stone that rested on the mantel.

Carefully, as though it were some priceless work of art, he handed it to Anna. 'Etruscan! That was dug up from the foundations. The castello was built on the site of an Etruscan Temple.'

'Oh, I'm beginning to understand your interest in the Venice exhibition. Sorry, Fabio, I'd have shown a little more interest if I'd known.' Anna clearly felt wrong-footed.

He bowed theatrically. 'I have no doubt you will come to feel the same way about them as I do. They will get to you—I think that is the expression you would use?'

Anna didn't reply. Fabio could be a little overwhelming at times,

24

thought Francesca. The last thing she wanted was for Fabio to alienate the girl so soon.

'Get to me?' Anna shrugged her shoulders. 'I think that's a bit unlikely. They've been a long time gone.' She laughed.

Hurriedly, the older woman interjected, 'So, is it really my forty-ninth that brings you back, Fabio?' Francesca sounded like any other possessive Italian mamma and she saw that the girl was amused.

Fabio smiled indulgently, his every movement exaggerated as he walked over to where Francesca had seated herself and bent to kiss the older woman on the cheek.

'You may not be my birth mother, but, you cannot be more loved. Of course I have come to celebrate your anniversary. Your every birthday is important to me.'

Fabio was acting for the girl, his words and gestures mannered and carefully chosen, playing to the audience as he always did. Fabio laughed, 'Though I am deeply glad, dear Francesca, you do not celebrate your seventieth year. The Etruscans believed that after that it was no longer possible to receive signs from the gods— in other words—'and he drew his hand across his throat.

'What nonsense you do talk, Fabio, though I'm glad to hear I've got some time left. That's a real relief!' Francesca's laugh was forced.

'Indeed, dear Francesca, what would I do without you and the castello? It is my home.'

'Naturally, you are the place. After all, I found you together, didn't I?'

'Oh?' Anna moved to the window seat beside her hostess and there was silence as she sipped the cool drink served unobtrusively by house keeper Catarina.

Fabio looked irritated. 'It's an old family story much repeated.'

'It's taken you a long time to get bored with it, Fabio.' Francesca pointedly turned her back on him and addressed Anna. 'One day, tired of the crowds in San Gimignano, I came out into the countryside. I could see this ruin isolated up on its hill and I was drawn to it.'

Anna looked encouraging, and in-spite of himself, Fabio moved back towards them.

Francesca smiled triumphantly, knowing well his need to hear the story, his nonchalance skin-deep. She could see the girl was impressed by this façade.

'I walked up the track, never once losing sight of the building. It shouts its presence. It's arrogant. I'm here, and have been for hundreds of years. And long before I reached the great gate lying unhinged and broken I was smitten.' Francesca's face was radiant. 'There was music, a plaintive pipe leading me on, and in the courtyard was a boy surrounded by goats. I could see only his head, and I thought of the god Pan. It was a strange coincidence. I knew then I had come home.'

Anna sat silent. Francesca eyed her audience, noting the girl was quick, that she did not have to spell out that the boy had been Fabio and they had shared the castello virtually from that day on. The girl's mobile face showed she was affected by the story and

Francesca felt an instinctive liking for the stranger brought to their castello by the one-time shepherd boy Fabio.

Fabio put his hand in his pocket and drew out a small musical pipe. The melody filled the room, the notes sublime. The girl and Francesca followed him across the courtyard, out of the great gate, out beyond the high walls, drawn irrevocably onward by the music.

Unlike the inward looking castello, the entrance to its adjoining church faced the world, opening out on to the ancient track and still accessible to climbing feet. Yet now it offered hollow comfort. The decline of the castle and its linked church had been mutual, although the church, unlike the castello, had not been restored. Steep steps climbed to a building now open to the elements. But still, the western sun bathed it in a deep orange glow lighting upon the altar within the eastern apse. There was an overwhelming feeling of peace.

Francesca gestured to Fabio to stop playing. His pipe had an alien sound in this Christian building. He stopped mid-phrase in a gentle sigh.

Anna looked about her. Although no longer a consecrated church, there were the trappings still. The stone altar stood high above the chancel steps: behind it ascended the peeling blue and white ceiling of the domed apse. A drape of white sheeting covered one side wall: the workmen had been in and gone. On the south wall two intricate family tombs were now a sad display of marble, stucco and today's dust. Francesca pointed to a small vase of flowers before each one. 'Catarina still heeds her ancestors and her links with the valley.'

'Do you have any plans for the church?' The girl appeared fascinated whilst Fabio only hovered, out of place in the dilapidation and obviously anxious to be gone.

Francesca nodded. 'Once the renovation of the castle is complete I shall turn my attention to the church, with the help of Catarina. She is a good Catholic. What do you think, Anna, I could do with the building?'

Their silence was companionable, the church small and intimate and already Francesca felt surprisingly at ease with her visitor.

Fabio had left them. 'Well, perhaps Fabio's pagan pipes are out of place, but I would love to hear music played here. Bach perhaps or Albione.'

'A small concert hall, that's a good idea. Are you a musician, or perhaps from a musical family?' Francesca took her hand and together they walked out into the evening sun. She felt the girl tense.

'I was adopted,' she added tersely, 'so I haven't a clue.' Then she said, 'I grew up with a new family in a little town in Kent. They aren't interested in music.' The small snippet of information was grudging.

Francesca made no comment and she found herself regretting tomorrow and the incursion of new arrivals. It would have been good to have had Anna to herself for a little longer. She studied her averted profile. The girl reminded her of herself at that age. She could have been her daughter. Anna must be twenty, twenty one?

Anna sighed. 'It's so beautiful here. How can you ever bear to leave?'

'I leave the castello rarely. Though Fabio likes to imagine it without me.'

Their intimate dinner on the terrace was a silent affair, although Anna made a valiant effort. Fabio was very quiet. Francesca pondered whether the girl had repeated her throw-away comment to him or if something else filled his thoughts, and afterwards she reached the seclusion of her tower with relief, removed once more from the demanding world. To emphasise the fact she drew the shutters with a satisfying resound of wood, not really necessary when summer still lingered, but at this moment she wanted nothing of the outside. Soon enough it would intrude. Tomorrow her home would be filled with intrusive feet. People who haunted her still, after twenty years and who she had no wish to see.

It sounded like an army invading the wood, dodging and hiding, losing, finding friend or stranger in the dark, claustrophobic world. She hated it from the first steps. The others shrieked and laughed and played the intended bonding game, discovery, retreat, fumbling and groping, the girls moving on to another tree and another grasp. All part of the Art College weekend away in the depths of Kent, so they could get to know each other, the rookie first years and the sophisticates about to graduate. Had the term 'bonding' been coined in those days? Discovering ones fellow students but also one's self. Why bother?

29

Already she knew herself, Frances Green, gifted artist, self-sufficient, not interested one jot in the others or what they thought of her. They're young, immature, whilst she was a mature first year and misfit from the start.

She hadn't even bothered to learn their names, the girls and boys in their tight jeans all eager for infantile horse-play, left in the wood to find their way back to base. October and the days were short, a feel of dusk though they had only just had lunch. The pub had been warm and friendly, the students unenthusiastic about the project devised by a sadistic tutor in the comfort of his office. Frances on the other hand wished for nothing more than to escape the bar-stool chat. Sole child of elderly parents, she was probably top of the list for the bonding scheme. Only she had no intention of playing their games.

'Come on, Fran—it is Fran Green isn't it?

'Frances actually."

'Okay, Fran, do keep up or you'll get lost. She had noticed fresher Sue Simpson was a natural leader, just the type they were looking for. Out-going, gregarious. Already she knew everyone's names: 'Keep your eyes on Greg Pearson, the third year striding ahead.' Not difficult even Frances knew his name, having noted his dark dramatic pictures in the College Exhibition and unconsciously acknowledging him to be well out of her reach, literally and metaphorically.

She slowed her step and soon she was alone, the tall beech interspersed with the oak, silent allies in her quest to stay apart from the group. After twenty minutes, she could hear them ahead. They

30

had stopped. The wood was thinning, and there were low bushes beside the track, rhododendron, laurel and small conifer. Grey sky filtered the green canopy. They were out in a clearing and there was a house, low and clinging to the forest floor, its growth stunted. Instinctively, Frances halted, seeking cover under a spreading fir tree. She waited for the challenge.

    'This house isn't on our map. How strange, perhaps it grew up overnight.' Sue smiled up at Greg Pearson. There was appreciative laughter from the rest.

    'What a weird name, 'The House of Pan'. Looks a bit creepy. Shame we haven't got time to explore. Has anyone seen Fran Green?' Sue was annoyed.

    'Don't worry, I'll wait for her.' Sue looked about to protest, decided against it and the party and their self-appointed leader disappeared from view. Greg, the handsome third-year student stood by the gate to the house, his back to Frances. She watched the others go, a mixture of emotions.

    'You can come out now, the coast is clear.' Greg turned and smiled straight at her hiding place, flaunting the look of a fellow conspirator as he held the branches apart to make her appearance as dignified as possible. Frances scrambled out on to the path, brushing off stray needles from the tree.

    Greg Pearson studied her intently. 'Tell me, do I address the nymph Pitys?' he questioned solemnly as he indicated the house name on the gate—'THE HOUSE OF PAN'. 'Remember when the God Pan tried to violate the chaste nymph of the said name, she escaped by turning herself into a fir tree.'

31

'A good disguise,' Frances said stiffly, not liking to be wrong-footed yet immediately intrigued by his classical knowledge. 'I really didn't mean to be a nuisance. I just thought—thought.' She strove to regain her composure. Her initial judgement of him had been right. This accomplished artist was not to be identified with the rest of the group.

'Fine by me.' Greg Pearson was nonchalant. 'I don't like being herded either. While we're here, why don't we take a look inside the house. It looks empty.' He lifted the latch and she followed. On to the wooden veranda, up to the front door, he tried the handle.

And now, twenty years later, here she was. And here he would be. Greg Pearson the artist of international repute was coming to her castello.

THREE

ANNA

Early morning and the castello's giant portal was shut fast against the night hours. But beside Anna's courtyard room a flight of stone steps led down on to the terrace, where they had dined the previous evening. From there, another few steps brought her out into the garden.

Supper had been a simple meal, but good. Peppers, tomatoes and the chard she'd been told had all been grown at the castello. Now she could see for herself the natural store cupboard. It sloped away on a gentle southern aspect in an orderly profusion; aubergines to zucchini would all appear on future menus.

She picked a cherry tomato, both sweet and bitter, a piquant mixture. She took another. There was the same dissension. Yet somehow the difference united the flavour. She moved away from temptation, brushing her fingers instead on a low hedge of rosemary that ran along the eastern range of buildings open to the first rays of morning sun. Her sense of smell overtook her sense of taste. Rosemary hedge and terracotta pots filled with basil, pungent and vibrant green. She pressed the leaves between her fingers and closed her eyes and the perfume was a heady fix. She could almost taste the tomato and basil soup for lunch. What lucky chance had brought her to Chiesa a Castello? She could hardly believe her good fortune.

A castle in Tuscany on a hot summer morning, it doesn't get much better than that. She stood, taking it all in, amazed by her daring. What would the family say if they knew? Thankfully, they didn't. The Tuscan landscape stretched to the horizon and the view made her fingers itch for her canvas and paint. Here were new subjects that just asked to be painted.

The castello's face was intriguing: good portrait material, aged, assured, a little pompous, with a knowledge of the world that was enviable. She crushed the basil, her eager fingers quickly releasing its bouquet. Already she knew the castello would be different. This subject would be her master and she would paint only the face it wished to reveal.

Now it was the turn of her eyes to be blasted as a high wall of brilliant orange fruit blocked her way; it hung in gaudy profusion, cluttering and violating the mellow stone of the castello. 'Gracious!' she said out loud. 'What on earth is that?' She wasn't expecting a reply, but she got one.

'Look at the flowers at the top. You'll recognise those even if you've never seen the fruit before.'

Anna stepped into the vegetation to find the voice. 'It's passion fruit,' she said to the figure of Matt Grant as she parted the foliage. 'Shit,' and she stopped in her tracks, amazement written all over her face. He looked back at her, unblinking. 'B…But I thought you…' She could only stare; Matt Grant was the very last person she had expected to see.

'Hi, Anna.'

'Hi, Anna?' she exploded. 'Is that all you've got to say for yourself?'

'I told you I had a summer school in Italy.' He shrugged.

'Come off it. You were cagey. It could have been anywhere.

34

Do you really mean it's actually here in Francesca's castello? I—I can't—' She paused to regain her composure. 'And you told me not to c—come.'

Matt's face was expressionless but incredulity loosened her tongue and her words were accusing. She glared at him, a mixture of emotions. 'So tell me exactly, why didn't you want me here? Come to think of it, I might easily feel the same about you.' His turning up at the castello could ruin everything; her early morning euphoria was fast disappearing. Five minutes ago everything about the morning had appeared idyllic. Matt Grant was nothing but an interloper, his big feet treading on her patch.

'Well, now seeing as you are here, Anna, why don't you come and join us?' He retreated backwards into a hidden bower, peremptorily indicating Anna should follow. Catarina was sitting at a wooden table and on it were two coffee cups. Surprise after surprise, she was obviously breaking up a cosy little pre-breakfast rendezvous between her art tutor and Francesca's housekeeper. When had he arrived? He looked as though he'd been here forever. Catarina smiled her beautiful white–teeth smile and rose to her feet, indicating she would fetch another cup and Anna did not resist. Her need at this moment was for some very strong Italian coffee.

'Why didn't you tell me you were coming here? That you really knew Fabio already? Why on earth the big secret for Heaven's sake?'

Matt was silent, but he raised his eyebrows and she knew his initial discomfort had already disappeared; any more accusations from her at this moment and she would sound peevish. She'd have to bide her time to find out his reason, but she would. She was a terrier not a lapdog.

Matt took a long drink, quenching any further comment, so that Catarina was back with the fresh percolator before Anna had achieved a glimmer of satisfaction.

She took the proffered cup from Catarina and smiled her thanks, turning her back on Matt in a gesture aimed to put him in his place. She was glad of the opportunity to study Catarina at close quarters.

Anna had hardly seen the housekeeper since her arrival the day before. The older woman had been in and out of the shadows, here and there, in no place very long, busy preparing for the awaited new arrivals. She had not dined with them; apparently Catarina had gone to visit her family, who lived locally. This morning, however, she looked to have all the time in the world just to sit and enjoy the sun and chat with Matt.

Catarina could bear scrutiny. Hard to tell her age, slight, her youthful figure exuded natural energy. Her small, lively face was framed by a mass of untamed auburn hair and Anna found herself wondering where that placed her in the Etruscan scheme of things, was she wife or courtesan? Her dark eyes interrogated, and they were fixed on Anna. Already she sensed that little would escape Catarina's notice or interest. Perhaps a few years younger than Francesca, in assurance she was way ahead, no innate self-doubt had caused early forehead wrinkles to spoil her flawless skin.

'Tell me, Anna, do you like our home?' Her voice was warm. Surprisingly, she seemed to await the answer with as much

36

eagerness as if she had been Francesca.

'It's very beautiful. I think already it has cast a spell.' She'd given the expected answer, but it was the truth. Anna glared at Matt. 'And he wanted to keep me from it. I'll not forgive him in a hurry.' She frowned, how had she ever thought he had her best interests at heart?

Catarina smiled serenely. 'You will enjoy your stay here, Anna, after all, you will be part of a small, very select group. We have seven guests this week.'

There was that number again. For a foolish moment Anna found herself wondering if Fabio had asked her just to make up the magic total.

'For the Etruscan weeks our groups usually range between eighteen and twenty. But this week is special. Friends come to mark the Signora's birthday.'

'Oh dear, that makes me the interloper.' Anna felt herself flushing; immediately seeing it had never been in Matt's place to invite her as guest to someone else's birthday party.

As though reading her thoughts, Catarina said, putting a hand on her arm, 'We are so happy that Fabio invited you to the castello, Anna.'

The girl grinned gratefully. She glanced at Matt and he returned her look with his usual raise of eyebrows; his eyes were friendly. 'Ditto, of course we are.'

Anna took a large gulp of coffee. She had recovered her equilibrium, Matt had never lost his; he stretched out his long legs from under the table, rested his hands behind his head. He looked totally at home, then why shouldn't he?

He said languidly, 'We're planning to give Francesca a birthday to remember. So, Anna, now you find yourself included in the group you'll be able to make yourself useful.'

'Really? Oh, thank goodness for that! Tell me what I can do?' She turned to Catarina, finding herself copying Matt's raising of the eyebrows, but Catarina's face was blank.

Matt was openly amused. 'Which of your many talents, Anna, do you think will be required?' He was teasing her.

'Put me out of my misery, I haven't a clue.'

He turned to Catarina. 'Anna is an artist.'

'Ah, that is good. 'Catarina nodded.

'Yes, undoubtedly as we're here to give Francesca a present. Not just any old present, but something she'll treasure for the rest of her life, and beyond that, something to stand the test of time.' He looked and sounded smug.

Catarina's eyes lit up, her smile expansive. Both she and Matt exuded an air of quiet satisfaction. 'The Signora, I know, will be delighted.'

Matt nodded. 'No question. Anything to enhance her beloved castello, and this most certainly will. Hopefully it will be the finishing touch to all this.' He indicated the castello. 'She's done a wonderful job here. How awful to leave this all behind.'

'*Malocchio*!' Catarina's bright smile vanished, hurriedly she made a strange gesture with her thumb and index finger.

Matt laughed at her obvious concern. 'She's warding off the evil eye. Our dear Catarina is the veritable mixed-up catholic-come-pagan. Even hinting at death can bring bad luck.'

Catarina forced a smile at his amusement, but her morning pleasure had visibly gone. She rose to her feet and Matt laughed again. 'You're right, my dear Catarina. There are better things to think about. Like breakfast. I'm starving. Come on, Anna.'

She was already several paces behind her companion, a man now focused on a more urgent mission. 'You haven't told me what Francesca's present is to be or my part in it.' He stopped and looked back at her.

'It's a painting of course. That's why all the other guests are artists.'

'Why didn't I think of that?'

She followed Matt, hurriedly digesting the information. He'd said she could be useful; she was an artist after all. But, she hadn't been on his original list, never part of the invited clique.

The perfume of rosemary jogged her memory. She had Fabio to thank for her being here, even though she had angled for the invitation. *And what a place to be*—too bad about Matt's presence and his apparent reluctance to include her in it.

The table on the upper terrace was loaded with a fantastic spread. Anna helped herself to the feast, yoghurt, honey, peaches, home-made bread, cherry jam, fruit salad and more coffee. She ate it all sitting beside Matt, looking south over the Tuscan countryside. It lay in long sinuous lines, like somnambulant snakes awaiting the day's heat to raise them from their stupor. There was neither movement nor sound. Anna sighed happily. Fabio was right. She would have no problem trying her hand at landscapes in such a place. She would have been a fool not to come.

'We could go out and do some sketching if you like.' Matt was trying to please. And her first instinct was to decline his offer, but she didn't.

'That would be great.'

She returned to her room, feeling rather like the Cheshire cat. After the heat of the morning it was cool and welcoming and the stillness almost tangible. Yet beyond the castello, the morning sun beckoned and she felt a rising excitement. To get the chance to paint with Matt Grant was luck indeed, however she had achieved it. Venice already seemed a long time ago. Hurriedly, she opened up her painting gear and there amongst all the tubes was not the proverbial grinning feline, but the Etruscan chimera.

She'd forgotten the strange figure that Fabio had given her. She sat the facsimile in full view on the windowsill. It should feel at home here in the Etruscan countryside. Against the sleeping serpent landscape the bronze monster no longer looked grotesque. Flippantly, she patted it on one of its three heads; the goat seemed the safest bet. She knew that when she closed the door she could leave it behind. Its eyes would not follow her here.

Matt was waiting outside her door in the courtyard. In the shaded light it felt like monastery cloisters, joining castle with church.

'I have the cell next to yours.' Matt indicated the door on the other side of the stone steps.

'Cell?'

'Yes, after the Etruscans came the Lombards and this

40

became a convent for nuns.'

'That explains the atmosphere. I share a common wall with the church apse. So I wouldn't have had far to go for night prayers.' Eyes were watching them. Anna glanced up at the tower and a figure stepped back into the shadows. It had to be Francesca, but she made no indication she had seen them. Francesca was introspective; they would get to know each other only in the older woman's time.

From the well-worn steps they circled the garden out on to the village track which dropped steeply onto a sunken hollow way. The stony path became a soft sward that cushioned their sandaled feet. They walked in companionable silence. On this first morning Anna was happy to fill her senses. Everything was perfect. Besides, Grant's silence was nothing new. She'd seen him taciturn before.

But he was keen to talk. 'T—This is the ancient salt route between Volterra and Siena. Can you hear the travellers' voices from the last two and a half thousand years?'

She knew immediately what he meant. There in the shadows around them the past hovered. She was seeing a new, unexpected side of him.

They were deep now into the wood. 'These forests hold a few surprises. You often stumble across bygone human activity like huts for drying chestnuts, piles of charcoal or scattered limekilns. They weren't the empty places they are today.'

It was cool and pleasant under the Holm oaks. Walking rather than sketching seemed to be her companion's mission and Anna was happy to follow. She had only a sketch book and charcoal in her cotton backpack. There was purpose in his long strides as they put the castello behind them.

Onwards and upwards. Their view was obscured by trees and hills, and from the sun's position, they appeared to have come almost full circle. Then suddenly they had a wide expansive view. The vista was so much like the background in Giorgione's Accademia painting that her smile was as wide as the scenery.

'Wow!' One word said it all. High on the skyline were walls and towers now bathed in morning sun; there were no dark thunder clouds on the horizon, no hovering storm to threaten the scene.

Anna stood spellbound, gazing at the familiar framed landscape. So easy to picture the figures of mother and child sitting under a tree and Grant as Giorgione's man, watching and waiting.

He smiled down at her. 'I've often wondered if Giorgione's background was Monteriggione, it easily could have been. The village you see up on the hill was old even in the fifteenth century. He indicated a rocky outcrop under a tree for them to sit and admire the view.

'Thank you for this.'

'I knew you'd recognise it.' He smiled at her obvious pleasure. 'And we are not the first to admire it. Dante called the Monteriggione towers 'Giants standing in a circle'. It's a nice analogy I think. He saw that places can become characters in a story, a bit like our castello.'

Anna felt a rush of gratitude. This friendly giant beside her was trying hard to make up for his lukewarm welcome. She took out her pad and pencil and began to sketch; straight stone towers and walls zigzagged up and down the hillside. That was the background, but for Anna all-important would be mother and child holding centre stage in the scene. Who might be their models? The comfortable form of Francesca would make a good mother figure but there were new arrivals soon to join the group. How would they fit into her picture?'

'In painting I always think it's important to see things in relation rather than in isolation but then I suppose that's true of life in general,' Matt Grant's words cut across her thoughts as he sat down beside her. 'However, it's difficult to see things quite like that at Francesca's castello. We're isolated here in a very inward-looking world. It's not just the surrounding woods that are haunted. You can hear the voices of the early inhabitants of the castello from three thousand years ago.' He grinned sheepishly and the face he turned to her was quite unlike any he had shown before. 'Don't quote me.'

'So you thought I wouldn't fit into such a world?'

'Only too well. That's why I knew you should stay away.'

'Really, why's that?'

Instead of answering Matt picked up a stick and began agitating the earth so that the umber soil and stones flew in all directions. He said, 'Francesca is a complex character.'

'I've already worked that out for myself.'

'And the castello quickly weaves its spell.'

'Oh, come on.' Anna laughed out loud. 'What on earth do you mean by that?'

He didn't reply; later she would remember his comments but for now the immediate scene was all that she could ask. She concentrated on her sketch.

43

Occasionally, he got up and walked off into the long grass on the hillside, as though his legs needed to uncoil. Then he was back again and looking appraisingly at her work. At last, Anna put down her charcoal, aware that Matt had sat himself down on the boulder beside her again and was regarding her rather than her sketch.

'Did Fabio know you were an artist when he invited you here?' he said.

'Yes—No— I can't remember. Why do you ask?'

'O, nothing. But just be careful, Anna. Fabio likes to enjoy himself with little regard—'

Anna laughed. 'I can assure you I'm only here to draw and paint. I've hardly set eyes on him since our arrival. He has other interests I think. But, thanks, for the warning.'

They headed home. This time it was easy walking on the unshaded side of the hill, tracing rows and rows of vines, making the most of aspect. A deep purple haze coloured the slope. Heavy, straining bunches of grapes lent earthward as though tired of the restraint of gravity. The fruit was profuse and her companion stopped to pick three large grapes. She put her hand out for one; the juice promising in its bouquet. The ancient vines stretched as far as the eye could see and the dark swathes promised a good harvest.

'This could be the garden of Eden.' Anna laughed, 'And no sign anywhere of a serpent lurking in the undergrowth.'

'Could be well hidden; beware hot sunny dry spots, in fact the walls of the castello are just the place. Remember that, Anna.'

Then they were down amongst the newer vines, young and

44

spindly and the grapes poorer. Matt pointed to the rows. 'See, a rose bush has been planted at the end of every line? They're put there as a warning. If they shrivel and die, the farmer knows the dreaded aphids are about and ready to strike the vines next. It's always roses they go for first.'

'Who would think that roses carry a warning? Next time I'm sent a bouquet I might question the sentiment behind it.' Anna grinned.

'You could be right.'

They stood in silence, reluctant to leave the sunny side of the hill. The valley below lay in deep shadow and within it the castello slumbered, a crouching animal. Anna gazed at the ancient dark building. 'Its walls shut out the world whilst church and castle are linked like mother and child, tied together with umbilical cord. It's as though nothing else exists.'

'You're beginning to understand.'

A sudden shaft of sunlight pierced the castle tower, round, solid and seemly impenetrable where narrow windows repelled. Yet there was warmth in the mellow tiled roof that anchored it to its Romanesque church now side-lined; the feet of the faithful no longer seeking its sanctuary.

Anna and Matt peered at small shapes moving below. The other guests had arrived: for the moment diminutive and unknown. 'Should we have been there to greet the new arrivals?' Anna frowned, feeling guilty. 'Will Francesca mind our absence?' All morning she had had the weird feeling that Matt was leading her away from the castello on purpose; how crazy was that?

'Of course not.' Matt was brusque. Yet Anna stared down at the antlike creatures and somehow knew they would figure large in her life before her stay at the castello had ended. A group of people, whatever the number, was bound to set up an eddy, however quiet the stream.

'I hope you will be happy at the castello.' Matt's words broke into her reverie.

She laughed, 'How could I be otherwise. It seems like heaven on earth.'

'Can there ever be such a place?'

FOUR

FRANCESCA

Handcrafted chestnut shutters at her tower window both hide and reveal. Francesca stood and watched as the new arrivals moved into the courtyard, their voices hushed, reverential. It hadn't taken long for them to get the feel of the place. No eyes were raised, no one sensed the unseen presence. All were fixed on the slim, elegant Catarina, her smile warm and friendly. The watching woman felt again her envy of her Italian friend's natural charm. Catarina could make anyone feel welcome. So it was good that Catarina was always the first to greet the minibus, when it came to a crunching halt before the massive wooden gate of Chiesa a Castello. She was the one they would want to see: a stunning, gracious Italian, quite beautiful; only later did they come to accept the unremarkable English woman who stood in the shadows and manipulated the strings. Moving figures held in the trance of Tuscany.

The travellers were weary, transported into another world. Kidnapped from chilly England, they rubbed tired eyes, looking around at the unfamiliar scene: focusing, taking in details as their blindfolds were removed. Did they want to come? They will be loath to leave. Once over the threshold the castello had that effect. The heavy castle gate was clamped to the wall, held open to invite them into the protecting walls of tufa and travertine that were ochre yellow, warm and haphazard.

The group stood in the searchlight of sun that had found the base of Francesca's tower. She moved nearer to the window, relishing the fact she'd not been included, not yet part of the scene. She had long since learned that people were predictable. Soon they would move out of the unrelenting sun, to the cool of the umbrellas, where on the slatted tables was the tangible castello's welcome: sparkling glasses and a large jug of iced-peach tea. This first drink would find its place high on any travel company questionnaire. She and Catarina had worked hard to make the holiday perfect.

The newcomers accepted the drink offering gratefully, and then moved back to the sun. Yes, they were like puppets, and for the moment Francesca would move the strings. But this group was very different from her usual guests. It was small and select, and they were no strangers. She knew them all.

In the early days, it had been necessity that had forced her to share her home with eager visitors. Because of the intruders she was able to live at the castello and she felt a grudging gratitude. Every head counted meant another wall raised, another roof tiled, another room habitable. It had been like living with the in-laws so she could be married. Only, of course, she was a free entity. After dinner she would show them the scrap book that recorded her labour of the last twenty years. They would not fail to be impressed, envying her foresight and luck. They would not see how hard it had been.

Anna came into the courtyard. There was slight hesitation and then she joined the others. They welcomed her with smiles. Perhaps it was the girl's youth, her prettiness, even her vulnerability. Paul Bradley made room for her beside him and pressed a glass into her hand. Typical of him, he liked an attractive girl. But he'd been to the castello many times before and saw it as his second home.

'Paul Bradley,' his voice boomed in greeting. Paul stood out in the group, small in stature but large in personality. The feted academic, used to dominating the scene, had taken the role his hostess should be filling. He took the mantel with ease, used to others listening to his pearls of wisdom, if delivered only over a pre-dinner drink. 'Authority on all things Etruscan. Shall I bore you before or after dinner?'

Anna grinned, 'There's no answer to that.'

'Very diplomatic. Have to tell you I'm at my most pedantic on a full stomach. What about over coffee?'

'A date.' Anna nodded. She looked about her, perplexed by the absence of their hostess, as no doubt were the others?

Francesca stood irresolute at the top of the steps to her tower. It was a long way down to the courtyard. Years and distance had kept her apart. She peered down into the group. Sue Simpson was standing there below her. Francesca sighed, knowing she must leave her refuge and greet Sue and the man beside her.

Years had eclipsed the pain. Now it was just numb memory. It had taken the day for Francesca to control her emotion. No puppeteer could have shaking fingers. She made her way down to where Fabio was waiting for her at the base of the tower. Francesca placed a steady hand on his arm and together they joined her guests under the umbrellas. Did he know her mixed emotions, her trepidation, her hardly contained excitement? Her guests moved towards her, clutching their glasses of Prosecco. She had watched from the shadows, noted each individual, absorbed their mood and knew how each would react.

Their sudden silence was unnerving. It had been a noisy group, Paul attentive to Anna, Catarina sharing some joke with the others. Now her entrance was like a switch being abruptly turned off on a radio. Young Anna smiled kindly, a little aloof now from the rest of them. But she was too young to have the social confidence needed to carry the moment. Besides, it was not for her to play the part of Francesca who was the hostess, the one supposed to put everyone else at their ease. Easy enough to say a word of greeting yet her mouth was dry and no words came. She knew that if she tried to say anything she would stutter like a child.

Of course, it was Sue Simpson who took control. 'Fran, I must say how wonderful it is to see you after all this time, and what a transformation since the last time I was here! We just love the castello and what you have done to it.' Her voice dropped to emphasize the point, anxious to get off on the right foot, to ingratiate herself. Then she turned to the man at her side. 'You remember Greg?'

Every word just right, just enough, and of course she knew Francesca remembered him. Greg smiled his easy smile and self-consciously gave her a hug. Her arms hung by her sides. He had changed of course, it was like squinting at a painting so true colour goes and just the tone is left. His tone was the same as it had always been: a handsome relaxed, affable figure; a mixture of the best colours on the early palette, but softer now. Unsurprisingly, Sue still had bold colour, strawberry blonde hair and red outfit to complement; the blonde had been well stirred and mixed.

Later, Francesca would question what she had managed to say, too many thoughts running through her head, wanting desperately to appear composed; after all those years she needed them to see her new persona. She smiled at Sue and the man beside her, and inclined her head. Tongue-tied, she moved on to the older, smaller man. Perhaps because she was on an eye-level with Paul but her shoulders dropped and immediately she was more relaxed.

Paul Bradley gave her a hug and a peck on the cheek. 'Good old Paul, good to see you again,' she said.

Bradley looked surprised at the warmth of her greeting. 'Yes, I'm back yet again, Francesca.' There was no apology in his voice.

'It's always good to see you, Paul.' At that moment Francesca meant it. She was used to Paul and his eccentricity. He made no demands on her emotions and he had been around in the intervening years, like a faithful spaniel. He came and went as he liked; if one morning he turned up at breakfast then an extra plate was laid and a lively discussion followed. He seemed to know everything, becoming her eyes on the world, allowing her to remain informed at Chiesa a Castello.

'I return as often as I can.' He turned to Anna. 'I'm sure you can see why. The place bewitches. Don't you agree?'

'I still feel like pinching myself at my good luck.' The girl turned to her hostess and smiled her gratitude. 'It's very kind of Francesca to invite me—or rather, let me stay in her home. I rather invited myself.'

51

Her hostess laughed. 'Hardly, my dear, it was Fabio who saw your suitability.' The half-smile aimed at putting the girl at her ease. Paul looked at Anna, his face serious, and Francesca could sense a 'Paulism' coming on. She wondered what the girl would make of him. Paul could be a bit of an acquired taste.

He smiled, 'Don't worry, my dear, it's in Francesca's own interests to have us share her home, otherwise she might annoy the gods. One's only chance against fate is to be humble, so that the ultimate ending can be postponed. So thankfully Francesca must share her possession, opening her gates to all and sundry.'

'Hardly all and sundry. Besides, enough, Paul,' Francesca admonished. 'Forget about all that fate business, you are not leading an Etruscan study group now.'

Sue Simpson laughed. 'It certainly sounds like an opportunist reading of the facts, Paul, but I will drink to it. We all gain from such fatalistic beliefs.' She sipped her wine. 'Glad to see you serve Italian sparkling wine and not Champagne, Fran.'

It hadn't taken Sue long to be totally at ease with her surroundings and the assembled group. 'How can I have left it so long to taste again the pleasures of Fran's Castello?' Sue repeated the English form of Francesca's name, putting her hostess in her place, reminding the rest of the assembled company that Francesca in her Italian castello was just a fantasy. In reality she was still plain Fran Green.

Francesca smiled stiffly. Sue's visit to Tuscany was long overdue, but still the distance between them remained other than miles.

52

'Anna, have you been introduced to Sue?' Francesca took the girl's arm. 'This is Sue Simpson. You may have heard of her.'

'I don't think so.' The girl's response was quick and emphatic.

'Oh,' and the older woman hid a smile. 'Sue is a very well-known artist.'

An embarrassed Anna said, 'Sorry, I've heard of her of course. I just meant I've n- never been this close.' Pink cheeks showed her confusion.

'Well, here's your chance.' Francesca smiled.

Sue shook her head. 'I think we've met, my dear, but don't know where. Of course, I do visit a lot of art schools.' She was already turning away towards Matt.

'Hello, Sue! You haven't deigned to visit our college yet. We live in hope.' Matt Grant indicated Anna. 'Our top student! You must show Sue your work, Anna. Where's Catarina gone. I must say it's food rather than art I'm interested in at this precise moment.' He added, 'You'll see why any minute now.'

'Matt, all you can think about is food.' Francesca sighed, 'How do you manage to stay so lean? Beware, Catarina could be about to change that.'

Francesca noted her housekeeper retreating to the kitchen; the hub of the castello that she had so lovingly restored at such personal cost. Catarina had been there through thick and thin, gratefully acknowledging what the building owed to its English owner. She had seen many people come and go, yet the castello's stout walls would be here long after they had all gone. Did Catarina include the castello's present owner in that dismissal? Francesca didn't doubt her housekeeper's loyalty but she knew the building came first with the passionate Italian. Catarina was integral to the place, moving as speedily as a shadow in the movement of the sun, her absence hardly to be noted before she was there bringing back the light. This time it was a double shadow. Catarina had brought with her Rita, the cook. They stood together, an unlikely duo, yet they complemented in a duet: as good as any heard in the local theatre, Catarina in perfect English, Rita in Italian. 'Buona sera, Signor, Signora. I have to tell you your dinner tonight.'

Rita was dressed in white from head to foot. A tight cap imprisoned her dark wiry hair. Only her smooth face and thick ankles showed she was other than a starched apron, though a tiny gold necklace brightened her bare neck and large gold hoops pierced her ears. She was dressed for dinner. Their dinner. She stood, earnest and unsmiling. Pale cheeks held no tell-tale flush to show she had toiled in the kitchen for hours. She had the cool assurance of someone who knew their craft. Her eyes were alert, but they looked beyond her audience, all she saw before her was the food she so lovingly promoted.

'Zuchini risotto, con vino bianco.' She paused.

Now it was Catarina's turn to continue the love story. In a short scarlet dress halfway up her lovely legs and her auburn hair massed on her shoulders, she was a flame beside the white of the cook.

'Ladies and gentlemen, Rita has cooked for you the simple food of the region found here for many centuries. Our food is of the

54

Etruscans,' Catarina rehearsed her usual introduction, ignoring the fact that for this group the ancient Etruscans had little significance.

'The ingredients are plain, herbs and vegetables from our garden that have been freshly gathered. It is the truth I did so this morning.' Catarina's voice caressed each ingredient and there was the vision of tomatoes picked from the vine, and the cabbage sliced from its root, chosen to complement the rabbit. 'The hunter comes often to the castello gates, *il cacciatore* an ever present shadow in the woods.'

Their guests smiled appreciatively. By the time Rita had reached the hot egg custard and strawberries Catarina's translation was superfluous. In their eagerness the listeners had entered the Tower of Babel, savouring the taste of words.

Francesca cast her eye around the group. There would be no constraint of language in their confined world, yet alienating factors lay trapped within it. The past lay darkly between Sue and Greg, and herself. And now there was the recent behaviour of Fabio. She could sense him moving away from her. She frowned, Fabio filling her thoughts. Seeds of discord had sprouted between them in the past months. His temperament did not sit easily under her quiet determination to dominate. He was resentful of the power she had over him, through the castello. Yet in the end, Francesca knew she had nothing to fear: no blood ties held them together just as no cement bound the castle stones. But while tufa block stood on travertine brick, Fabio would stay attentive.

Tonight he was making a valiant effort to be everything she asked of him and more, fitting easily into the role of host. Catarina and Rita had disappeared back into the confines of the kitchen and there was a murmur of expectancy. Fabio had moved to stand beside Anna, and Francesca looked from one to the other. She had Fabio to thank for the fact that Anna stood in the courtyard; this slight girl who wore her vulnerability for all to see, though she herself was unaware. But tonight she had piled up her long fair hair away from her face in an attempt at sophistication. She looked older, more self-assured, and her plain dress completed the image. She looked relaxed. Francesca sighed; tonight it all looked so uncomplicated; a clear view across the valley, yet she well knew the speed of sudden storms in the surrounding hills.

For now, Anna had Fabio's full attention, and Matt, in conversation with Greg, had one eye on them. Anna was teasing Fabio and he was taking it surprisingly well. Seldom frivolous, his rule was that any joke should only be of his choosing. As a boy, he could not bear for Francesca to laugh at him and this tendency had not diminished. To be fair, he did not look a figure of fun, but one chosen by the gods.

Catarina was now handing round a plate of antipasto: small pieces of aubergine lightly sautéed in batter, and bite sized pieces of pizza. Fabio had a piece of pizza in his mouth and one in either hand. Anna was ribbing him. 'Fabio, I had you up on a pedestal in Venice, thought you would look good as a city equestrian statue. I might have to change my ideas if you go on eating like that. I can almost hear the poor horse groaning in the Piazza Giorgio e Paulo. His back would have quite a curve if you climbed on him now.'

Oh, how would he take that public put-down? Francesca

waited for Fabio's reaction. He shrugged, 'There is not a problem. I have always eaten like a horse, haven't I, Francesca?' He seized another piece of pizza from Catarina's proffered plate, then scooped another into his hand to prove his point, and smiled across at the girl. 'I like that you look up to me.'

Matt joined them. 'Don't hog that plate, Fabio. There are others who like the aubergine.' He turned to Anna. 'This is only the beginning you know. A feast awaits in the baptistery'.

'Baptistery?' Anna looked surprised.

'Yes, our hostess has restored it to its former glory. Only now it makes the most spectacular dining room. Doesn't it, Francesca?'

'I'm happy you feel that too, Matt. I like to think it's a room fit for Rita's gastronomic delights.' As she spoke, lights came on in the courtyard and a subtle warmth invaded the surrounding walls. 'Come then, it is time to show Anna my favourite room of the castello.' Francesca took hold of the girl's hand, gratified to have someone new to impress, and they walked towards the faint shimmering light emanating from the baptistery.

Low voices, but as the visitor's eyes became accustomed there was an awed silence; this was a splendid room with its remote ceiling as high as the heavens, and as unadorned, except for tiny lights that pinpricked the cool dark of the interior like distant stars. A long glass-topped table stood on the stone floor, set with silver, white china and fine glass. It dazzled against the room, its light Sienna brown walls moulded into bare plastered alcoves. Stark, it still had an unfinished look; something Francesca sensed every time she entered.

Anna was charmed, as Francesca knew she would be. The girl gasped, as did Greg. And even the others who had seen it before were silently impressed.

Fabio caught hold of Francesca's arm, startling her back into reality, reminding her it was she who must take command. There were no name cards. It would have been hard to allot place to person. She would have got it wrong and she wanted so much for this first meal to be a success. She must take head of table. Solicitous Fabio moved back her chair. She sat down gratefully and gestured to the others. 'Do please sit where you like, we do not stand on ceremony, and feel free to move around other evenings. I wouldn't want to bore the same person every time.'

She had never been a party animal, happiest in this, her confined world. Fabio took the chair beside her, saying, 'But that's simply not true, I never cease to be amazed at your fund of stories. For someone who leads such a cloistered life you know an awful lot about what goes on around here.'

Matt agreed. 'Be warned, she seems to know what is going to happen before it does.' He looked to take the seat on her other side but Fabio interrupted.

'You're right, Grant. Francesca has already chosen Greg to sit there.'

Francesca protested, 'Of course I haven't,' and she flushed. But Fabio had guessed her wish and he looked pleased with himself. 'Francesca is dying to tell Greg all about the castello's conversion from ruin to this.' He knew her need to boast of her castle to fresh ears. She was thankful that could be all that lay behind his manoeuvring.

So they're fighting to be near her. She was amused. Fabio should really be sitting amongst the guests. Matt had taken his demotion with good grace. Francesca watched him seat Anna and Sue before he took his place between them: a remarkably uncomplicated young man with a good deal of common sense. If only all men were like him.

Greg sat beside her. She wondered if her pleasure was so noticeable to the others? People were talking, not watching her. Voices rose and fell as speaker changed to listener and then back to raconteur. Fabio, seated on the other side of Francesca, turned immediately to Sue. She and Greg were left in their separate world, as contrived as that last time in the House of Pan.

She clasped her hands tightly together under the table and breathed deeply, praying she would be able to talk in something like a normal voice.

'It's a long time since our last meeting.' Greg was anxious to get the acknowledgement over so they could transcend the intervening years as effortlessly as skaters gliding over ice. 'You've obviously had quite a project here, creating your home from a ruin, F—Francesca. I can't think how you knew where to start.'

And in the next breath he had turned away from her and was questioning Catarina on her garden, and congratulating her on the zucchini. Francesca, left at the table end, felt her isolation. Paul Bradley came to her rescue. 'Francesca, so which one of us is extra to requirements?'

Francesca frowned, unsure of his implication. The room fell into silence. 'What do you mean, Paul?'

'Well, surely we should be seven, not eight. All things Etruscan you know. Seven was their auspicious number. So it's not hard to calculate there's one too many seated around this table.'

'Oh, dear, and I'm probably to blame.' Anna's cheeks flushed in the dim light.

'Of course not!' Francesca did not try to keep the annoyance out of her voice, but it was with Paul not the girl. 'I have told you, Paul, this is not an Etruscan week. You know—'

Matt rose from his seat, his tall frame seeming to ape the lofty walls. 'It's perhaps the right time to explain to Francesca why we are all gathered here.' There was a murmur of interest. 'Yes, we have come to celebrate your birthday.' He held up his hand to stop Francesca's protest. 'Yes, we know it is still another week away, Francesca, but it will take all of that time.'

'Naughty boy, I said no presents.' She wagged a finger at him, belying her smile of affection. Matt was another of her 'adoptees'. She had known him since he was a young lad. A couple of years older than Fabio, they were very different. 'You know...' and she looked concerned.

'No buts—collectively, we want to give you a memorable present, one that you will treasure.'

Someone thumped the table in support and Matt grinned, 'You won't be able to refuse when you hear what it is. I've known you long enough to know it will please you, besides, it wasn't me but Catarina who came up with the brilliant idea.'

60

Francesca looked across at her friend and housekeeper, and even before she knew what their present was to be, she felt a rush of gratitude. She and Catarina were very different, yet they understood that difference. Whatever she had chosen would be right. Sometimes Catarina knew her better than she knew herself. How foolish, just a moment ago she had felt so isolated, and yet in reality she was surrounded by friends, all anxious to please.

Sue lent forward across the table. 'Haven't you guessed why the group is as it is? Surely, Fran, you must have questioned my inclusion for instance, and of course that of Greg?'

'But you're a friend, Sue, and have been for a long time, and you run the London end of our Castello Holiday business. Isn't that as important in its way as the Italian side?' She smiled her reassurance. She wasn't going to give Sue the benefit of knowing she'd questioned the other woman's part in her celebrations. So, she thought, it was Catarina who had chosen the group. It was only by chance that Greg was here.

'Right, Francesca. What do we all have in common?' Matt was enjoying the moment, 'besides being your friends and admirers.'

'I've been trying to figure it out.' Francesca smiled. 'But without much success.'

'We can all wield a paintbrush.'

'So you've all turned into painters and decorators. If so, you're more than welcome, there's plenty still to do.'

'Well, we'll need ladders.' Matt waved his arms to encompass the room. 'But we are all bone fide artists at the end of

61

the day, and our plan is to paint a mural for you on the baptistery walls.'

They waited. They all knew that to please their hostess could be a hit and miss affair.

'O, what a splendid idea. Thank you.' Her smile was genuine. 'How clever of you, Catarina. I cannot think of anything I would like more.'

Catarina moved to stand beside Francesca and took her hand. 'I knew that it would please you, but it is Matt who has organised it. He knew exactly who to invite.' She laughed, 'However, do not worry that Fabio and I will be included in the artistic part of the present.' Catarina was now smiling broadly. 'We shall help in the preparation of the walls, and then our involvement will be purely to keep your gifted friends happy with constant refreshment. We know our place, do we not, Fabio?'

'You have thought of everything. I don't know what to say.' Francesca's voice was tremulous. Smiles all round. But when she glanced across at Anna she saw the girl was still biting her lip.

'So, Anna, you must see you are very much needed on this project. Clever Fabio must have smelt the oil paint on you when he sat beside you on the vaporetta.'

Anna laughed, her relief genuine. 'It could have been the turpentine.'

Fabio winked at the girl. 'But of course. It is my favourite perfume.' He folded his napkin carefully. 'So when do we start? Straight after the strawberries?

Matt coughed. 'Time enough after breakfast, I think. We

shall need to spend most of the evening discussing what form the fresco will take. I've already made a few sketches, and perhaps Francesca can choose her favourite.'

'So it's serious business this week.' Paul Bradley grinned. 'There are some superb Etruscan banqueting scenes we could copy. I can take you all to Tarquinia tomorrow, and you will see for yourselves what I mean.'

'But this is a Christian building.' Catarina had returned to her seat but was quickly on her feet again at Paul's suggestion. 'The Etruscans had an obsession with death. Theirs was a religion of fear and superstition.' She crossed herself.

'And you talk about superstition and fear!' Paul was scathing.

Catarina ignored the jibe. 'I will take you to the Cistercian Abbey Church to show you the mural we must copy.'

'Dissension already. What do you say, Francesca? After all, it is your wall and your mural.' Matt's usually quiet voice was strained.

Francesca sighed, 'Give me time to think about it. Now let us drink to the eight of us, to the artist in us all.'

FIVE

ANNA

Anna enjoyed the meal in the baptistery. The wine flowed. Was it a libation to the gods, whichever God they followed? Did they need a deity for excuse? Anna felt grateful to whichever one had included her in the magic of Chiesa a Castello. Intoxicated by the place, the people and the wine, she felt a euphoria that did not depend on potent drink.

Catarina had chosen well, she knew her wine. To complement the risotto there were bottles of Falaghina from Campania, for the rabbit, Chianti Collee Senesi. No connoisseur, Anna guessed no young cheap grape was allowed here; the age of the wine surely in keeping with the place. And with each bottle, Catarina explained her choice with as much passion and conviction as she had denounced any suggestion of an Etruscan mural. Each accompanying wine was lovingly introduced and Anna thought fleetingly that Paul would find it harder to convince his audience. Catarina's attractive personality and appearance were in great contrast to his pedantry. Anna felt increasingly drawn to the bubbly, vivacious Italian woman, again so different from her serious, English employer. Yet Anna felt a growing sympathy for her hostess, whereas Paul—? She stole a glance at the man, he looked broad-shouldered enough to cope with any of her girl's negative vibes.

The academic Paul, blinkered scholar, would be her button-holing. She saw the evening stretching out ahead, if he were allowed to get on his hobby-horse. His deep voice held none of Catarina's charming cadence. So would the next day hold for them Pagan tomb or Christian shrine? Paul Bradley would have to use all of his powers of persuasion to overcome Catarina's voluble determination.

Poor Francesca, she'd need the wisdom of Solomon. Now she looked ill at ease. Her evening was no happy, relaxed gathering, for already dissension had reared its ugly head. One camp would be disappointed whatever her decision. From Catarina's reaction and Paul's stony silence, passion was clearly already running high. This introspective woman was being drawn into a dispute not of her making. A hornets nest agitated by the good intentions of Matt Grant.

Had Matt foreseen there would be a problem? Anna wondered how he viewed the different camps. On the surface he appeared undisturbed. She'd never seen him in such good form, even enjoying an exchange with Fabio. It hadn't taken much observation to see that both men eyed each other warily. Perhaps Matt enjoyed a challenge. Conversation wafted around her. She stared at the plain, blank wall of the baptistery. A scene waited to be painted. Someone would get their way, someone would be thwarted. She noted Francesca eyeing the space, a frown creasing her forehead.

Slowly, their hostess rose from the table and they immediately fell silent. The meal had been long, an important occasion in its own right. But now the older woman looked tired.

What had their hostess decided upon, Etruscan or Christian art?

'Ah, decision time.' Paul rose to his feet, but Catarina already stood beside the castello's owner. Francesca looked from one to the other, momentarily sought the edge of the table for support, then raised her eyes in bafflement to the lights twinkling in the ceiling.

Matt smiled at the older woman. 'Sleep on your decision if you want to, Francesca. After all, the mural should be what you want it to be.'

'Come follow me.' Francesca walked slowly to the door. Chair legs scraped on the stone flags and heels tapped on the stone courtyard, but no one spoke. Over the threshold of the great gate and out onto the Tuscan hillside it was infinitely black and still. But as their senses cleared, cicadas screamed their impatience and the indigo sky erupted into pinpricks of light, millions in a vast unfathomable pattern.

'This darkness is a cauldron of Christian belief and pagan disbelief,' Francesca said softly. 'Somewhere up there lies my decision. If only I could read the signs.' Away in the distance, the sinuous silhouettes of the hills coiled into the night, and in the village of Monteriggione the last sleepless inhabitants burnt the terminal night light.

'It's been like this for centuries, nothing has changed,' Anna whispered, affected by the primeval dark surrounding Chiesa a Castello: the Christian monument erect on its Etruscan foundations. Francesca stood, a small dark insignificant shape at its gate, guarded by Catarina on one side and Paul on the other.

Anna, close beside Matt, could sense his lack of fervour. He had no problem with the eventual outcome; the mural waited for Francesca to make up her mind, whatever it was to be. Anna felt in tune with Francesca. She could readily sympathise with the woman's angst. Their hostess had much to lose whereas Matt could just walk away from it at the end of the day. Get on with his life; whatever that was. She didn't know very much about him.

'Matt, what do you like other than painting?' her question a soft query, his answer as suddenly as important to her as Francesca's momentous pronouncement.

'Butterflies!' Matt sounded distinctly defensive.

'That is the right answer; you've won the prize on the top shelf.' Anna's chianti giggle echoed into the night sky and the cicadas shrieked their laughter.

In the dim light, butterflies, azure blue and yellow, vied with birds seeking a favoured place, the flute sigh calling them heavenward. Below them, the couple on the couch lay in passionate embrace. The bearded man, dark haired and bare-chested, rested on his bed. The girl, with elaborately coiffed hair and large drop earrings, reached out to him with bronzed arms. Dancers whirled, boys frolicked and a well fed cat crouched under the couch .The flute player played his funeral dirge on double pipes.

'Isn't it just splendid, this wonderful mixed metaphor of life and death together?' Paul was a changed man. 'What spontaneity and love of life. Note, he's leaving it with remarkable good will. This chap has got the right approach.' Enthusiasm lit the academic's face. Anna saw she had misjudged him. A scholar, yes, steeped in his subject, but more than eager to impart his knowledge to the group, who nodded obediently, mute spectators of the Etruscan tomb scene. 'Don't you just love the naivety of it? The man and his lady painted larger than life, their inferior retainers and servants appropriately small.' Paul grinned at the noticeable discrepancy. 'So my stature puts me firmly in my place in society,' he joked against himself. 'Plus the fact he has a lot more hair than me.'

They stood silent before the ancient artwork.

'So what do you think of the wall painting, Anna?' Paul turned to the girl beside him with a look of expectation. She gazed at the mural scene, a normal day, early morning, the couple engrossed in each other, their minions awaiting their every desire.

'It's great. It's not the highest art, but it's realistic. It looks just like any domestic scene.'

'A clever deception, they built their tombs to represent the dead man's home, creating for him his familiar surroundings. Home sweet home, in fact.' Paul was pleased at her perception.

Matt joined the discussion. 'We almost feel we can touch the man. Feel his arm resting on the couch and sense, like the woman, the warmth of his skin. But he is very dead.' He was as involved as Paul, both natural teachers. Anna felt a flicker of self-congratulation. How lucky to be looking at Etruscan art with two such companions.

Matt continued, 'And you don't need to be an artist to admire the scene. When D. H. Lawrence visited in 1927, he admired the naturalness of the painting. He was lucky. Then there was no glass partition between him and the walls.'

'Oh, well, it's easier to get here now.' Sue was matter of fact. 'Even so, it was quite a journey.'

'Yes, so we shouldn't leave Francesca alone too long.' Anna felt conscious stricken. It had been hours since they'd deserted the castello, and it felt like truancy. Only Greg had excused himself from the trip and had disappeared with sketchpad and pencil.

'So how many Etruscan tombs are there, Paul?' Sue's voice had a lazy edge. Was she really interested in his answer? Up to now she'd targeted every small detail with her digital camera. Its long memory making her snap happy, it was as though the camera could see the ancient world for her. For now, subject exhausted, the camera was back in its case. Anna sensed the woman couldn't care less whether an Etruscan or Christian depiction graced the wall of Francesca's Baptistery. She glanced at the woman artist and felt for the first time the chill of the tomb. It was not a happy scene.

Sue's style of painting was very different; precise and detailed, perhaps even pernickety, with little imagination. Anna had seen her work in London. Once she had liked it, even wanted to emulate the perfect watercolours. Not any more, thought the painter in oils, untidy and slapdash. Anna felt a growing affinity with the artisan tomb artists.

Intent on her deliberations, Anna realised she had missed Paul's answer. She repeated the question and was amazed at the man's reply.

'There are over six thousand tombs.'

'But that's incredible.'

Matt replied, 'Not all excavated I can assure you. So many were found in the nineteenth century that their artefacts were just destroyed in situ. But today, sites are still being unearthed, and the market is healthy. Isn't it Paul?' He turned to the older man with raised eyebrows.

Sue lost her bored expression. 'So, any chance of the real thing; wouldn't mind taking home a painted vase as a keepsake?'

'Not the question you should be asking Paul.' Matt grinned.

'So, lucky me, I've got the next best thing. Fabio has given me a really good facsimile of the Arrezo Chimera.' Anna threw in her limited knowledge of things Etruscan.

'Ah, a marvellous mixture of noble, timid and cunning beast with all their conflicting passions coming together under one roof, so to speak.' Paul was in his element.

'Yes, it's a real enigma.' Anna raised her eyes skyward.

'Why do you say that? It's no more difficult to read than human beings.' Paul shook his head. 'Even you, Anna, cannot be totally as you appear.' The small man peered at her through his thick spectacles, as though they had the ability to see some inner turmoil.

She laughed flippantly. 'Alright, so how do you see me then? Or would I prefer not to know?'

Paul surveyed her quizzically. 'In relation to the chimera do you mean? I think you are the goat.'

'That's as I see her.' Matt turned from the banqueting scene, immediately interested in Paul's present day character reading.

Paul was animated. 'But it's not the whole picture. You appear a gentle creature, but if roused I think you could more than stand up for yourself.'

Matt nodded in agreement. 'I wouldn't like to cross Anna.'

'O, you both make me sound a real horror.'

'Not at all, my dear, life is hard, one has to be able to fight for one's cause.' Paul gave her a friendly pat on the back and turned back to the wall-painting.

So Paul had noted her easily-summoned aggressive side. But Matt's comment? She was piqued, what had she done to merit his outspoken assessment. Suddenly, she'd had enough of the tomb and accompanying dark thoughts.

But Paul was still engrossed. 'Your crazy mixed-up beast, Anna was a favourite with the Etruscans. The chimera was a common offering. There were a lot of goats caught between lion and serpent.

'Scary.' Anna turned to the exit. 'I feel like some fresh air, too much introspection for one morning.'

Out in the midday heat, she climbed thankfully to the top of the mound above the tomb and plonked herself on the springy turf directly above, Matt and Paul still held in the underworld below. She thought of the couple on the couch, only the girl could get back into the world, whilst her lover lay forever in his subterranean prison. She felt an irrational sympathy for those figures trapped for ever in their grief. However homely they had tried to make the tomb, it was a poor substitute for the real world.

'O, there you are. You've had enough too?' Sue sat down beside her, not waiting for an invitation. Assured, immaculate in crease-resistant shorts and sleeveless top, she boasted a youthful

71

figure. Anna at close proximity noted that her arms were firm, Francesca wore sleeves. She could picture Sue in the gym at least three times a week. Again she felt antipathy. They'd hardly exchanged a word, let alone a conversation, since their introduction at the castello the previous day. Why should she hold the gym against the woman? Her own feeling of inertia was not something to applaud.

Anna was tongue-tied. Sue had not been overtly friendly, and up to now Anna had eyed her from the periphery of the group.

'Interesting figures in that tomb. I was wondering how they executed them.'

'O, didn't he just die—'Anna knew at once her gaffe.

'My dear, I meant what method of painting they used for the pictures, so they can still be seen today?'

Anna flushed scarlet at the put-down as the others emerged into the awkward pause and climbed up to join them.

'We are wondering how the figures were painted?' Sue smiled and patted the ground beside her. Peeved, Anna watched both men move to her side. That would please her companion. Somehow, like herself, she knew Sue was not averse to attention. But then Anna had her excuse.

'So, Sue, you see the Etruscans had very much your style of painting, big, bold, colourful.' Matt was enthusiastic. 'And you'd be quite at home with their techniques. They scratched the stucco with sharp nails, plastered on the colour with brushes. The result was bold imaginative work. Just like your canvases.'

Anna hadn't seen Sue's work in years. So now it was bold

72

and imaginative and Matt liked the woman's work. Anna was niggled.

She sat, her knees drawn up under her chin, letting the conversation wash over her, feeling the gate-crasher in a fan-club convention, strangely resentful that Sue had developed a dynamic style. She liked to think that was her prerogative.

'Matt,' her voice was low, but the urgency cut through their talk, like a neglected child interrupting grown-ups.

Hardly daring to move her lips, she said, 'There is a butterfly on the plant beside me.' She prayed hard she wouldn't frighten it away and the sighting be lost, so that instead of praise she got exasperation. She heard Matt's gasp of surprise. The others were silenced by their ignorance. It was delicate, like all butterflies, pale fluttering wings beating the noon air. To the rest of them it meant little, to Matt it was something else.

He whispered, 'It's a Two Tailed Pasha.' His voice held a reverence that impressed, even if the name had no significance for the rest of them. 'It's only the second one I've ever seen, and certainly never this far west in Italy. Thank you, Anna. I would have missed it. Seeing this Pasha has made my day.'

She basked in her moment of glory and watched as the butterfly rose into the air. Free to fly away, but caught in a collector's memory. They were all free to move but no one did. Anna said, 'Its flight to freedom is in contrast to the imprisoned world we saw below in the tomb.' She shuddered.

Paul shrugged his shoulders. 'Don't worry, my dear, death was no big deal for them as they believed in life after death. That's why they buried their dead furnished with everything needed for the afterlife: food, drink, clothing, ornaments and weapons.' He placed his hands together, as though in prayer. 'So, just remember, folks, when my time comes, make sure I get all those necessities. And don't forget to provide the couch and a beautiful girl, sitting pliant beside me.'

On the way home they picked up Fabio in the nearby town. He'd had business there, excusing himself from the tombs visit, but had asked for a lift back. Fabio carried a bundle and Anna wondered if it were artwork for his Venice Salon or a birthday present for Francesca. The great day was getting nearer and she was as yet empty-handed.

SIX

FRANCESCA

Francesca had the castello to herself; Catarina hovered in the background, but then she was part of the stonework. Their guests had gone on the tourist trail to see the Tarquinia tomb paintings, Francesca left the sole occupier of her world.

She'd not seen the minibus go at the crack of dawn, but she'd heard it as it disappeared down the track below her window, and the sound was like music to her ears. She had the next few hours to herself, without any compunction to please anyone, other than herself. Yet she was strangely unsettled. In the short time, she'd become used to having the others around. Illogically, today she'd rather have not been alone. Empty hours stretched before her. She could suggest to Catarina that they shared an early lunch under the walnut tree. The Italian would think she'd taken leave of her senses, and perhaps she had. She had never sought company, not when the alternative was undemanding seclusion.

Thoughts chased around in her head, conflicting ones that gave warning noises. The mural in the baptistery was an unimagined surprise. It was a complication, meaning she would displease either Catarina or Fabio; the two who had been behind the plans for her forty-ninth birthday celebrations. She had gone along with them. Bullied was perhaps too strong a word. Now, when she finally made up her mind about the mural, it would sow discord. She could discuss it now with her housekeeper, but she'd never liked confrontation, and the excitable Catarina held strong views; life-long catholic belief. And Fabio was as obsessed as Paul with all things Etruscan.

Francesca descended her tower steps to the *contadina*, the vast old kitchen. Catarina was nowhere to be seen. Unsettled, she returned to the hall, to the *madia*, the huge old wooden chest used originally in the castello's bread making. Now it was filled with bottles of water. The store was used to replenish bedroom fridges. Between them they had thought of everything for the comfort of their guests. No need to provide a complaint form for their visitors to fill in at the end of their stay.

Beside the chest, an old coat rack, free standing, going nowhere, held three languid straw hats waiting for heads. A pile of polished waist-high sticks idled against the wall, like day labourers waiting for hire. They would wait in vain, there would be no takers. There was silence and then she heard a gentle murmur. It wasn't the bees, for they were deep down in the valley, but Catarina and Rita preparing lunch. Francesca sought them out, glad of their comforting hum. The smaller kitchen was dark and intimate in its busy domestic scene. The two women exchanged their gossip and pulped peaches into the cold waiting tea. The pale liquid was burnt umber, as if it had gushed from the land. They smiled but did not stop: what they did was more important than gossip. A large pile of cannelloni beans awaited their shelling. Smiling, Francesca acknowledged the women with a wave of her hand. She went out into the morning heat, armed with her bottled water, sun hat and walking stick. Their

76

inconsequential murmur faded into the stones. She heard them laugh but it didn't offend. Theirs was optimism and humour in abundance, and she felt a rise in spirits.

There was a bench under the walnut tree. The great bending branches afforded almost complete shade from the morning sun, and would do so all through the day as the sun moved westward. The tree was like a giant floppy hat to fit any sized head. But today Francesca needed to walk. She had donned one of the wavy straw hats from the hall stand, essential for braving the outside heat. Catarina used one when she went into the garden, or Rita when she raided the basil pots. Now it was her turn. She could not remember when last she had one on her head. It fitted loosely above her hair, light and shady, and if she looked up through the brim, she could see a square patterned sky.

The hill above the castello was steep. The oak stick, fashioned expertly by Riccardo the gardener, aided her ascent. She stopped for breath, but looked upward, not behind. Francesca knew well the view of her home was breathtaking. She would savour it on her return. Today, she felt the impulse to turn her back on her confined world, above, the forest beckoned. She climbed again, stopped and glanced back, furtively, at the view spread below. In the valley, regular groups of umbrella pines, introduced by the Romans, were tell-tale signs of habitation. In the fields, tiny white dots moved in a long straight line: not random like the South Down sheep around her childhood home in England. These local sheep had long legs and pointed faces and were kept for milk. Yet now it was these animals that were part of her everyday life; the English crossbreeds, unfamiliar.

She reached the trees. Oak and holm oak and alder merged in ancient confusion to form an overhead twisted canopy. She stopped and glanced over her shoulder like a latter-day Lot's wife, back to the reassurance of her home now diminished from this high viewpoint, yet its honey coloured stone still shouted its presence. It had been there for ever, built on a pilgrim route, offering succour to the medieval traveller. What had it got in return? The isolated community exacted news and stories that widened their lives, just as she awaited Paul's return or Fabio from Venice. Their stories enlarged her world. Especially Fabio, who brought with him a different girl every time: castle cat with captured mouse, dropped, teased, caught again. He played, then quickly lost interest, like a child wanting a new toy. Perhaps, this time Anna would be different. Yet he had had little time for her since the first evening, even though he appeared pleased with this choice. How clever of him to find an artist for this special visit. She thought of Anna and smiled. Drawn to this girl, for once she had shown it. Would it make Fabio resentful?

It was cool amongst the trees. One could forget the heat of jealousy under this protecting parasol. The leaves of the oak had started to fall, and they carpeted the hard ground. Filtering sunlight made a jazzy pattern, circling and spiralling in random design. No repeat motif here, but scattered leaves, twigs and branches, and animal droppings. Evidence that other feet had trod this way; the wild boar had been here before her. In addition there were strange, long cylindrical shapes strung out along the track. Caught in the

78

dried mud ridges, they looked like route markers. She halted and gingerly picked one up. Its point was sharp. Menace for the unguarded, porcupine quills held deadly poison. She had never seen so many, the animal must surely have been killed, or at least badly injured. But who could be the predator? The dried tracks disappeared off into the trees. Some vehicle had been up here and caught its victim; no nobility of chase here between hunter and hunted. Francesca eyed the tell-tale signs. Why would a vehicle venture up so deep into the forest?

A noise in the undergrowth broke her reverie and immediately she felt the fear of the hunted, instant and knowing. Had she cornered the injured porcupine? She turned to run, but it was neither animal nor hunter who blocked her path.

'Oh, am I glad it's you' She laughed with relief as the quizzical face of Greg Pearson peered out from the bushes.

'Ditto. This wood seems to be filled with wild animals. The animal droppings are huge. Can't possibly imagine what has produced them.'

'The wild boar. Quite impressive isn't it, which can't be said about our topic of conversation?' She sounded prudish, words and tone.

'How are you, Fran? We haven't had much of a chance to talk.' He indicated a large fallen tree trunk, and they sat side by side.

'You've been avoiding me, Greg, that's the simple answer.' Her forced laughter echoed his. 'Still the same old Greg, aren't you? Still, you're safe now. Sue is out of harm's way, off in the minibus hunting Etruscan culture, if only for her photograph album.'

Greg smiled ruefully, and as if to confirm the truth of her words, leant over and planted a light kiss on her forehead. She drew away from him, feeling his proximity as keenly as if the years had never been.

'Romeo, Greg, they called you. Quite a hit with us girls.'

'Quite a name to fill. I wasn't as bad as that, was I?'

'Probably worse.'

'Come off it, Fran, you never included yourself in all of that.'

'All of what?'

'The harmless student flirting!' Greg smiled, a hint of embarrassment colouring his face.

'How little you knew me.'

He looked at her and sighed. 'You were too nice to hurt, much too vulnerable. Not like Sue, who had the skin of a—'

'Was hurt the inevitable result?'

'I early vowed to plough the lonely furrow.' His face was a blank canvas. Was there a hint of regret in his voice? She turned away from him, picking the bark from the tree trunk in quick angry scalping. Harmful desecration, if the chestnut hadn't already been dead.

'Francesca. There was good reason. Good reason why I could never commit to family life.'

Silence. She waited for the explanation from the middle-aged man for his misspent youth. The reason, for why the handsome, charming Greg Pearson had ruined her life. Her thumb nail caught a resistant piece of bark and she imagined she could hear the break. A

80

dark line of dirt was now embedded in her manicured fingers. She stabbed at the intrusion. Even now he could leave his mark. For the flippancy of youth read mature indifference?

She looked at him through lowered eyelashes. Already his short time at the castello had worked its magic, the gaunt paleness changed now to the bronzed fine-boned face she so well remembered. His long artistic fingers looked as though they could wield a woodman's axe as easily as any sable brush. She closed her eyes. His voice hadn't changed and it had the same effect on her. How could they be sitting here now as though nothing had happened?

'Why didn't you go on the trip with the others?' Her voice held the same chiding, childish pique.

'I did intend to but then, at the last minute, I just fancied my own company. Sorry, I didn't mean that. I'm glad we've met. I had forgotten how much I enjoy being with you.'

She laughed. He sounded convincing, then he always did. She'd not ask him why he'd come here. Was it to be with Sue?

'Do you know anything about wild boar?' It was an innocuous subject. Anything to keep covered her memories, as thinly concealed as the first forest leaf-fall of the year.

'No—tell me all about your Tuscan wild boar. You're a good raconteur. I remember us discussing the god Pan so that I ended up actually sensing his presence in that house.'

So he remembered. No time lapse could eclipse for her that madness, that insanity.

- - - - - - - - - -- -- -- -- - - - - - - - - -- - - -- -- - - - - - - - - - - - -

It's a shared conspiracy, trespassing like thieves into the House of Pan. But, our youthful feet violate no ordinary house; it's as though we can hear the very pipes of the God, and they lead us on. We are running as we reach the verandah and the verdant green door. Greg turns the handle and the door swings open.

'It's like stepping straight into a fairy tale.' Greg laughs out loud as we gaze at the Goldilocks interior. Table and benches, though there are no half-empty bowls.

'Did you hear Sue say the house must have literally sprung out of the ground?' He sounds impressed. 'Surprisingly poetic from down-to-earth Sue Simpson.'

'Yes, it's as though the wooden staves are rooted deep down into the forest underworld.' Frances is not to be outdone.

'Lucky devil whoever is the owner. It must be a holiday retreat, no one can possibly live here.' Greg is back down to earth, unlike Frances.

She says breathlessly, 'I can't even try to picture the real inmates, can you?'

A narrow plank stair leads up into the eaves. She steps on to the first rung but Greg puts out a restraining hand.

'Perhaps the three bears are still in their beds.'

'But the Pan pipes are calling us up, can't you hear them?'

'No, but then you are the nymph, I'm just a mere mortal.' He takes hold of her hand. 'I don't think we should trespass any further, any moment I expect the wicked fairy, or the three bears to return home and find us.' Greg is now grinning from ear to ear. 'What do you think our punishment will be? Sue not speaking to us *for a week?' He's enjoying himself. 'Oh, well, who minds her?' But it's obvious he does. 'We'd better go, nymph, but we can return. Tonight the three bears will surely be out foraging in the forest.'*

'So you've got wild boar in your wood? but no three bears alas.' His eyes laughed down at her. His memory was as good as hers. Only the interpretation of the story was different, depending on the teller.

'No bears. But the boar are almost as dangerous. They can be quite ferocious if cornered.'

'Who couldn't?'

'We have frequent boar hunts in the forest. They're exciting, but can be gruesome. I remember one chase in particular; the cornered sow turned nasty, caught one of the hunting dogs on its tusks and ripped open its stomach. I can hear the scream, see the blood even now.'

'Then perhaps we should change the subject.'

She laughed, 'Surprisingly, the story had a happy ending. A vet in the party linked a piece of pasta into the stomach, until he could get the dog to the operating table: it was probably *cannelloni*.'

'I like it. It's believable here in Italy. In England that story would stretch credulity.'

'Of course it sounds right here. This is a country of happy endings.'

'Do you know, Fran, I think you could be right.' He caught hold of her hand. 'It's never too late, I'm different from my irresponsible youth, you'll see.'

Francesca got to her feet, momentarily steadying herself on

the nearest branch. She looked down at him and smiled. If he had changed then so had she. It would be harder this time for him to impress her. But there was time to show his intent.

She walked away, back on the path she had come along, retracing her steps on the animal track. Soon she was lost. She stopped and there ahead was a glimmer of sunlight. She broke cover, unprepared for the potent light of the heat-filled day out beyond the forest. She blinked like a released prisoner. Turner, the artist, had locked himself in his cellar for three days so when he emerged he could experience the true intensity of light. And now Francesca had the same sensation. A moment of blindness and then, like the great landscape painter himself, she had new eyes. The castello and its landscape lay before her, bathed in its noon spotlight. She stood in the rutted track and fixed her eyes on her converted home, the highlighted subject on a revealing canvas. It was as though lemon yellow, Naples yellow and white paint had been squeezed from their tubes. She stood, remembering the other time when she had emerged from a wood, dazed and besotted by fellow student Greg. Then the dark October afternoon had been as bright as summer. Now, the days ahead were full of promise.

SEVEN

ANNA

The minibus made good time home, Matt driving and navigator as well, though Fabio, sitting beside him, could be consulted at any point of indecision. Anna sat between Paul and Sue on the back seat. She disliked the close contact, but there was no room to move away. Their conversation flowed around her and she was content to listen.

Her first sight of Etruscan art had left her intrigued, and her two close companions were more than knowledgeable, discussing the wonders of the Etruscan exhibits in the Museo Julio in Rome. Matt was listening from the front.

'But what about Volterra? Who was it that said, "Envy not the man who can walk through Volterra Museum without feeling a tear rise in his eye"? Was it D.H.Lawrence?' He turned his head and Anna looked away. His lack of attention was nerve racking on the winding roads.

'No, it wasn't Lawrence, but he did like the Museum, you're right, Matt. He said he got more pleasure from its Etruscan ash chests than he did the Parthenon frieze.' Paul was positively beaming at the captive audience: more than happy to discuss his lifelong passion. Anna found herself wondering what would have filled his life if he hadn't found the Etruscans for soul mates.

'So I presume ash chests were for the dead?' Anna joined in.

'Their final resting place. Look out Grant, or we might all

need one sooner than we think.' Matt's driving was likewise concerning Paul. Once back on the right side of the road, Paul continued his tutoring. 'You know it was the Etruscans not the Greeks who first gave men and women serpent legs and wings. They could see what a mixed up lot we humans are.'

'You speak for yourself, Bradley.' Fabio, without turning his head, made his contribution to the back-seat conversation. Anna hoped, if Matt had any other comment to make, he would follow the Italian's example.

'We've already had a similar conversation back at the tomb.' Matt laughed over his shoulder. 'Paul was assessing our characters and I have to tell you Anna came out of it rather badly. Didn't you?' This time he turned his head and gave her a huge wink. Her answering smile was feeble. It was good to see Matt so laid back, but not when hairpin bends were involved. Still, the conspiratorial gesture pleased her, perhaps now he had accepted her presence at the castello. Sometime she would ask the reason for his initial reluctance.

Fabio's eyes were fixed on the road ahead. 'So what problems do you have with Anna, Paul?'

'None at all. I like her a lot.'

'That wasn't what you said.' Matt was in stirring mood. Was he trying to make the journey home less boring or was he trying to be difficult? Anna was back wondering what his real attitude to her was.

Sue sought to defuse the discussion. 'We're all complex characters, aren't we? Don't start on me, Paul. I already know you can list my faults.'

'Look, all I said was that Anna could stand up for herself, even though her slight frame belies her ability to do so. What is wrong with that?'

Fabio said over his shoulder, 'So do any of you know Anna's reason for coming to the castello?'

'O, come on, Fabio,' protested Anna. 'You practically got down on your bended knee outside the Palazzo Grassi.' She was strident.

'Oh no, you invited yourself, if you remember? When we were at Torcello. At the time, I thought it was because you found me irresistible'. He did not have to turn round for her to see the smirk on his face.

'Then I don't think much of her taste.' Matt kept his eyes on the road, manoeuvred an almost impossible corner and the last few miles were completed in silence. They were all ready for their very late lunch.

At the castello, they piled out of the minibus. It was good to be back. The warmth of the place welcomed them, vivid passion fruit orange vying with the intense red of the geraniums in their terracotta pots. The colour was almost suffocating. Like their group's colourful characters, now returned to the claustrophobia of Francesca's home.

Anna needed to be alone. She'd help herself to some food from the buffet and then go off to a quiet spot. Under the walnut tree looked inviting; there she wouldn't need to inflict her company on any of the others. Had the former convent inmates got on each other's nerves? If so, there was not much chance for this little group. By no stretch of the imagination could they be mistaken for saints.

'See those geraniums.' Paul pointed to the splash of colour in the pots about their feet. Still his pedantic self in spite of the long morning. 'They are also chimeras. Two genetically distinct tissues, one growing inside the other. Hence the variegated leaves.'

Matt sighed, 'Are you trying to tell us that we're surrounded by mixed up plants as well as everything else?' His voice was a mixture of amusement and exasperation, but his feet were already heading in the direction of the lunch terrace. Anna looked at him disappearing in a cloud of dust and thought he was the only normal one; every group should have a Matt. She was not so sure about intense Paul, but she fell behind to walk with the older man. She couldn't just leave him talking to himself.

'Of course, they're complex.' Paul went on, 'That geranium is a composite of two plants. One has chlorophyll in it, which gives the green in the leaf, the other doesn't. It's like a green finger in a white glove.' Satisfied he had made his point, they walked companionably to the terrace.

Anna, impressed, said, 'I'm beginning to think there isn't much you don't know,' and thought, he isn't boring at all. If the man like the geranium was complex, then that could be levelled at her. Of course Paul had been around long enough to know what made him tick. She still had some way to go to fathom herself out.

'Well, I could do with a cold beer.' Paul was back in the real world, deftly removing the top from the iced bottle and pouring the umber liquid into a pint glass.

The Chianti Classico looked inviting, deep red tending to garnet, old and venerable, a perfect mixture, just like the geraniums. But Anna chose a bottle of ice cold water. She helped herself to a large bowl of salad, rich colours of ripe purple figs, pink prosciutto and ruby-toned radicchio, with the crunch of fennel and a sprinkling of mint. She felt inordinately hungry. She took a hunk of fresh homemade bread and a delicious looking mix of beans. Sue had taken a delicate helping of green salad and found a seat on the terrace. She smiled at Anna. But Anna beat a hasty retreat. Strange how little things had begun to grate. Certainly she had no desire to be pleasant to Sue or Fabio at this precise moment. How could he distort the truth about her presence at the castello, putting her in a bad light with the others?

She headed straight for the shade of the walnut tree. '*Do not pursue*' was obvious for all to read from her erect back and purposeful strides, and thankfully she heard no following footsteps. So intent was she on the plates and glass in her hands, that she reached her destination to find she had been beaten to it. Someone had already sought the tree's seclusion and, embarrassed, Anna saw it was Francesca. Her apology was stuttered, Francesca's wish for solitude obvious to them all.

'I'm so sorry, I didn't see you under the tree.' She looked back at the terrace. Fabio, sipping his wine, was gazing intently in their direction, waiting no doubt to enjoy the sight of her ignominious retreat? Anna turned her back on him.

Francesca was smiling. 'Please stay, Anna. How did you like the tombs?'

Awkwardly, Anna placed her plate on the ground and took the place beside her hostess. She was pleased that Francesca actually appeared to welcome the interruption, and relieved they already had a topic of conversation. The last thing she wanted was long awkward silences.

'Ferragosta, the feast of the Assumption on August the fifteenth usually brings change to the weather. This year was different.' Francesca's voice was earnest, not waiting for Anna's opinion on the Etruscan Tombs. 'Everything is cyclical or it should be.' Her words were staccato, and Anna stole a sideways glance at her. The woman was distracted; her face a busy sky with scurrying clouds.

'O, so it's hotter than normal?' Did she really want to talk about the weather? Surprised that Francesca took heed of saints days.

'What? Oh, yes. It is quite airless; I think we could be in for a storm.' Francesca wiped her forehead once and then repeated the action. Her skin was clear and any perspiration illusory, but her hand removed the wisps of hair that fell untidily about her face. In the heat, Anna had already scraped her hair back in a tight bun.

There was a faint stirring in the walnut tree and a sudden breeze eddied the dust about their feet. Perhaps Francesca was right about the storm. To her it seemed a perfect day, but Francesca had lived at the castello long enough to read the signs. Besides, a storm might clear the air: it could be just what was needed. There was a definite tetchiness about the group, and not just between Fabio and herself. It would be less than gracious to fall out so early in their stay in Francesca's idyllic home. She vowed to make a concerted effort to be nice to Fabio, especially as he seemed to think she owed her place at the castello to him. Then of course she did. It would have been impossible to have got here without him. But why had he asked her? He'd hardly recognised her existence since their arrival.

'Have you had a good morning without us all under your feet?' Anna smiled.

'O yes, but you haven't replied to my question. What do you think of Etruscan art?' Then before the girl could answer, 'Greg says he doesn't like it, too stark, too dramatic. Funny, I always think of his style as just that. Perhaps even his ideas on art are changing with age.'

Francesca fell silent and Anna said nothing; Francesca could not really be interested in her view of Etruscan art. Already the woman was being pummelled on all sides by differing opinions. Yet at the end of the day, Francesca would do exactly what she wanted. Why not? It was her birthday present and her baptistery wall.

'Anna, you must have some opinion on what you saw this morning. I defy anyone not to be moved by it.' Francesca's tone was urgent.

So she does care. 'Yes, it's so colourful, so full of movement, so atmospheric, and in the end, so very sad.'

Francesca seized the girl's hand. 'Yes, it's sad alright and rather unsettling. It makes me realize how helpless we are against fate.'

'Do you really believe that?'

'Don't you feel it?' Francesca still had hold of her hand.

'Anna, you must believe in fate, it was what brought you here.'

Anna eyed her companion. 'I don't much go along with that sort of thing.' She was intrigued. 'After all, do I really want to believe fate dealt me a poor hand from the very beginning?' She took a long drink of her water. 'No, I'm optimistic in spite of all that, I definitely believe I control my own destiny.'

'It's easy to believe that when you're young. But I've spent half a lifetime knowing I wasn't dealt a hand of trumps.'

Anna lowered her gaze. On the surface Francesca appeared to have everything, yet she did not appear content. Why had the woman shut herself away? She herself would never have confined herself in such a narrow world. She began to gather up the dishes and put them onto the tray. The terrace was empty, the others had disappeared.

'Don't go.' Francesca put out a restraining hand. 'Perhaps you still have choice.'

Anna forced a smile. 'I would hope so,' and she paused. 'I admitted to you when we first met that my mother had abandoned me. I often wonder if my mother considered the options. Did she live to regret her action? I would love to—' What an outburst; her companion's vulnerability had brought her own doubts, embarrassingly, out into the open. 'Sorry, I shouldn't have said all that.'

'Why not?' The older woman's face softened. 'I began the soul searching. I live in my own little world; it's good to be reminded there are others.' Her hazel eyes smiled encouragement.

'Do you know anything of your mother? She must have

been distraught when she did it.' Her voice shook when she then added, 'I—it is terrible to lose a child.' Her eyes filled with tears. 'You know I would have liked you for a daughter, Anna .I think we are alike.' She wiped her cheek, straightened her skirt and rose from the bench. Anna was surprised to note she had made a positive effort with her appearance. Instead of the flowing black that usually hid her frame, she was dressed in soft mauve, and it suited her. A soft pink tinged her usual pale cheeks.

Anna watched her cross the scorched grass in her out-of-place high-heeled sandals.

Fabio was waiting for Francesca by the terrace, their exchange brief, and then he was striding out towards Anna over the baked earth towards the walnut tree. Anna sighed, forced to wait and take whatever his mood had to offer, but he was smiling and she grinned back at him, in relief. She'd had quite enough soul searching for one day.

But Fabio wasn't one to wear his heart on his sleeve, making it hard to know what he thought. Reluctantly, she indicated the bench, but he shook his head and put out his hands to raise her to her feet. 'It's time for you to escape the castle, I think.'

'Escape? but I love it here.'

'That is obvious.'

'So where are we going? I could do with some retail therapy. I think I should buy Francesca a present.'

'There's no need. Our mural will be more than adequate.' Fabio was dismissive.

'I would still like to get something small.'

'First things first I think.'

'What's more important?'

'You'll see.' He kept hold of her hand as they retraced Francesca's footsteps, but instead of retreating into the dark coolness of the castello, they walked to Fabio's car which was parked in the full heat of the afternoon. The mini-bus stood beside it, Matt busy tinkering under the bonnet. He looked hot and bothered.

'Mad dogs and—' Fabio did not complete the saying and Matt gave no indication he had heard. Anna climbed into the car. Fabio could be very annoying. He must have read her thoughts for, as he bent to kiss her fleetingly on the cheek, he complimented, 'And you are quite the English Rose today.'

'Be careful of the aphids,' Matt called. He wiped his grubby hands on an equally dirty, oily rag and watched them drive out of sight.

EIGHT

FRANCESCA

Was the girl happy here? Had the others accepted this unsure girl with feisty overtones? How she had enjoyed sharing confidences with her young guest: at last, refreshingly uninhibited with her hostess. The vulnerable girl reminded her of another impressionable ingénue of twenty years before.

What did Anna make of them all? What of the morning trip, ancient tomb and Paul on his hobbyhorse? In some ways Anna was old for her years. Even so, a great gap yawned between her and stuffed-shirt Paul. The girl's smile was less ready than on her first evening. Did she find the castello oppressive? Except for Fabio and Matt they were old enough to be her parents.

Deep in thought, Francesca almost collided with Fabio as she reached the herb path below the terrace. She stopped in her tracks, a loud exclamation of surprise echoed by her adopted son. As she put out her hand to steady herself, he caught her arm to save her from falling. How inappropriate on the parched earth were her designer sandals. Sharp spikes of dry grass had pierced her bare heels, chastising her foolishness. Had Anna noticed her ridiculous footwear? Probably, the girl hadn't looked directly at her throughout their tryst.

A few terse words, then she watched Fabio, hand in hand with Anna, walk to his car for their escape from the castello. That was how he would view the visit she had suggested. More and more he was moving away from her, she knew that. And to fuel her doubts was her night's dream, vividly brought back at the sight of Fabio on the path. The night terrors had lingered with her, potent as the reality of day.

As dawn had come through her window she'd had a dream so compelling she'd been startled awake, bathed in sweat. She'd opened the shutters to let in the light, but to little effect. The somnolent countryside slept under a white veil of mist: known contours, yet the hills were blurred. On such a morning, like her jumbled thoughts, nothing was defined except for the long white serpent river that slithered in its valley, a tell tale feature in an obscured world.

The night image was with her and she shuddered. To dream of snakes was a foreboding of evil. In the cold light of day she relived the nightmare, struggling to make half sense of it.

The snake had emerged from thick foliage; she had stepped aside and it had slithered past her. But when she'd returned along the same path, she saw it approaching her again, and this time it was growing in size. Now it was enormous. She had fought it long and hard, and only with difficulty had she escaped its venom.

Now she stood on the very spot where she thought she'd seen the monster serpent. Did her beloved home harbour a hidden viper? No, it could not possibly be. The vegetation here struggled, the foliage in the dream much more the prolific greenery of England. Did her nightmare warn of trouble ahead from her newly arrived guests? She relived her sensation of terror. It had threatened malice long after the menace had passed. Perhaps the path was one she had not yet trod? She had almost told Anna of the visitation, but the girl would have questioned her sanity. She had not told Greg.

She could have confessed it to Fabio, as he pulled her on to the rosemary path. His size hadn't altered. How foolish even to consider him, the person who meant most to her in the world, though she sometimes wondered about his feelings for her. But his smile showed him in good mood: he'd even got time for small talk. Not something he indulged in very often.

'Have you had a good lunch, with Anna?'

'I hear you had a profitable visit this morning.' She avoided the allusion to her tete a tete with Anna.

'Yes. The Etruscans lived up to expectations. Anna seemed particularly impressed.' It was half question, half statement; he wanted to know what her conversation with the girl had been all about.

'Take her to San Galgano.' It sounded an order and he took it as such. Without a second's hesitation Fabio had made his way to the girl, still seated under the tree. And again Francesca experienced the sensation of pulling the strings. Yes, long years and distance separated Frances Green, art student, from Francesca, mistress of a Tuscan castello. No dream of snakes was going to unseat her.

From the stifling heat of the early afternoon she entered the calm of her stout walled home, solid, protective and reassuring. She went to the kitchen where she would find her ultimate comfort, Catarina with her peasant sense. For all her outward sophistication, her sojourn in America, she had not moved far from her original country roots. She looked now a picture of cool confidence, unworried by the afternoon heat, only her vibrant hair sultry in the dark interior.

Catarina was surprised by her visitor, but her smile was instant. No more than Francesca would have expected, Catarina had long been her certainty. It was her half day today, but Francesca knew she would still be there checking everything was in place, before she left Rita in charge. The cook was able, but there would be no entertaining translation of the menu in the courtyard this evening. Catarina's absence would be felt. Francesca knew she herself was a poor substitute at reading out the wine list that Catarina had chosen to accompany the dinner.

Now, Francesca made the list her excuse for invading the Italian's domain. 'Do you have any instructions for dinner that you want me to pass on to our guests? It's time you were off home.'

'Thank you, Francesca. That is kind of you. I would have brought the list to you.'

'I know that.' The silence hung between them.

'I would have hurried if I had thought you were waiting for it.' Catarina was concerned.

'No-no.' Then, 'I met Fabio on the rosemary path. Has he been in here?' Still she could not let go of her dream.

'Yes.' Catarina smiled, but did not elaborate.

'The Etruscan tombs obviously appealed to the party.'

Catarina didn't reply and Francesca knew by the set of her mouth that a retort was on her lips, but would not express it; strange for the usually voluble Catarina. Normally, open and spontaneous, it was obvious Catarina knew she would say too much if pressed.

She was busying herself now, but doing nothing. Her plans were already detailed for the day, nothing ever left to chance. If something did go wrong during her absence, it would be someone else's fault. Francesca surveyed the trim, slight figure that held so well her large personality. She was like a brimming flagon of wine, yet somehow there was no wasteful overflow. Standing close beside her, Francesca instinctively placed her companion on her serpent path. They were abreast, but the Italian did not grow into some unseemly creature. Rather, Francesca felt Catarina's steady gaze diminishing herself. Catarina could read her thoughts?

'Catarina, one more task before you go.'

'What is it? Have I forgotten something?' She was surprised, for she shared Francesca's confidence in her ability.

'You know about dreams?'

'Of course.' Ah, as expected, here was just the person to explain away her baseless fears.

Francesca smiled at her trustworthy friend. 'I had a dream last night. It was surprisingly v-vivid...' The housekeeper waited. 'I—I dreamed I met a snake.'

'Ah.' Catarina had a drying cloth in her hand; she did not wait to put it down. She did a hurried sign of the cross. 'They are evil.'

'I guessed that.' Francesca frowned, she'd not wanted her fears confirmed quite so emphatically.

'What was it doing?' Catarina was involved, in spite of herself.

'I was walking along a path and a serpent appeared, then, as I walked back, it reappeared. It grew into an enormous monster.' Put into words, it sounded foolish. 'Oh, forget it. My imagination is working overtime.'

'O, but it's a common dream.' Catarina hung the cloth slowly and deliberately back on the hook on the door. 'Did you lose sight of it?'

'Yes, it disappeared.'

'It has gone. But from now on you will remember. You will wonder when it will return.' She paused. 'It warns that you are being disobeyed, that there are forces gathering against you.'

The kitchen was oppressive, as though an oven had come up to temperature yet no switch had been pressed. Catarina was back to looking unruffled, but Francesca could feel a deep flush stain her cheeks.

It was just a few steps through the arch, across the courtyard and to the refuge she needed. Sue was waiting at the base of the tower, on the fourth step, looking down at her hostess, a sentinel obstructing Francesca's way. Dismayed, Francesca squinted into the intense sunlight striking the travertine blocks of her sanctuary; emerging from the day-dark confines of the castle, she was temporarily disadvantaged. Sue looked giant-sized; shaken by Catarina's dream reading, emotions raw edged, Francesca halted in her tracks.

'Sue, you gave me quite a shock. I wasn't expecting to see you.' She refrained from saying you're the one I least want to talk to at this moment. She hadn't spoken to Sue alone since her arrival. It seemed a long time ago, but in reality was only two days.

'Fran. At last! I knew I would catch you sooner or later.' Her voice was casual but Francesca heard the almost imperceptible emphasis on the word *catch*, though a smile played around Sue's lips. Francesca forced herself to smile back, though doubting it looked any more genuine than that of the woman herself. She knew that smile from of old.

'We haven't had a chance to catch up.' Slowly Sue descended to courtyard level and only then did she return to being smaller than her hostess. They stood awkwardly, already having said all they had to say to each other.

As always, clever Sue found the safe ground. 'You've no idea how lovely it is to be back in the restored castello. It's even better than the brochure. On paper you don't get the smell of herbs, the tangible warmth of the stone and of course the wonderful food. What a combination Catarina and Rita make. Last night in the baptistery was the ultimate experience. You have a gem in Catarina.'

'Yes' Then childishly Francesca added, 'Of course, it's I who have worked hard to make Chiesa a Castello such a success.'

'Oh, of course, Fran. It is obviously your baby.' The tone was calculated, vindictive. The past and present kept them enemies. Francesca clasped her hands together. How far had she climbed Francesca's steps? though a locked door would have spoilt any intended invasion of her privacy. She'd been thwarted and Sue was never pleasant when she failed to get what she wanted. Why had she come? What did she want? Was it still Greg, or did she just play with the toy of the moment?

She produced her camera from behind her back. 'I've been taking some photographs. On long winter evenings it will be nice for Greg and me to reminisce about your castle, hidden away in the middle of nowhere. Though in winter I can imagine even a castle in Tuscany isn't that much fun.'

Francesca stepped aside to let her pass. She watched her out of the courtyard. She had no need to watch if Sue would return, grown to monster size. How could this woman seriously be part of her celebrations?

NINE

ANNA

Anna looked back over her shoulder; Chiesa a Castello stood impregnable and safe yet she had opted to leave its protective walls.

'Thanks, Fabio, I need to get away. The place is beginning to get claustrophobic. It might have Etruscan beginnings but it feels more like the convent to me.'

Fabio smiled; an attractive smile, rationed it looked sincere. 'So are you saying you want to throw off your nun's habit—yes?'

'I'm ready to let my hair down, as the saying goes.'

'Then there is no knowing what I might expect.' His smile had become a grin.

'Try me,' and she fluttered her eyelashes. 'So what dastardly plan do you have in mind?'

'Can you not guess?'

'No, should I be able to?' They were playing cat and mouse again, Fabio's favourite game but he'd chosen the wrong person.

As though he could read her thoughts, he said, 'In English you call it cat and mouse, in Italian we do not have such a good phrase. I think it sums up you and I. You enjoy being in and out of the shadows, and I like to tease.' He looked down at her. 'But sometimes the roles can be reversed?'

'Perhaps by the end of the game we shall have discovered which is which.'

'You mean who will be the winner, who will be the loser?'

'Something like that.'

'It seems I shall have to raise the stakes then.' Fabio was gleeful, ever combative. He liked nothing better than a war of words, English or Italian. She guessed he didn't get one with Francesca.

'I never gamble.' She wagged her finger at him to emphasize the point.

'But you did when you decided to trust a complete stranger? Why? Now that I know you better I am surprised you were not more cir-circumspect.'

She didn't reply. First points to Fabio.

Why indeed had she been prepared to come to an unknown place with someone she had only just met? It had been a lucky break meeting Fabio. If Matt had had his way, she wouldn't be here now. What a killjoy he was.

Fabio's car was low, fast and expensive. She wondered, fleetingly, if it was a gift from a benevolent Francesca. Then she remembered Francesca had told her of Fabio's art gallery in Venice. It must be quite something if it could finance such an expensive plaything. His clothes were expensive too, more than likely purchased in Milan. Francesca seemed to be the most likely source. It was easy to see that she would do anything for the handsome young Italian. He was understandably more than happy to be on the receiving end. According to him, there was always a winner, and he, Fabio, surely fitted the bill. She glanced at his profile, and suddenly it seemed a long time ago when a rain soaked skyline in Venice had been backcloth to his star good looks. Yes, it had been a lucky chance meeting.

She anticipated the afternoon ahead alone with him. It was another hot dry day but a strange light hovered in the west and the atmosphere was oppressive. 'Francesca was saying she thought there might be a storm. If so, your sports car could be exciting. Where are you taking me?'

'Do we have to have a particular place to go? I thought to get away from the rest and spend some time together. You seemed this morning to have had enough of the group. It's understandable.'

'That's very discerning of you. Thanks.'

'Well, we young ones should stick together, the others are the previous generation.'

'Certainly, Francesca thinks of you as her son, along with Matt, another of her 'non-children'?

'I'm the one who matters most.'

'I can understand your 'non-sibling rivalry'.' Anna grinned sympathetically.

Fabio laughed. 'She can have as many imagined children as she likes, but I'm the one who is closest to her.' Fabio glanced into the rear view mirror and smoothed his already immaculate hair. 'It is physically impossible to have two mothers, but I have.'

'Well, that's something we have in common. I had two. One that didn't want to be a mother and one that tried too hard to be.'

'So neither was right?'

'My reply will be 'no' but in all honesty the second one persisted in spite of me.' Anna pulled a face and laughed. 'My second mother always said making faces would give me wrinkles. Again, on reflection, I think perhaps it wasn't unkindly meant. Whatever the poor woman said was taken the wrong way by number one ungrateful daughter.'

'So it's confession time, is it?'

'Yes, Friar Fabio, let me admit to always wanting something just out of reach.'

'That is not bad, I think. One should always strive for the top. I knew that truth by the time I was eight years old. I played my pipes and they brought Francesca. I knew then she was my bread ticket. Is that the right expression?'

'I think it probably is.'

'You sound condemning. I feel no guilt. Francesca needs me as I need her. More so her I think; I have no need of her money. But the castello is different. I love it. One day it will be mine.' His voice was clipped, taut. She wondered if, seeing her under the walnut tree with Francesca, he had felt aggrieved enough to put her in the picture: hence the trip out in the car. Could he really be that jealous? Silence; the mood had sobered again. Why had Fabio invited her to Castello a Chiesa? The meeting appeared opportunistic for them both, and yet—? Perhaps he had fancied her, but she was beginning to doubt that.

'So, Fabio, do you make a habit of stalking the Venice Vaporetta for girls? Do a blonde and a fast car go together in your imaginings?'

'Of course, after antiques they are my main pastime.' With that he slammed on the car brakes. They came to an undignified halt in the middle of the road. He laughed at her consternation, and

106

catching hold of her, kissed her long and hard.

It was a pleasant sensation, Fabio's lips on hers. Taken by surprise, she had mixed emotions. Fabio's attraction was obvious, but above all was the relief they were not on the Autostrada Sud. There was no torn metal, just a spiralling of dust where the roadside verge rose into the already darkening sky. Her surprise was only that he had waited so long.

As they scrambled out of the car, she said flippantly, 'You're wonderful, Fabio. You think of everything. You have even provided the priest.' No other road user was involved but a small stout man stood at gates that opened onto a drive leading up to a church. By the man's garb he was the incumbent.

Fabio, immediately picking up on her joke, laughed. 'Miscusi, padre, siamo in ritardo.' And he moved purposefully towards the onlooker, explaining over his shoulder to Anna, 'I said we are the couple ready for his services.'

'Hey, steady on, I was only joking about our elopement.' Anna giggled.

'So who now is the cat, who the mouse?' And Fabio seized her hand, opened the church gate and nodded again at their witness. She pulled back in exaggerated terror.

'I have you worried, I think.' Fabio winked but let go of her arm. 'Come, Anna, it was Francesca who told me to bring you here, I have no ulterior motive, I assure you.'

Ah, so she had guessed correctly. 'Why did Francesca suggest this venue?'

'Have you forgotten the burning issue of the moment?

Surprisingly enough, it isn't you and me. It's a matter of art. I think she wanted you to see the rival art to the Etruscan, so you could compare both contenders for the baptistery walls.' He shrugged. 'Somehow your opinion matters to her.'

'O, that's nice, it's good to be included.' Did Fabio always do Francesca's bidding? She took hold of his hand and said, 'So I'm safe to walk into the church. There's truly no shot-gun-wedding scenario?'

'No. If it means what I think it does. It's another good English expression.' He squeezed her hand, his good mood obvious. 'Come, you will love the church.'

So they were there only because Fabio was carrying out Francesca's orders. Anna had seen the brief exchange after lunch that had assigned him as escort. It had not been his idea. Had the kiss been his volition or had Francesca ordered that as well? It seemed crazy, but not so strange.

They walked up the tree-lined avenue. It was coolly shaded, the crowded cypress an erect fire-guard shutting out the oppressive heat of the afternoon. At the far end of the avenue, in the illusion of fire from the embers of the sun, stood a glowing building.

'Oh, it's beautiful.'

'The Rotunda of San Galgano, fourteenth century burial place of a young hermit.'

'It's a strange building for a church.' Circular, it looked like an enormous beehive. The sun's rays lit up the top terracotta brick layers, leaving the grey base in shadow. Higher up, the stone sandwiched between rows of brick formed a geometric pattern. On

108

the terracotta tiled roof stood a simple cross.

'It is beautiful,' she said again.

'Wait until you see inside.'

The cupola climbed above them in an ascending spiral, up and up and up, the cool serenity contrasting starkly with the heat outside: incense was added balm.

'The height portrays man rising towards his creator.' Her immaculate Venice guide was back; a role that suited him. 'The circular nature of the building is considered to be the symbol of infinity and perfection. You see it has no angles, and before you try to count them, I will tell you there are forty-eight alternating circles of terracotta and stone.'

'It's awe-inspiring.' Reluctantly, she ceased her gaze heavenward and turned to face Fabio. 'It couldn't be more different from the Etruscan tomb.'

'But it's like an Etruscan tomb; the medieval Christians used the same shape for San Galgano's final resting place.'

'Yes, the Etruscans knew a thing or two. So, is there artwork here, and does it stand comparison?'

'Come to the chapel and see for yourself.'

She followed a purposeful Fabio, wondering what his biased take would be on the Christian alternative.

If the rotunda was beautiful, the chapel had none of its appeal: the adjoining squat building lacked the radiant light of the church. But as her accustoming eyes adjusted to the Gothic addition, she saw what Fabio had brought her to see. The chapel was wall to wall fresco.

She turned to him for help. He would be more than keen to air his knowledge.

'This Maesta is very famous. It's the oldest known example. Centre stage is the enthroned virgin with child, as you would expect, surrounded by angels and saints.' Already, he was the talking guide book. 'But this one is unique because of the two female figures at Mary's feet. The woman with the basket represents practical charity, the woman holding the heart is divine love.'

It was cosy fourteenth century religion and Anna felt its uncomplicated appeal. Her family Sundays had involved the local Anglican church.

'So who's that?' She moved closer to the wall. 'It looks like there's an interloper.' In the very centre of the scene, low down, a strange woman was caught in a beam of light. The Virgin Mary lay in shadow.

'Who's the other woman? She looks modern, as though she has positioned herself there to have her photograph taken, just like any tourist.'

'It's Eve.'

'But she shouldn't be part of the scene.' Anna frowned. 'And everyone else is turned to Mother and child, but she faces in the opposite direction.' Dressed in a simple white dress there was nothing virginal about her. Anna stared at the intruder. 'And what's that round the woman's shoulders?' From her goatskin cloak wriggled a writhing serpent.

'But the intended contrast is obvious. Eve is the cause of original sin and the mother of death, Mary, mother of Christ, is the source of life.' Fabio was strangely involved, but then he was never happier than when comparing black with white.

'So it's a matter of life and death whether you're in medieval Tuscany or Etruscan Etruria. Take your pick.'

'Yes. Francesca has an impossible choice.' He sounded neutral. 'Then, the castello started Etruscan. That fact alone should be more than enough for Francesca.' He scowled for the first time that afternoon.

Anna grinned, 'What about a compromise? We could put Eve in with the Etruscans. She would sort them out.'

'Indeed.' Fabio almost looked as though he liked her idea.

Anna said, 'I have to confess, the more I get to know that ancient lot, the more I like them. I felt really close to the couple in the Tomb of Bulls this morning, I could sense the woman's sadness.' Her gaze was drawn back to Eve, fresh-faced, her hair in long fair plaits, her dress sparkling white. 'Mind, this one does ooze innocence, doesn't she? But how can she be so blameless when they say she was responsible for the sins of the world?'

'We mustn't spoil the baptistery.' Anna and Fabio were standing out on the Hermit's hill, gazing out over the surrounding country, a vast uncomplicated panorama of fields and woods and dotted farmhouses. 'We've got to be very careful with the mural. I see now it's important to make the right decision.' Anna glanced at Fabio. How had this outing helped the conundrum when Francesca herself did not know what she wanted? If she did, she was keeping her cards very close to her chest.

'Fabio, just one more good turn. I see there's a little gift shop. Do you mind if I go and buy some postcards to send home? I won't be five minutes.' She hadn't thought of any of the family for days. How would she ever be able to explain to them this time at the castello. But at least she could let them know where she was.

'Of course.'

'I'll not be long. The weather looks a bit dodgy. Looks like there's a storm brewing.'

'Yes. I'll go down to the car and put up the hood. Take as long as you like. It is quite a spectacle here, the thunder and lightning. You're not worried are you? You will find a Tuscan storm memorable.'

Fabio's long strides soon had him out of sight. She turned back towards the rotunda, the heavy atmosphere combining with her guilt that she hadn't been in touch with her family. It didn't take much to send a postcard, though she was glad she had left her mobile phone at home.

A smiling woman behind the counter welcomed Anna, her sole customer. She looked about her. A few cards and stamps would meet her needs. But she'd forgotten the Catholic love of image. The counter was covered in little plaster figures, naive and utterly appealing. The woman noted the girl's pleasure and picked up the Virgin.

'O no thank you. It's Eve I like.'

'Eve?' The assistant shrugged and turned her attention to a newly arrived group of tourists. Anna, left to her own devices, delved amongst the figures. And there, hidden by a serene Mary, was the confrontational face of Eve. Anna picked her up, and then another and then another. Seven, and she had cleared the display. One of the group would have to do without.

When she got back to the car, Fabio didn't hide his amusement. 'What made you buy her, and why so many?'

'But she's a wonderful example of naive art, so let's say it's my way of trying to influence the rest of the group. She would look wonderful on our baptistery wall.'

'So now it is *our* baptistery?' Fabio raised his eyebrows but it wasn't the appealing gesture of Matt.

She hurried to explain herself. 'I'm totally committed to Francesca's birthday project. I do so want her to love it.'

'Let's face it, Francesca doesn't love anything or anybody, least of all herself.'

'Oh that's nonsense and you know it.'

'Perhaps.'

'And at the end of the day it will be you to whom Francesca listens.'

'Do you think so?' Fabio started the car engine, but not before the first clap of thunder rolled across the sky.

'You mean an awful lot to her. How fortunate for you both that you were playing your pipes in the courtyard the day she found the castello. It was meant.'

'Yes. There is no such thing as chance. The Etruscans knew that and so of course did my family. My parents saw their opportunity as soon as I told them about Francesca and the castello.'

'You mean you were not an orphan?'

113

'No, Francesca bought me from them. She paid good money.'

TEN
FRANCESCA

They sat on the terrace even though the remnants of afternoon tea had long been cleared away. Long gaps in the conversation interspersed by spasmodic talk; Francesca considered if it was because she had joined the party. Her guests would question her sudden sociability, then so did she. Dinner would be soon enough for them to discuss and come to a decision about the mural. Anna could sing the praises of San Galgano. Where had the girl and Fabio got to? They'd be caught in the approaching storm if they didn't hurry?

Those remaining balanced on the edges of their seats. Waiting for what, the storm? The atmosphere had the feel of a doctor's waiting room, only no one's name had been called. Greg was seated beside Sue, his hands idle. Sue was reading, Francesca had the week's menus to go over, and Matt had paper and a 2B pencil and was doing a number of quick sketches. Francesca, glancing over at him, noted he looked hot and out of sorts. He'd spent some time looking at the minibus's engine and had come late for tea. He sipped only occasionally at the stewed brew, his pencil taking his undivided attention. Fidgety Paul was occupied with the heavens, leaning over the terrace rail, gazing skyward and then sweeping the valley in both directions as though he expected a visitation.

For the rest of them the impending storm had had an enervating effect, only Paul couldn't sit still. He walked impatiently up and down in the confined space, glasses off and on, as though they might make some difference to his reading of the weather. Distant rumbles had given early warning; Sue looked up from her book. She caught Francesca's glance and flashed the fleeting smile expected from guest to host. Then back to her novel, a withdrawn disdain hovering still about her lowered face. Sue was transparent if nothing else.

And what of Greg? He and Sue sat side by side without the necessity to talk. There has been no intimation that their paths had crossed only recently after years of no contact. Or so Greg had been at great pains to tell his host. Francesca thought of the animal tracks in the wood, crossing and re-crossing as if tracing all their lives: their separations, occasional sightings before each stumbled on into the dark forest alone once more. Why had Sue brought Greg to her castello? Why involve him in the birthday celebrations? Was she the hunter flaunting her prize? Francesca thought if that woman stands up to go he will follow and the others will automatically leave as well. For now she was staying put; so the others remained.

An angry rumble of thunder and a spluttering of rain on the awning announced both the storm and the return of Anna and Fabio. They appeared, breathless, laughing and exhilarated from their dash to escape the elements; their arrival as noisy as the thunder and as obvious.

'You're just in time. Did you see that flash of lightning?' Paul was triumphant.

116

Sue said, 'For goodness sake, you're like a child, Paul.' She didn't bother to raise her head from the book for the comment, or to greet the new arrivals. The book couldn't be that fascinating.

Paul ignored her. 'That thunder clap shows that the gods are angry.'

Sue groaned, loudly snapping closed her book.

Fabio interrupted, 'The gods are not angry, Paul. There is a much more simple explanation. Here, when it thunders, we say the gods have been eating too many Tuscan beans.' His face was deadpan, but his remark had the desired effect.

'Thank you, Fabio, for lowering the tone,' Francesca reproved but was smiling, grateful for his immediate lightening of the mood. Anna laughed appreciatively, as did Greg; Sue's expression did not change.

Paul looked daggers. 'You should take note, Fabio, you may very well regret not heeding the omen.'

'What could it possibly mean?' Anna was sceptical. Francesca looked at the girl, her outing with Fabio had had the desired effect. Then she knew only too well that the castello could become oppressive, and she did so want the girl to stay. She hoped Fabio would show more interest in her than he had in all the other girls up to now. Oh dear, how trying Paul was becoming.

'The interpretation of divine intent is always shown through signs from the heavens.' Paul was at his most ponderous.

'It might have been for the Etruscans, but not now, no one can possibly believe that.' Anna was dismissive.

Paul ignored her interruption. 'LIBRI FULQULARES was

the interpretation of lightning and its significance. Lightening is caused by clouds colliding.'

'So, we all know that.' Matt was to be counted amongst the sceptics.

'Nature is controlled by the gods. We just have to heed the signs to discover the divine message.' Paul raised his voice. 'If the storm comes from the east, which is the source of life, it is good. But from the west comes only evil.' As he spoke there was a great flash of light along the valley and a cymbal crash of thunder. Instinctively, they all looked westward and Paul turned to face his captive audience in undisguised triumph. 'As you can see, the portent is evil.'

'I'm not going to listen to any more of your insane ramblings, I've got better things to do,' and Sue rose from her chair. 'You're deluded. I'm going out to take some photographs of that colourful sky.' She threw a parting remark at the prophet of doom. 'You never know, Paul, I might catch one of your gods on my camera. That would be a real scoop, and then we might all start believing in your nonsense.'

They watched her go, no one remonstrating that she shouldn't be going out in such a storm. Greg stayed in his seat. Anna and Fabio sat down by the replenished teapot. They were not going anywhere either.

'Well, don't say I haven't warned you,' Paul shouted at Sue's retreating back. 'And I wouldn't shelter under a tree if I were you, or you might find yourself fatally struck down by the displeased deities.'

'O, come on, Paul.' Matt, remarkably restrained up to this point, yawned pointedly. 'We none of us can take you seriously.' He turned to Anna. 'Did you have a good trip?'

'O, yes.' She brightened. 'Do you know the Galgano Rotunda?'

'Yes, Francesca took me there once. How do you like the murals?'

'I love Eve.'

'Eve?' Francesca interrupted. 'What about Mary? She dominates the chapel. I can't say I've ever noticed Eve.'

Matt agreed. 'Yes, Mary was the cult figure in the fourteenth century. Pilgrims used to flock to the shrine to pray for her intercession.'

Francesca nodded. 'Preg…pregnant women came to pray for safe delivery, as did the barren praying for fertili—' She stopped, embarrassed.

Fabio, quiet during the exchange, now looked smug. 'So then, Anna, it is time to give out your presents I think. Have you forgotten the plastic mementoes you so kindly bought for everyone?' His tone was provocative. The girl looked hesitant and he seized the paper bag from her grasp and threw the images on to the table. Paul, not waiting for an invitation, seized one of the replicas.

'If none of you believe in Etruscan portents, how about a medieval message to convince you? Anna has brought no cosy Virgin Mary, but Eve, the progenitor of death.' He wafted the tiny figure in his hand. 'You know Eve would be much more to the

119

ancients liking, she knew that physical forces build the soul and then destroy it.'

Matt unwound his long legs and stood up. 'Well, that's enough nonsense for one afternoon.'

'Aren't you going to take a figure? Anna will be so disappointed.' Fabio was openly enjoying himself.

'Yes,' Anna grinned, picking up an Eve and handing it to him, 'I brought one especially for you, Matt.'

'What a shame she could only get seven, someone will have to do without. The unlucky ones are Catarina or Sue. So there you are, too few keepsakes or are we one too many in the group?' Paul was triumphant.

Francesca sighed, 'Paul, you really are obsessed. I keep reminding you this is no Etruscan week, so there is no need to keep up your ridiculous pretence.'

'I can assure you, Francesca, I am deadly serious.' And Paul stressed the word 'deadly'.

Matt studied the figure resting in his hand with exaggerated interest. 'It's quite sexy. She might have a simple white dress, her long golden hair demurely plaited, but her gaze is definitely provocative.' His good humour, never far away, was restored. 'I bet the artist used his girlfriend as the model. She could be a medieval Catarina. In fact, why didn't I think of it before?' Matt grinned triumphantly. 'Real models are so much more believable. Why don't we capture our group for posterity in the baptistery mural?' Deliberately, he picked up his sketches and tore them in two.

'Well, as long as you don't give us snakes in our hair.'

'What do you mean, Anna?' Francesca's morning dream was still very vivid.

'Haven't you noticed that Eve holds a snake. That coil isn't a continuation of her plait you know.'

Francesca shuddered

But at that moment a monumental clap of thunder echoed above their heads. Sue's blue-cum-black sky had merged with the land, opaque hills and clouds rolling together over and over in giant malignant puffballs, only to be dramatically severed by a fork of lightning. Francesca saw the look of exhilaration on Paul's expressive face and surprisingly it was reflected in the girl's eyes.

'I wouldn't have missed this for anything. It's the best storm ever. I wish I was out in it.'

'You ain't seen nothing yet.' Paul was in his element. 'Nine gods were granted the right to create lightning, so there'll be pyrotechnics well into the night.'

'Paul Bradley, have you ever been told you are a crashing bore?' Greg had joined the anti-Etruscan brigade.

'I'm inclined to agree.' Francesca was trying to contain her rising anger.

'Well, I stand by everything I've said. The gods are telling us something and that something is very obvious. Our group is one too many—and our friend Anna thinks the same, or why only bring seven figures?'

His words were drowned by the rain. It came suddenly and fiercely, cascading on to the awning in Niagara proportions.

'Where's Sue? She'll be drenched, if nothing else.' Greg

121

frowned as they all moved back instinctively to the far wall of the loggia and watched the rain fall in vertical tinsel streams reflecting back the weird light. It seemed any moment the awning would blow inside out like an unmanageable umbrella.

'I hope Sue is alright.' Anna was perturbed, which surprised Francesca. It seemed the girl avoided Sue. But then, she thought the girl probably preferred men's company. From early days she had learnt not to trust the female of the species.

'Perhaps someone should go and look for Sue,' Anna persisted.

Matt sighed, 'Anna, do stop fussing. Sue is old enough to look after herself. Can't you find something to do? It's a long time before dinner.' Equable Matt was beginning to sound impatient again.

'Now, now, children.' Paul was enjoying the contretemps. 'The devil finds work for idle hands you know, so if you don't have anything better to do I could give my acclaimed lecture on the Etruscans.'

'God forbid.' Greg looked horrified and they all laughed, including Paul, as it had the effect of getting the languid Greg out of his seat.

Francesca said hurriedly, 'Anna, how about you entertaining us all?' and as the girl looked blank, 'I'm sure we would all love to watch you paint a self-portrait. Matt tells me you are very gifted.'

'Sorry, Francesca, I think Paul's lecture is a much better bet.'

'Brilliant idea, Francesca. Here's your chance, Anna, to

show the rest of us how it should be done.' Matt was smiling.

Francesca said authoritatively, 'I want to see how a young modern artist works.' And as an afterthought, 'will you be recognisable or not?'

Anna grinned, in spite of herself.

'That's my girl, besides, you'll have a head start over the rest of us. You can use it for the mural.' Matt was animated for the first time that day.

'That's a crying shame. I rather fancied painting Anna myself.' Paul frowned, 'much better if we paint each other in the mural. In fact, I've made a few sketches of her already.'

'Have you indeed? I hope they are fully clothed.' Fabio glowered, and then with an elaborate flourish that none could miss, put a protective arm round the girl and they led the way from the terrace.

'See you in half an hour in the church.' Francesca had raised her voice so all could hear. Greg moved to her side and slipped his arm about her waist. She felt a rush of pleasure. He said, 'I should think Sue is safely back in the castello by now.'

ELEVEN

ANNA

It wasn't just the storm that had excited Anna. Everything about the day had left her in a heady state. She felt a weird mix of emotions as she returned to her room for her paints. Here at the castello she was amongst friends, fellow artists keen to see her work. Eagerly, she grabbed her brushes from the windowsill, the Etruscan chimera still there beside them. It seemed an age since Fabio had given it to her. She had replied by giving him Eve, was that a fair return?

Hurriedly, she assembled the tools of her trade, brushes, a small canvas and a few paints, the colour choice not hard, limited palette marked her pictures. She'd been reluctant to pick up her brushes in the last few weeks but now she was eager to create. She remembered Francesca's words 'Matthew says you are very talented'. His approbation meant a lot.

The group were in the church waiting for her. They had voted with their feet. Any nervousness disappeared when she saw their collected backs ranged in a friendly circle in front of the altar. Matt turned as he heard her feet on the marble floor, and rose to greet her.

'Your master class awaits you.'

'Oh, dear.' With their backs towards her she'd felt confident, but being under their close scrutiny would be something else. They might be friends but she preferred an audience of strangers. The circle was smaller than at first appeared, Catarina no longer in the castello, and where was Sue? Surely not still hunting photographs? Anna was disappointed.

'Let me introduce the college's star pupil.' So Sue missed Matt's introduction.

Polite clapping as she set up her easel. Matt had thought of everything. A mirror, positioned carefully on the redundant altar, reflected back her anxious, red-cheeked face. This could be a disaster. She said, appealing to Matt, 'Couldn't I paint someone else, I'm more used to having someone in front of me?' His blank face made her turn to Francesca. 'I'd really like to paint you.'

'No.' Francesca's response was short and sharp.

'Come on, Anna.' Matt's voice was encouraging. 'I'm fascinated to see how you see yourself. And no holding back, remember our conversation in Venice. No profile, we want the real Anna, so start with the eyes.'

To stop her unsteady hands she took the top off the nearest tube of paint. It felt plump and reassuring, oozing smoothly like a snake slithering over a hot rock. She watched the Naples yellow coil onto the waiting palette, chrome yellow followed; she said apologetically, 'Non artists are always perplexed by the hues for face tone, but of course you know otherwise.'

She peered into the mirror. Her cheeks redder than normal, did she really want to show them her insecurity? She added some magenta, and then two or three other colours. Starting was the hardest part. With the first stroke she felt the tension slipping away, like the storm outside. Already it was a faint murmur in the church, and a distant grumble down in the valley. The gods had digested their beans.

125

'Explain yourself, Grant, what did you mean, you're interested to see how Anna sees herself?' To her relief Fabio broke the silence, preferring that their undivided attention was not fixed on her. Of course, she reflected Fabio was no artist and he'd bore very quickly.

Matt nodded. 'When you paint someone's portrait, you enter the world of that person. So a self-portrait will reveal things about yourself you may not have been fully aware of. That is why I'm interested in what Anna will show. I think I know her. Perhaps I don't.' He'd lost his guarded look; his eyes showed total commitment. She remembered the first time she'd noticed his chocolate brown eyes: in the Venice Trattoria. Then he hadn't shown any inclination to bring her to Francesca's intimate little group. Did he really believe his spoken words of approval? The doubt brought back her unease. She had to restrain the impulse to get up and run out of the chiesa door, and off down the village track.

Greg spoke into the silence: 'That's why I only ever painted one self-portrait, it ended up as me looking the mirror image of my father.' Greg's voice was bitter. 'God forbid.'

Renewed silence. Anna started to mix a strong undercoat. She turned away from Matt to Fabio. 'Faces aren't like fingerprints where no two are alike. Faces fall into types. We all have a twin or at least a brother or sister in looks.'

'Ah, that's why people mistake me for Leonardo di Caprio?' Fabio preened.

'You've got a good opinion of yourself, Fabio Renaldi. Perhaps Anna should be painting you.' Paul was cutting.

126

'Well, he might not be too pleased with how Anna sees him,' Matt answered Paul's rejoinder with a knowing grin. 'Is it Picasso or Freud you favour?'

'Of course art is a metaphor for life, Anna's finished picture will reveal her to be the beautiful girl we all see.' Paul raised his voice above the groans that met his remark. 'Even though she may paint herself as a goat with a twisted head.'

'That might stretch our imaginations a little. Come on, Anna, we can't wait to see the finished result.' Matt sought to steer the talk away from Paul's bizarre ideas.

Anna peered into the mirror. Her face was a blank canvas but reflected behind her, in the altar mirror, stood Sue. She had weathered the storm and was looking impossibly elegant. There could be no mirror image there; Anna resisted the tempting idea to put the woman's likeness into her self-portrait.

Sue joined the others without saying a word and with her arrival there was a distinct change in atmosphere; like—watching ice-skaters and waiting for the fall.

Anna worked on in silence. Once or twice she flicked back her unruly hair, but otherwise she remained engrossed. The emerging image looked back at her from the canvas. Every face is a complex mix of features, of nuances, of expressions: but surely she had become someone else. Startled, she rested her brush. An older woman stared back at her. An older Anna or— Shit, she hesitated to accept the dawning conclusion. Was she looking at her mother? Had their talk of someone else being reflected in a portrait made her ultra-fanciful? In all the years of wondering and longing, she had never thought she could summon up that lost face with her paint brush.

Shaken, she broke the silence: 'When I look at a face I always see two faces. The sitter and someone else, like Greg and his father. Or perhaps even some one glimpsed in the newspaper or on television. Or as Fabio says, in a film.'

'Who do you think Grant looks like?' Fabio was struggling to mask his boredom. 'Can't see any film-star in him.'

'Oh, I don't know...' Anna grinned.

'You must have your rose coloured spectacles on.' Matt threw a spanner in the works. 'So, Anna, perhaps you see yourself as a raving beauty?'

'Raving, without a doubt!' Sue's mouth twisted. Anna stopped, her brush poised in mid-air, and peered through the mirror at her openly hostile detractor. The celebrated artist had a strange look on her face. How easy to understand Francesca's dislike of Sue, though their host thought she hid it.

Anna seethed inwardly. A large blob of mauve paint appeared on the left cheek. There would be no fairy-tale princess on this canvas; no smooth pink cheeks, no pretty blonde hair, no simpering smile. The mauve spread thickly under the lower lip. She could see Matt out of the corner of her eye, beginning to rock on his chair. That calmed her. He was the one who mattered; she wanted his seal of approval more than any other.

Yet her hair was changing colour, as though blonde was no longer correct; there were dark roots. 'If we didn't know you better, we would think you're a frustrated brunette.' Francesca had been quiet up to now, absorbed in the painting. Or had it been other matters on her mind, concerned that Fabio and Catarina, essential in her life, were in opposite camps; even though Fabio outwardly ridiculed Paul's obsession?

Anna squinted at her painting; the face on the canvas was no chocolate box representation, no smooth unlined cheeks, no blonde curls, no Virgin blue eyes. She had not painted herself. It was someone else.

Footsteps! The altar mirror revealed a new figure, Catarina stood momentarily silhouetted against the late afternoon returned sun and then she was amongst them.

'Let's take a break, Anna. You've certainly earned one.' Matt looked across at her with a quick smile and then turned to the rest of the group. 'Aperitif time already.'

Catarina had brought a tray of drinks.

'Catarina, I thought you were off until tomorrow morning.' Francesca rose from her seat.

'I came back. The storm was severe. The village is without electricity and therefore the castello.'

'Oh, we've been so absorbed in Anna's painting we didn't notice. How kind of you, Catarina, to think of us. Quite beyond the call of duty.'

Catarina smiled, 'Rita has everything under control, the menu is already altered.'

'Oh, what a team I've got! Has everyone got a drink? Anna, you haven't and you have been doing all the work.'

But Anna declined, eager to work on, her brush no longer

under her control. The group, glasses in hands, moved to be in a circle around her, their eyes focusing in the now noticeable gloom.

'Sorry, Anna, we can't switch on a light to help us see your portrait.' Francesca put a hand on the girl's shoulder. 'Gracious', and her exclamation was out before she could stop it. There was a loud murmur of surprise from the rest.

Fabio frowned, 'I thought it was supposed to be a self-portrait of Anna.'

Across the silence, Sue challenged, 'You've painted Fran— well, a mixed up version of her, combined with some of your young features.'

There was a chorus of agreement. 'And it's warts and all Fran, even to the scar on your left cheek.' Sue looked from Francesca to Anna. 'Perhaps a combination of the two of you will produce a complete whole.'

Anna sat stunned; Francesca's square face, not her own oval one, filled the canvas, and though Anna's almond-shaped eyes gazed out at the viewer, they were brown not blue. Anna's innocent smile hovered about Francesca's thin lips.

'Well, to be really true to life, Anna, you'll have to acquire plumper cheeks, my dear, so it's lots of pasta for you tonight.' Sue turned her back on the portrait.

Fabio was scathing. 'I didn't think your explanation of two people in a portrait would be quite so literal in the interpretation. Why have you merged with Francesca?'

Anna shook her head, bewildered. 'I don't know. I didn't know I was doing it.' Head down, she ran from the chiesa and out

130

onto the track.

TWELVE
FRANCESCA

There had been a real feeling of wellbeing when they'd entered the church and settled down for Anna's painting session. The storm had gone and in the late afternoon, with the return of the sun, normality seemed to have returned. Gold shafts of light picked out chosen corners whilst far niches lay in shadow. Francesca noted how it played on the girl's fair hair as she sat in front of the empty canvas. Calm after the storm. Quietly, she congratulated herself on her inspired idea. All of them knew each other's artistic abilities, probably none had seen Anna's work, except for Matt. Certainly the girl had glowed at his praise. Then, it was obvious she needed all the encouragement she could get as far as her art was concerned. And besides her art?

And now, after Anna's master class, they dispersed from the church, intrigued, and what besides? Anna's golden curls had become her own dark brown straight, severe style and the innocent face had aged. The portrait filled her thoughts; the face on the canvas, and the meaning behind it. Was she reading more into it than she needed to? Francesca well knew her own weakness; her over reaction to any situation that was beyond her control.

Unsteadily, she descended the steps of the chiesa and out into the post-storm gloom. She was only too aware, as she left the Christian comfort of the old church, of entering back into the darker world of pagan belief as she crossed over the threshold of the castello. The western rays of light did not enter here and no welcoming lights flickered in the courtyard. Everyone groped in the void. Francesca sighed; Anna's performance had broken her fragile ease, though the others would have already put it from their mind: contemplating only how to find their rooms in the dark maze of the castle, and the foreseen difficulty of dressing for dinner.

She felt an arm go round her waist. Paul was close beside her, but it would not be him offering comfort. She caught hold of Greg's supportive hand.

'Francesca, have you ever stopped to question why your castle faces east?'

'No, Paul.' She tried to keep the irritation from her voice.

'Purely Etruscan reasons. They always orientated their buildings in that direction.' The arm tightened around her. How good, someone cared about her feelings, sensing she was troubled by trouble-maker Paul's efforts to get under her skin.

Sudden lights sparkled, as glow-worms at first and then like fiesta torches. 'O-oh.' They reacted like children as Catarina came from the underworld with a tray of candles.

'Catarina, you're always in the right place at the right time.' Paul said what she should have said amidst the murmurs of agreement from the others.

'O, I don't know. I was rather enjoying the hide and seek atmosphere.' Greg withdrew his arm, fearing the light and what it might reveal as surely as he'd shunned self-portrait revelations. What was it he had not wanted to see replicated from father to son?

133

And as he moved away from her, Catarina stepped quickly to take his place; hardly noticed. But Francesca did; was Catarina flaunting to the rest of them the English woman's obvious dependence? The flickering shadows and Greg's wandering attention were making her edgy. Was she recognizing her own insecurity in that of Anna's? Surely that neediness was the explanation for her strange portrait.

Catarina was now busy handing round the candles. As she gave Francesca her own, Francesca squeezed her hand in gratitude. Catarina inclined her head. 'Do you think, Senora, we will not change for dinner? It is already quite late and it will be difficult.'

'What a good idea.' Fabio had overheard. 'I know Rita has planned an alternative feast but I hope it is more than a salad.' He turned to the girl. 'How about you, Anna, has all your hard work given you an appetite? Or have your weird thoughts driven it away?'

Matt interrupted. 'See you at dinner, Anna, and may I book the seat next to you? I want to discuss with you what your plans are after Italy.'

'Is there life after Chiesa a Castello?' Anna questioned, her laugh forced.

'Both of you come and sit with me at the meal.' Francesca raised her voice so they could all hear. 'We must make a decision on the mural.'

'It is your decision alone.' Fabio followed her across the courtyard.

As she began to climb the tower steps, she turned, towering above him, 'Don't worry, Fabio. You will hear along with all the others.' She mounted the rest of the steps two at a time.

The tower's seclusion welcomed, the coal black held no fear for her. No window on the western side let in the last light of day; the solitary window faced east, awaiting the return of morning. Paul was right. She closed the door behind her. She needn't have dismissed Fabio quite so fiercely but he needed to know his place. She gazed out into the gloom. Moving shadows in the courtyard made his figure loom. Was he becoming too big for his boots, threatening her tenure at Chiesa a Castello?

She placed her candle in the window. Everyone now dispersed to their rooms, their candles casting hidden shadows, all except Anna's. The flickering light in her cloister cell shivered across the courtyard. She imagined the girl alone in her narrow room, stewing over her performance. The individual cells, so convenient for the tourist weeks, meant no single supplement here. And this resident group, all of them single units. Even Sue and Greg at the moment still uncommitted? How much all of them reflected present day society; so much for bonding. Sue and Greg, have they become an item? She felt the stab of envy.

Hastily, she turned her thoughts to Anna. Had her behaviour been blatant? The girl's performance was strange to say the least. Her eyes looking out of the older woman's face, like mother, like daughter? The impossible thought she had struggled to keep out acknowledged at last. It could not possibly be and yet she knew she was capable of believing anything she wanted.

The knock at the door was loud and cut through her reverie. Catarina's face was anxious in the light held close up to her chin, revealing surely nothing but the Italian's total commitment to her. Commitment was not a bad word.

'Catarina, come in.' She wouldn't say that to anyone else. Her room her sanctuary, but Catarina—was different? With a shock she remembered her earlier thoughts about all of them being single entities. Not so Catarina, she was married. How could she have forgotten? Easily, because Catarina needed her to think just that; the Italian's married status never intruded into her work world.

'Catarina, you should not be here.'

'Signora, forgive me.' She moved back towards the door.

'I mean it's your day off, your night off.' But the thought of an irate husband alone in his dark house, fuming that his wife felt duty-bound to come back to her, gave her an odd feeling of pleasure. 'G...Giuseppi...'she could hardly put a name to him, 'will be cursing me,' she said aloud, but inwardly thought Catarina should not be invading this, her bolt hole.

'Cursing? I think not. He knows I am wanted here.'

Is she? Could they have managed without her? She'd brought the drinks to the church, equipped them all with candles, and now she had a bottle of gin in her hand; Francesca had taken an empty one down to the kitchen that morning; the refill a good enough reason to invade her privacy? It had never been done before. Catarina placed the new bottle on the table but made no attempt to leave, something on her mind other than Francesca's comfort drink.

'The painting, I was wondering—'

'O, that! I think it was meant as a joke. Anna was trying to keep us entertained, her way of livening up the proceedings. She's young, remember. Anyway, it obviously worked, judging from Fabio's reaction. I found it amusing. Though a combination of Anna and myself certainly didn't produce a beauty. Did it?'

'No.' Catarina was disinterested. 'I was not thinking of that, I was thinking about the mural for the baptistery wall.'

'O, my fresco. O, that is very much more important.'

'Yes.' One word, and it was meant. Catarina could be voluble when she wanted to be, but equally terse when she felt aggrieved.

'Christian or pagan art. I don't have to ask your opinion, Catarina, I know what you will say?'

'It is a Christian building.'

'Yes, it was part of a consecrated church as you say, but no longer. So really there is no appropriate painting for this day and age.' Her voice was steady, yet who was she kidding? She might try to swim against the tide but in the end she would go with the flow. She always had.

'So you wish to please Fabio? Not to mention Paul. Their obsession with the Etruscan world is bad for Chiesa a Castello.'

'It's our bread and butter. That is how we keep the place going. People crave themed holidays, and you have to admit that scholar Paul Bradley brings them in. Not to forget Fabio's Etruscan facsimiles, to be bought as keepsakes, so funding his expensive habits.'

'But if you only knew—'

'Knew what?'

Catarina did not reply, but she was close enough for

Francesca to feel the woman's agitation. The candle in the window flickered, and for a moment Francesca feared total darkness again. The housekeeper's torch was instantly there, its beam direct on her face. Their two shadows were large upon the wall.

'Don't worry, Catarina, the baptistery will have its Christian painting.'

No show of gratitude, just, 'Which figure will the girl paint? Her style is odd. I cannot see any resemblance between you and her.'

So, Catarina had noted the afternoon painting session.

Normality had returned with the electricity. Both the village and the castello could get on with living.

'I do hate the dark, especially in Italian castles. It's not what you see but what you imagine you can see.' Sue's comment greeted Francesca as she joined the evening assembly. 'Still, I was glad to have Greg close by.'

Francesca chose to ignore her, walking straight past her to Anna standing a little apart from the rest of the guests. 'I'd like you to have these.' She thrust a large bunch of late roses into the girl's hand. 'Just to say thank you for this afternoon. In front of such an exacting audience I think you did brilliantly.' Her approbation was very public, as it was meant to be.

Anna's grin of relief was obvious. 'Oh, that's so kind of you, Francesca, they're my favourite flower.'

'And in return for the roses I would like to have the portrait to keep.'

Fabio looked askance.

Paul moved toward the girl. 'Ah, roses, my dear Anna, you are in good company. Roses were sacred to the goddess Aphrodite. Then they were conveniently transferred to the cult of the Virgin Mary.'

'So, Paul, we should all be as adaptable, and I include you in that.' Francesca wagged her finger at him.

'Like you, you mean, English Fran become Italian Francesca?' Paul's voice held the sneer his face concealed.

Silence greeted the remark. The others had quickly learnt not to react to Paul's latest stuffed-shirt contribution to the proceedings. Had he always been so pedantic and had she always just let it flow over her? Whilst now, in this group, he appeared irksome.

Matt said casually, 'Roses are not just props for goddesses and virgins, but grown alongside vines, they warn of aphids, so there you are, Paul, a dead rose is another omen to add to your list.'

Before Paul could think up a reply Francesca said, 'I have made my decision about my birthday mural.' It was a throwaway remark just as Catarina joined the group to tell them dinner was served. But before the housekeeper could open her mouth, Francesca placed her hand on her arm to restrain her.

'A moment, Catarina, I am just about to tell them about the mural.'

Silence. 'I have decided that a Christian painting will be most appropriate.'

Catarina's face was impassive. She did not smile.

Fabio turned away, no expected outburst from him. Just a laconic smile. 'So let us go and eat. Just as long as I don't have to sit next to Bradley; I don't want my evening totally ruined. Anna, come and explain your afternoon's painting to a Philistine.'

They took their allotted places like children in class. Rita had produced wonderful food. A delicious cold tomato soup to start, followed by an impressive platter of cold meats, served with sweet and sour cucumber, rocket and bean salad.

Francesca did not look in Fabio's direction. The evening fare would not satisfy his taste nor his hunger. And what of her choice of mural? Fabio was being thwarted at every turn.

She watched her other guests succumb as the ingredients suffused into a feeling of wellbeing. Applause greeted the Chianti. Deliberately chosen by Catarina to mark her victory? The choice tonight was very good and very expensive. How could they improve on that for her birthday banquet? There was nothing better left in their cellar. Catarina had seen fit to celebrate the Christian victory rather than Francesca's Etruscan forty-ninth birthday.

THIRTEEN

ANNA

Over dinner, everyone was on their best behaviour. Francesca seemed remarkably relaxed. And the roses? Anna pondered the gesture from Francesca that had pleased her far beyond the simple act or value of the gift. There could not have been a more public demonstration that her host had not been offended by the master class.

The meal followed in a haze and when Matt tried to nail Anna on her intended movements after the castello she refused to be drawn. This was an idyllic interlude that she did not want to end. Why think of tomorrow when today was everything she had ever dreamed of?

And Francesca? She looked almost pretty. Anna remembered the first evening, the stilted silent meal, the isolation that had wrapped itself around their hostess, as though she were a Trappist nun. The change in their hostess was profound, could it be just the expensive wine she was consuming as though there was no tomorrow? It was exceptionally good and Anna readily accepted another glass then had to drink it with unnecessary haste as chairs were moved back and the others rose from the table.

The party was breaking up. It was already tomorrow and there was a feeling of anticipation. In a few hours' time their reason for being at the castello would begin to have meaning. Today, work would begin on the fresco. Anna was wide awake. She and Matt walked across the starlit courtyard to their respective cells, whilst the others disappeared deep into the castle.

'Anna, are you tired?'

'No.'

'Then how about giving me the value of your opinion?'

'Haven't you had enough of me for one evening?'

'Of course not.'

'Then yes.'

'Good. I'd like you to see my sketch for the mural. See you in five minutes back in the baptistery.'

Time to place the bouquet of roses in water, put a comb through her hair. The mirror reflected a happy face; her eyes sparkled like Chianti bubbles.

There was a light in the baptistery as she re-crossed the courtyard, Matt had beaten her to it. Eagerly, she pushed open the glass door and there was Sue sitting curled up in one of the alcoves.

'Anna.' She was surprised. 'So you don't feel like sleep either? Too much food I think for me. What is it with you? Do you have something on your conscience?'

'Of course. I have endless evil thoughts.' She didn't bother to laugh.

'I thought so. For someone so young you seem a little inward looking. Were you trying to upset Fran this afternoon? It doesn't take much you know.'

'Really?' She didn't need this woman to tell her that their hostess teetered on the brink. She'd already worked that out for herself. Everyone in the group must recognise in Francesca a natural loner, on the outside longing to come in. After all, she herself could fit into those shoes with a pinch; the need to be accepted never very far away. But this woman in front of her was the very last person with whom to discuss it. Where was Matt when he was needed?

Close to, Sue looked older, her sun glasses, usually part of her face, were back in their case, and the obvious crows' feet about her eyes were deep etched. Anna thought of Francesca and her almost childlike skin.

Sue was staring at her and Anna could sense the hostility.

'I found your performance this afternoon intriguing. Were you just trying to be clever or did you intend revealing some dark secret?'

'Hardly,' Anna laughed. 'I don't have any dark secrets and I'm sure no one else here does, either.'

'I think we could all come up with something, if pressed.' Sue's laugh echoed round the vaulted ceiling. 'Even the soft Greg could entertain us on that score. You should get him to tell you some time about his brutal father.' Anna didn't react. 'Perhaps it could be the group ploy for the next wet afternoon? As the thunder and lightning crash about us, we could all vie to tell our worst guilty revelation.'

Anna waited for the poison words, knowing Sue's pause was just for impact. 'Fran would win hands down.'

'I don't want to hear. You—We are her friends.'

'O, everyone knew, twenty odd years ago it got the whole college talking. Though we did wonder how she became pregnant

143

when she wasn't with a man.'

Anna turned to the door.

'Such a shame it brought a promising career to an end. So, my dear, you can see why I'm so intrigued. Might you be the lost child?' Malice was written all over her face and Anna had an inordinate desire to hit her.

'You must be twisted if you think that. I have only just met Francesca and then purely by chance.' Furious, she caught hold of the door handle just as Matt loomed behind the glass panel. He looked flustered as he pushed past her.

'Sorry, Anna. I was waylaid by Fabio, but I've managed to get rid of him.'

'Ah,' Sue pounced, 'an assignation; more intrigue. The castello is positively oozing with it. Well, I can tell when I'm not wanted.'

'That's right, Sue. See you at breakfast. Has she been annoying you?' Matt queried as the door banged behind her.

'She isn't my favourite person round here. Why does Fran— I mean Francesca,' she quickly changed to the Italian form, Sue's English version derogatory, 'think she is a pal of hers?'

'Think?'

'Yes. She's a back-stabber.'

'O, I can imagine what she's been saying. She is quite free with that scandal. Strange that Francesca ever got involved with her again. Bossy Sue must have really browbeaten Francesca for her to make her head of the Holiday Company in England.'

'Poor Francesca.'

'Why do you say that?'

'She seems so vulnerable.'

Matt shook his head. 'Oh, she can look after herself. She is tougher than people give her credit for. She's survived this long and prospered. Don't you waste any sleep over her. However, you are another matter.'

'Me?'

'Take care. All the rest of us are older and—'

'You must be only six or seven years older than me. Besides, I'm not stupid, you know.'

'I didn't say you were. If I didn't value you highly, I wouldn't be here now.' His face relaxed. 'I want to show you my sketch. But, let's have a glass of wine first. Any opened bottles remaining from dinner are left here overnight. Just in case anyone has a thirst before morning.'

'Oh gracious, they think of everything.' Glasses and two bottles waited on the table at the far end of the room.

'Red or white?'

'Red, please. Is there anything they've forgotten?'

'No, so that's why we owe it to Francesca to produce a fresco for the castello that will crown her restoration. She has worked long and hard. I would like this to be the cherry on the cake.'

'Couldn't have put it better myself.'

'So come over here and see what you think.' He had his glass in one hand, a large scroll of paper in the other. She followed him to the alcove opposite the door.

145

'On this wall, the mural will have greatest impact on entry.'
Carefully, Matt unwound the sketch, stuck Blu-Tack in each corner
and fixed it to the wall. Then he pulled her down beside him.
'Comfortable?'

'O, yes.'

'Good. So tell me what you think of it.'

She'd always admired her tutor's work. Forceful, with
flashes of Stanley Spencer, so that there was depth alongside close-
to-the-surface humour. His sketch hugged the wall. There was
Matt's version of Georgione's 'Tempesta', Chiesa a Castello the
back ground, whilst wild turbulent sky with scurrying clouds and
lightning revealed the Virgin and child seated by the passion fruit
and geraniums in their pots. Francesca stood on her tower steps,
Catarina was at the kitchen door. In the fore ground Fabio and Matt
watched, and on the other side, Sue, Greg and Paul stood together.
For a brief moment Anna questioned her place. Had Matt left her
out, the interloper? And then she saw.

'What do you think?'

'It's wonderful. Except for—'

'I know what you're going to say. But it's alright. The
virgin had to be young and innocent and you were the obvious
choice. Besides, it was Francesca's idea and I think it's brilliant. So
no protests.'

'Then it's lovely.'

'Anything to add?'

'Why not put in some roses? This Madonna likes roses.'

'Okay.'

'And a butterfly or two.'

'Of course.'

They gazed at the sketch, at the bare piece of wall, and imagined the finished mural as they enjoyed the wine. When both the red and white bottles were empty, Matt clambered to his feet and held out his hands to her. As they stood close, he whispered, 'No more games, Anna.'

'What do you mean?'

'I don't need to explain. Come on, it's been a long day.'

'I can hardly remember the beginning.' Suddenly she was exhausted.

'You can a have a bit of a lie-in tomorrow. Paul is an early riser and he's promised to start off proceedings by coating the lime wash on the wall.'

They crossed the silent courtyard. At her door, Matt squeezed her hand and abruptly turned away. But instead of retreating to his cell, he took the garden stairs that separated their rooms. He called over his shoulder, 'I'm going for a walk, I'm wide awake still. Promise no more games.'

His goodnight drifted up from the bottom of the steps. He had descended into deep black and she wondered how he could possibly find his way. It had been hard enough to find the handle of her door. There was no moon, they were in the darkest part of the night before first light would crack the eastern sky. Paul could have something to say about that. She peered eastward. There was not even a small chink to light Matt on his way, but then, he did know the castello well. For town-girl Anna there was nothing as absolute as country black. Groping, at last her hand found the door handle and it turned easily. No locks on the doors here, a fact emphasised on their arrival.

The room was pitch-black even though the curtains were not yet drawn. She fumbled for the light switch. Light flooded the room, as though a full harvest moon had broken through the clouds into her convent cell. It was filled with a beautiful scent of roses.

Francesca's bouquet was standing on the chestnut sill. The flowers were no longer in her tooth glass. Someone must have been in and made the change; her need catered for even before the request. The new bowl was Madonna blue, the roses cream and yellow and they stood out against the rich colour of the wood; perfection. Anna breathed in the heady scent, and the image of her as the Madonna surrounded by roses filled her vision. She was to be Matt's Madonna and now she desperately wanted to tell him of her pleasure. Had she appeared reluctant? She'd wait up for his return, to tell him how she really felt.

She sat on the end of the bed, listening for his steps, wide awake, through and beyond her earlier fatigue. How beautiful was the bowl of roses. Beside it the chimera was overshadowed, the goat no longer looked vulnerable, the lion and the serpent no longer menaced.

At last there was a noise. Anna sat bolt upright. She must have fallen back upon the bed and slept. How long she didn't know. Struggling to sit up, she remembered she was foolishly waiting for Matt's return. Good, he must be back. She was compos mentis enough to know she'd been worried about him roaming in the dark.

148

The light was still on in the room, so there was no fumbling to find the door and handle and no key to turn. She opened it a crack and peered out, hoping to see Matt. Disappointment, there was no one. But she had heard something. A noise had woken her. She moved out into the courtyard and as she did so her bare feet trod on something lying on the step. She stifled a cry of pain.

At that moment, eastern light erupted beyond the castello. Looking down, she let out a cry of disbelief, and bent to pick up a bouquet of roses. But in this one all the blooms were dead.

FOURTEEN

FRANCESCA

Usually, early in the week she'd yearn for the departure of the visitor group, to have her beloved home to herself. But this time it was different. For a start, Fabio hadn't been around for such a long period in years, Venice always calling him back to girls who came and went. What of Anna? How she would have liked that relationship to develop. And the girl herself? The previous night at dinner she would not be drawn when Matt questioned her future movements. She would make a lovely Madonna, her idea inspirational.

Busy thoughts. She was on a see-saw, high and happy, yet she knew only a small jerk could send her plummeting. She thought of Greg and her in the dark courtyard, his arm about her. She had never ceased to want him.

Her breakfast tray had lain untouched, Catarina's kindness rebuffed. She should have eaten something, but she wasn't hungry. The others would be having breakfast now on the terrace: it was not too late to join them. Only that would be too much out of character. They would think she had taken leave of her senses; perhaps she had.

The bottle of expensive Chianti she'd taken back with her to the tower the previous night was not quite empty. She could squeeze out one more glass perhaps? Her unsteady hand poured the reassuring liquid: the trusted way to keep her see-saw going up and up—

Today work would begin on her mural. Surely, a day in the castello's history to be recorded in her scrapbook? She would ask Sue to take the photographs. How good the mural would look in their newsletter! Modern Christian art adorning an eighth-century baptistery wall. An Etruscan fresco would have been more relevant. It was the precursors of the Romans who brought the punters here. Would Anna have looked as good reclining on a funeral couch?

It was a perfect August morning, the sun warm and inviting as she crossed the courtyard; it would play happily on the mural wall, heating backs as her fellow artists began their labours. She had no intention of wielding a brush, hadn't publically lifted one since her arrival in Italy. She could be an involved spectator. The sun was already shining on the baptistery glass door and it was ajar. Golden light streamed into the room. Paul had been hard at work putting on the lime wash. The wall was stark and white and so was Paul.

The man wielding the brush was naked, his buttocks sharply defined against the bare wall.

Francesca halted on the threshold, rooted to the spot. 'Gracious, Paul, w—what on earth are you doing?' Her shock was evident in her stutter. There were new voices in the yard, expectant, eager now to be involved in the project. She heard Fabio's raucous exclamation of surprise, Anna's sharp intake of breath, then they were all about her. Paul had not moved, intent on his task. Red-faced, Francesca turned to face the others, and there was a flash as Sue's camera recorded the scene.

151

Sue's triumphant, 'Thanks, Fran and Paul. That will make a really good one for the castello newsletter.'

Greg let out a roar of approval. 'Why not take another one, Sue, just in case. Do you want one of yourself?'

'Why not?' She handed him the camera.

'Enough, enough, children. You have all had your fun, and that includes Paul. But before it descends into utter farce, let's remember we're not here to paint a holiday- postcard scene. Here, Paul, put this on now.' Matt grinned as he handed Paul his robe. Francesca sighed with relief, glad he'd taken charge, whilst she had been left speechless and stupidly upset.

'Are you alright, Francesca?' Catarina was beside her, her face a study. 'You should have called for help.'

'Help. Why on earth would she need help? Do you really think she hasn't seen a naked man before? You can't honestly think I would try it on with her do you?' There was disbelief in Paul's voice. He turned and faced them. The robe was all consuming. 'What is all the fuss about?' He was genuinely nonplussed. 'I always paint in the nude. Didn't you know?'

No one bothered to answer, staring at him as though they were seeing him for the first time: and now in a very new light. 'Francesca, you must know.' The unlikely streaker turned to her, seeking to implicate her in his eccentric habit.

'Of course she didn't know.' Catarina was furious. 'And if I had realised, I would have stopped you.' It took a lot to get Catarina ruffled, known for her earthy sense of humour, but now she was visibly agitated.

'So why do you do it?' Greg, roused from his usual lassitude, was intrigued by the antics of the older man.

'Blame the Catholic church.'

'What in God's name do you mean by that?' Catarina's voice was rasping as she crossed herself, oblivious she'd blasphemed in her dismay.

Paul stared back at her long and hard, his face contorted. 'If you are really interested, in my youth I trained for the priesthood.' He shook his head. 'Would you believe we weren't even allowed to look at our own bodies. What's wrong with looking at one's own willy for goodness sake?' He looked skyward in his disbelief. 'Well, the church thought it was an unpardonable sin! So when we took a bath we were forced to do it under a cover. Hardly surprising then that when I renounced the Church I gave up, with it, all their false modesty nonsense. I chose to go to the other extreme.'

Paul's explanation was greeted in silence, unease tangible. His nudity now seemed acceptable, the reason for his behaviour far more disturbing than the sight of his bare buttocks.

'Okay, Paul, but in future just tell us where and when you are going to paint. Then we can either avoid you or come and seek you out; whatever appeals to the individual,' Matt joked amidst good natured amusement from the rest. All except Catarina.

Sue said lazily, 'Well, all I can say, Fran, is what a good job you employ him as an authority on the Etruscans and not as resident artist. Mind you, every week would be a sell-out. He might be getting on a bit, but he's beautifully preserved.'

'Thank you, Sue, for that backhanded compliment.' There

was more laughter and this time Francesca joined in. No harm done and the others were entertained, though she could see Catarina was un-amused at Paul's very open criticism of the church. Thank goodness she'd had the good sense to choose a Christian mural. That in the end would placate her friend.

'I have better things to do than stand around here. You know where I am if you want me, Signora.' Catarina turned on her heel and Francesca watched as she stormed to the door. Being busy would be her antidote; gathering vegetables and herbs from the garden would help calm the volatile Italian.

'Thank you, Catarina.' Francesca called after her.

'Prego.' She managed to find a smile.

The others watched her departure, enjoying her discomfort, and Francesca was relieved to see that included Anna. Momentarily, she had wondered how the girl would react to Paul. She was young of course and would have been to life classes. She glanced again at the girl. Below the giggles, tell-tale black circles lined her eyes. Then she'd stayed up late with Matt.

'Seeing Paul like that reminds me of the Giorgeone painting.' A grinning Anna turned to Matt. 'Perhaps some bare flesh would bring Renaissance reality into our present-day scene.'

'Okay, let's keep him in the picture like that. Come on, Paul, you can disrobe again.' Matt was mock serious.

'That way, Paul, you can get your own back on the church.' Anna was flippant.

Francesca raised her eyebrows, thankful Catarina was not there to hear the girl's blasphemous remark.

'Okay, fine by me. Perhaps by the end others will be joining me.'

'Why not, Paul?' Fabio, quiet up to now, entered the banter. 'I am more than confident I could challenge you in a reveal-all beauty competition.'

'Right, to the job in hand,' and Matt held up his hands. 'We're all here to make our mark on Francesca's wall. To paint something beautiful and lasting so that when tourists come to see it in six hundred years, as they do at San Galgano, they will be bowled over.'

'Thank you, Matteo, I could not have put it better myself.' Francesca was moved. 'You understand me so well. The mural will hold a unique place in my restoration.'

'You know, Fran,' annoyingly, Greg was still following Sue's English form of her name, 'we shall love doing it for you. I must say I feel as though I'm just setting out, and am poised to paint my first masterpiece. The next one is always going to be the one, isn't it?' His tone was wistful.

'O for goodness sake, Greg. You speak for yourself. I am quite happy with what I have turned out.'

'Thought for a minute you were going to say churned out, Sue.' Paul grinned at her, and the calm achieved by Matt was ready to evaporate again.

'Right, concentrate, guys. Could all of you look at my sketch. I'll take any suggestions.'

Francesca said, 'Matteo has spent time and considerable thought on the drawing, so there shouldn't be any dissension.'

Matt spread the large sheet of paper, left propped up by the wall, and Anna moved to help display the sketch. There were cries of assent. The pencil drawing had become a pastel picture, the vibrant colours of the medium in bold display.

Francesca felt tears pricking her eyes. 'It's perfect.'

The others' silence showed their approval. Anna was the Virgin. She was dressed in the simple blue dress she'd worn the night before. Her fair hair, in long tresses, reached down to the holy infant. Innocence and strength were equally portrayed. Francesca marvelled afresh at Matt's assured touch. A simple, modern scene; it could have been any mother and child. It must surely have pleased Anna. Her cheeks were prettily flushed.

'Perfect; couldn't have done better myself.' Paul gave his approval. He seemed to have accepted Francesca's non-Etruscan decision.

'You've made a few changes besides adding the colour.' Francesca moved closer to the picture.

'Yes, I've added the roses round the Madonna. Paul did say it's both a pagan and Christian symbol.' Matt had been his conciliatory self.

'It's a terrific use of colour, red, orange, terracotta, pink, totally discordant, but it works.' Bold colourist Anna admired the palette.

'You've also added butterflies.' Paul fingered one of the delicate shapes.

'Yes, that was Anna's idea. What do you think?' Matt turned to the girl.

'Yes. It's great, Matt. Thank you for that. It's good to see you showing your soft side as well.'

He raised his eyebrows, then flexed his arms so that his taut muscles rippled under his shirt sleeves. 'Just to show I'm a force to be reckoned with. Wouldn't like you to think I've gone completely soft—any of you for that matter.'

'The Etruscans were big into butterflies. As harbingers of death, they carried away the souls of the departed.'

'Paul, do I have to remind you this is not Etruscan?' Matt sighed.

'No, perhaps not.'

'No "perhaps" about it. No discordant thoughts allowed now we've all sanctioned Matt's painting.' Francesca sounded reproving, though she forced herself to smile. 'Oh, there you are, Catarina.' The housekeeper had come back into the baptistery. She carried glasses and a jug, her composure returned to the ice cool of the cubes floating in the liquid refreshment. 'Come, my dear, and have a look at Matteo's sketch. I think you will like it.'

Catarina looked from Francesca to Matt and then moved to stand before the sketch. 'That is as it should be.' Her words were deliberate and heart-felt.

'There now, Matteo, you could not have better praise than that.'

'Great, so that's it then.' He smiled his appreciation at Catarina and took a glass from her. She was being as good as her word about keeping them fed and watered.

'Refreshment, though, not earned yet. So, let's get started,

157

background first, then the figures; who's painting whom?'

'I want to get my hands on Paul's buttocks.' Sue was her usual irreverent self.

'Be my guest, Sue. Then I can paint you with bared breasts. Pagan ladies always tore their bodices to show their grief. It was a mourning ritual with Egyptians, Minoans and any others you like to mention.'

'Ah but, Paul, I have a head start on you. You will just have to imagine my boobs. I have the real thing on my camera for my aide memoire.' So saying, Sue produced her camera and pressed the relevant recall button. 'Here we are, folks, all in brilliant technicolour and larger than life. I had the zoom lens working.'

Sue's words were greeted by shrieks of laughter. Francesca could feel tears of laughter running down her own cheeks. Both Paul and Sue could give as good as they got. But the woman had had the last word, as she always did. Sue always won any fight, though that was hardly the right word for this banter. Even Catarina was trying hard to hide her amusement and Francesca smiled to herself; no need to point out that Paul baring all could just be aping one of her church's cherubs.

'Paul,' Anna entered the fray. 'This isn't going to be a sad primeval scene with the women tearing their breasts. Our picture is much more hopeful.'

'O, no, that's where you're wrong, Anna. Hope is illusory. Sooner or later our little virgin will be tearing her breast and bewailing Man's folly. Christian and pagan alike have always read portents. Yesterday's storm said "watch this space!".'

Anna chose to ignore him. 'I hope no one objects to me being the Madonna.' She looked around the group.

'You can't dismiss me that easily, young lady,' and now Paul looked old. It was wrinkles, not laughter lines, that creased his face. Francesca felt a tinge of sympathy. His life had been one of obsessions and rejection. The result was a lonely man. His stark revelation about the priesthood, and his ultimate renunciation of it, showed someone deeply at odds with himself; a complex man who still carried a large dose of religious guilt below the surface.

Paul's face was flushed. 'Perhaps we might question whether you fit the role of innocent virgin?'

Anna frowned. 'Is that what you now think? Well, I didn't put myself forward for the role. It was Matt's idea.' Matt raised his eyebrows at that and Francesca wondered at the untruth. Anna knew very well the suggestion had come from her. She'd told Matt to tell her that. So why did she want the others to think otherwise?

'O, no, Anna,' Francesca interrupted, 'it was my idea, mine alone. You are the obvious choice.' Nods showed approval. 'So let's get started. You are a talented bunch and I can't wait.' The image of the finished work floated before her eyes. Her castello would be a worthy backcloth for the painted figures, about to be portrayed for posterity. Was that what she wanted? Did she really want to be reminded of them all?

FIFTEEN

ANNA

Chiaroscuro, in this case the light and shade of the Italian Renaissance would paint the castello scene: brilliant flashes of sunlight pitted by deep dark shadows. Others had placed Anna centre stage, but—and it was a big 'but'—someone didn't welcome her intrusion. In one short day she had basked in sunlight only to be cast out into gloom. Two bouquets of roses, one fresh and alive, the other withered and dead, showed the conflict. She had been warned. Of that there was no doubt.

During the long night hours, Anna had tried to calm her dismay caused by the withered roses, a local belief but surely not relevant to her. It could be no more than a cruel leg-pull, as was so much about the castello. After its discovery, she had pulled the duvet over her head and slept. But in the morning light all she could see was the dead bouquet and its emphatic rebuff. The rose thorns had well and truly pierced her growing happiness since coming to Chiesa a Castello. Could it be yet another place of rejection for her?

How was that for overreaction? By the time they had all assembled back in the baptistery and Paul had theatrically taken centre stage, she had retrieved her sense of proportion. After all, who was she to compete with ultimate show-stealer Paul? Him doing a moonie so publically had put her firmly where she wanted to be, in the shade.

She watched Matt begin the mural that would link this disparate group together for all time. Drawn together for the week, but in reality far apart.

Paul was of infinite interest. Who would have guessed such a character lurked in the small, arrogant man. No, for arrogant supplant mixed-up; his past still haunted his present. Anna acknowledged kinship with that dilemma.

When his involvement in the lime-washing of the wall was finished, and the empty glasses had been gathered, he followed Catarina out of the baptistery. Anna felt the man's isolation as though it were her own, and instinctively she went after him, out through the western portal and in to the church. In the infinite silence her steps were a loud intrusion. He turned and waited for her to join him.

'I knew it would be you. How nice.' He spread his arms, encompassing the building. 'You see, I always turn back to the Catholic Church when I need comfort. I suppose I always shall. You'll find me seeking absolution on my death bed.'

They stood in the void; no sound of psalms, no comfort of incense, no creaking joints as the congregation bent to pray, yet all of the past was about them.

'You know the Mural should be Etruscan, don't you?' Paul's comment broke her reverie.

'Why is that?'

'I would have thought you'd understand. No more church medieval mumbo jumbo, instead we need up-to-date reality. You're a modern girl.' He looked at her appraisingly in her short shorts and skimpy tee-shirt. 'The Etruscans knew how to treat women. They were never ever second class citizens, allowed to attend banquets, and they had their own servants.'

His face softened at the reflection and she saw again the handsome man with fine chiselled cheeks and long straight nose; a striking head on a toned body. It was as though having seen his bare back she was seeing him for the first time. His trunk was taut and muscular, as though his sculptor had been mean with the clay. His eyes held her gaze; a dark pool of blue that reflected deep self-knowledge. She'd wasted her time feeling sympathy for the man. He did not need it. A successful gambler, he had taken what he wanted out of life, and at the very end, he acknowledged, he would be free to change his mind. It was as simple as that. She laughed, and it echoed through the church, lifting the dust and scattering the calm.

'I don't need to feel sorry for you do I? Have you ever really felt guilt at rejecting your Church?' she asked boldly. Paul was right, the truth was too often hidden by needless reticence.

'No, of course not, it's important to use scales in this life. Weigh everything and then find the balance. Look what I found instead. A life interest in people who lived here over two thousand years ago, and yet who seem more real to me than our little group, gathered here in the castello.'

'But wasn't the Etruscan world as narrow as the monastery you rejected?' She was playing devil's advocate.

He ignored her question, but said instead, 'You know, my dear, it is freedom that you need. At the moment you drag shackles behind you. I can hear them on the bare floor and they are

162

deafening.'

It should have been her turn to find words of denial, but both knew he spoke the truth.

'You need no mother figure now, no coattails to tie yourself to. I nearly made the same mistake with the church. Thankfully, I saw the light. You can wander far when you have nothing to hold you back.' He stopped and looked at her apologetically. 'I would have been good in the confession box, don't you think?'

'You've missed your vocation.'

'It's always easier to see what is wrong with someone else. It's more difficult to look inward. Besides, I've the advantage of years, some sort of knowledge does come with the grey hairs.'

His hair was short cropped and the colour diffuse, so he could have been almost any age. How old was he? Could one ever retire from an obsession?

'Did the Etruscans have priests?' Paul had rejected his church calling, but it wouldn't be hard to see this lean aesthete in Etruscan priestly robes. 'I think you'd look rather good in a sacred sanctuary, doling out the comfort.'

He shook his head. 'I'm not sure there was any excess comfort. Easy to feel it here in this womb-like building, but out in a shady glade I think there would be greater awareness of the reality of life. We clutch at straws nowadays, then everyone was aware that cruel fate was waiting just around the corner.'

'So they didn't need priests then.'

'Oh, they existed alright, the elite Etruscan priesthood held considerable sway. Without a written language their oral tradition

163

was handed down from generation to generation.'

'Hence the mystery.'

'Secrecy means that only a few are in the know.'

'But you can't really believe in omens now?' She remembered his excitement at the previous day's storm and the fact it was seen to come from the west.

'Of course! Did you know they forecasted their own demise? Portents told them they would last only a thousand years. Along came the Romans and that was that.'

'What we know about them comes from the Romans. And they were the enemy.' Anna added her limited knowledge.

'Yes, so hence their bad press. It's like my reputation relying on an obituary written by Francesca.'

'Francesca?' She did not hide her surprise.

'She suffers me.'

'O, I'm sure you're wrong about Francesca.'

'Not many folk would want our hostess as their biographer.' Again Anna saw the embittered older man as he shrugged his shoulders. 'You know, Anna, there is no such thing as chance. Everything is ordained. The Etruscans fought without hope against the Romans, for they knew their end. As do I. It is useless to struggle against pre-destiny.' The finality of his words wrote years onto his parchment face.

'You know of course your destiny was to come to Chiesa a Castello. Although you think it was chance, your meeting with Fabio in Venice was meant. It was the gods that brought you here.'

'I'm not going to argue. I think so too.'

'Goodness, I was waiting for the scornful retort.' Paul was startled. 'So, Anna, you are more complex than even I thought. O, I know I remarked on that before when we were at the tombs. Sorry, it is an old man's prerogative to repeat himself.'

'But you're not old.' She sensed he wanted her to deny his age. 'You're amazing. You haven't an ounce of flab on you.'

Paul laughed. 'Glad you noticed. I certainly shocked a few. Did you see Francesca's face? Catarina wasn't amused either.'

'Did you do it to annoy your hostess?'

'Certainly not, young lady. I really do paint without the hindrance of clothes. Spilt paint is easier to remove from skin.' His eyes twinkled. 'If Francesca has never seen me it's because I mostly go off to some quiet spot to paint landscape. Figures in a church are not my usual subject matter. So why should I change habits of a lifetime for them?'

'I bet you don't do it in your native Northumberland. You'd catch your death, 'she teased, glad to see the little man out of his introspection.

'Haven't you ever heard of bubble wrap?'

'Oh what a sight that would be. I'm amazed I haven't read about you in the national press.'

'One day you will. It is only a matter of time.'

'So it's written in the stars?'

'Of course!' He was adamant and she was almost beginning to believe him. So why did he think her presence at the castello had been ordained? She felt a twinge of unease.

She turned round as Fabio came into the church. 'Hi, Fabio,

165

Paul was just saying our Venice meeting was ordained by the gods.'

He ignored her. 'There you are, Bradley, I've brought you this.'

'Is that the present for Francesca?' Paul held out his hand.

'Present?' Anna frowned.

'It's just a local artefact that she can put beside her Etruscan stone.' Fabio was less than expansive.

Anna, not to be so easily dismissed, said, 'Is it the real thing? Have there been many Etruscan finds in the area?'

'A few.'

'Perhaps you've got something that Anna could give her as a present?'

'I can't conjure up things from fresh air.' Fabio looked annoyed.

'Well, come on, let's see this one.' Fabio was holding a cardboard box carefully in both hands and Paul removed the lid, copying Fabio's caution. He smiled his appreciation at the content.

'Bucchero Sottile, isn't it beautiful?' A small bowl lay black and stark against the white tissue paper.

'Oh, Francesca will be delighted with that.' It was beautiful and Anna beamed her approval.

'I hope she likes it.' There was a hint of doubt in Fabio's voice.

'But why not? It's exquisite,' Anna exclaimed as Paul lifted the delicate bowl and placed it in her hands. 'This surely was far too fragile for daily use?'

'Of course. The sotille pottery was kept only for Funeral

Banquets.'

'Oh.' Immediately, she understood Fabio's concern. 'What's Francesca going to think about that?'

'No problem.' Fabio was flippant. 'Francesca is only going to be forty nine, so she's nowhere near contemplating her mortality. Not like someone I can mention.'

'By that I take it you are referring to me?' Paul scowled at the young man.

'Well, Bradley, the gods will be withdrawing their goodwill from you any day soon.' Fabio turned to Anna. 'I'm sure Paul won't mind me divulging his age. He is about to be seventy.'

SIXTEEN

FRANCESCA

So it had begun. The fresco took shape on the bare wall. The final act of restoration, and with it the last chapter in the long rebuilding of her life.

She stood in the shadows, watching as Matt painted the fresco backcloth, a tufa-walled castello that looked solid and set to last another thousand years. Frailty would appear only with the figures.

His sketch showed her on her tower steps, apart yet integral to the scene. She was the first figure to be portrayed. She braced herself to shake her head as Matt turned to her and indicated the wall; animated, he expected her to be the same. The lime-washed wall awaited her, and she breathed in deeply. Fear was such a negative emotion.

Fear, guilt, jealousy, and anger, all negative emotions she had had in abundance. But they belonged to the past. They'd not be revealed in her present-day painted figure. A closed book now, she was very different from that vulnerable, naïve girl she'd been on that student weekend in Kent all those years ago.

That night, Frances Green set out for the House of Pan, filled with one all-consuming emotion, enough to make her ignore the scurrying clouds, the cold flurries of rain and the almost impenetrable trees of the dark wood. The thought of Greg Pearson lures her as though she follows the music of Pan, harmonizing with the soft moan of the wind. For a town girl she is surprisingly surefooted, the black night a winter mantle, hugging her in its protective fleece.

The other students crowding the smoke-filled bar will be heedless of the non-appearance of the morose plain mouse .But they will miss him. One thing for certain, they will never link the two of them. The thought makes her want to laugh out loud. She could never merit Greg Pearson's attentions. And yet she has.

Sue had met them on their return from the afternoon exercise, breaking away from the group to come over and thank Greg for rounding up the waif and stray. 'I will see you later,' she had said pointedly to Greg, and he had nodded. 'See you later nymph Pytis,' he had said to Frances, winking so that Sue couldn't see, and had gone off to the bar to join the others.

There's a faint moon that beats as erratically as her heart, in, out, up, down as the clouds skim and dip. She gains entry into the house with ridiculous ease and leaves the door ajar for him. He'll not be long.

Inside, a milky darkness means there is no need to look for a light switch. The black is shot with fissures of light, like taffeta, and it moves and swirls like a ballgown in a Mecca Ballroom. She can feel his arms about her, strong and supportive, and she leans away, flouncing her skirt, knowing soon he will be here to hold her. But only later, much later will they dance the night away. Stairs lead

169

*from the room and she follows their tread, remembering his earlier
promise to seek the empty bedroom.*

*His mouth is warm and hard, more pleasurable than she could
imagine, and she responds as though she has been kissed like it
many times before. His hands are smooth and eager and work
quickly, moonlight highlighting the piled clothes, winter disrobing
so much more skilled than easy summer stripping. Flesh is curved
and tantalizing in the dim light, and the noise of love-making fills
the house. It reaches her on her stair-head viewpoint and at the
climax she feels a pain so intense she cries out like a trapped
animal, but they do not hear, they make their own pleasured sounds.*

*She is trapped, the voyeur watching every caress, hearing every
murmur as though some metal trap has her in its grip, forcing her to
feel his hands, his lips, though they are not for her. Her time, her
place has been high-jacked by another. And that girl is Sue Simpson.
That night, she climbed tower steps and never came down.*

The castello was Francesca. She was the castello; she wanted
nothing else. She'd worked hard at the relationship, put in her all so
that now there were no cracks in its walls or in her composure. Her
edifice stood dominant and self-confident above the countryside.
She must strive to be the same. This mural would be the climax of
her love affair with the castle. As the paint fused with the wet
plaster, the mural would tie them inextricably together forever. They
would never be parted.

Fabio sat on the stone floor, intent on her work. From the look on his face she knew he had sensed the change in her.

'You are happy, Francesca.' It was not a question but a statement of fact from her 'adopted son' and she didn't reply. Instead, she turned to Matt who was still there, unable to leave the proceedings. Dear Matteo, totally dedicated to her and the castello, so much so that he had persuaded her, against her better judgement, to pick up paint brush.

The others had disappeared for various reasons; Paul as soon as his task of preparing the wall was done and Anna quick to follow.

'Dear Matteo,' she slipped easily into her Italianate version of his name. 'Thank you for everything.' She pointed to the mural. 'You couldn't have thought of a better present for me. You know me so well.'

'Good old Matteo.' Fabio was sarcastic.

Matt didn't respond, continuing to mix the powdered pigments in water so she could immediately apply it to the wall. She had chosen to be shown not in her usual subdued colour, but in vivid purple; she'd be no shrinking violet. There must be no competition from Catarina in her vivid scarlet. Besides, she'd be standing at the kitchen door, so no mistaking who was the Signora.

'You're lucky in Tuscany to have the right climate for fresco.' Matt eyed the restored room. 'This baptistery just cries out for such painting.'

'You are right, Matteo, we are blessed, are we not?' Fabio still sounded niggled. 'Having the perfect weather for vine growing, for olives, and for wall paintings. Unlike foggy England?'

'Lucky, indeed.' The Englishman grinned, in his element; painting filled his life. Even more so, she surmised, since his failed marriage. He'd bombarded her with questions as to why she had stopped painting, and was now delighted he'd persuaded her to renew her early skill. And she felt a silent happiness that she had never expected to feel again. She could see a future. When all the others had gone, she and Anna would adorn all the other alcoves. That would keep Fabio close.

'There are no frescos in England then?' Fabio basked in the reflected glory of his homeland, already knowing the answer to his question. He had been to England once, and it had rained every day for a week, only to be followed by a pea-souper.

'Virtually none. You need a dry climate like Tuscany and then the mural will last forever. If damp penetrates the wall, the plaster will crumble and with it the paint. In fact, Fabio, even in your Venice there are few frescos. It's really too damp there for the medium.'

Francesca said smugly, 'So here in my castello this one will last forever.'

'Yes, which means all of us will be here for the duration. I rather like that thought.' Matt raised his eyebrows at Francesca.

'Hum,' Fabio was dubious. 'Do we really deserve to last for posterity, with our differences and quarrels? One good thing, our mouths will be permanently shut, so we can't fight like cat and dog all the time.'

'Why do you keep saying that?' Francesca snapped.

'My dear Francesca, we haven't been here a whole week yet. I wager another month and there would be murder.' Fabio rose to his feet and moved closer to the painting. 'Just like damp getting into this paint and plaster so that everything crumbles.'

Francesca controlled her annoyance. 'How tiresome you are. So what do you have against—' Francesca hesitated to name herself. 'What could you possibly have against Matteo, for instance?'

Fabio considered Matt long and hard and then shrugged. 'Of course I have it in for Grant, it is only a matter of time, and as for—' he turned as Greg came back into the baptistery. 'I think there are a number of old scores to be settled, wouldn't you agree, Francesca? Greg, on which side of the painting will you put your figure, Francesca's or Sue's?'

'Don't take any notice of him, Greg, for those who don't know Fabio it's difficult to know when he's being serious and when not.'

'O Francesca, I have never been more serious. And still we haven't considered Paul in the list of combatants.' He frowned, 'Then we all hate Paul, if only for showing us his warts and all.'

'What on earth was all that about?' Greg looked bemused as Fabio slammed out of the room.

'Fabio being Fabio. Anyway, Greg, what do you think of Francesca's effort?' Matt was looking smug.

Greg studied the wall. 'It's stunning. How clever of you to catch your great strength.'

'And what's that?'

'Your ability to stand apart.'

173

'The ideal onlooker?' Francesca laughed.

Matt said, 'I hope this is the start of a new painting career for you, Francesca. It has been too long since Frances Green picked up a brush. Look at the expression on your face. It says it all.'

Was he talking about her real or mural face? Could they see her conflicting emotions? Greg again put his hands on her waist and gazed admiringly above her head, at her fantasy figure on the wall. She could scarcely breath.

'You've worn well in real life.' Compliments were so easy for him.

'What is real life, what is fantasy?' Her voice was hard.

He'd no answer for that, then Greg had always had his feet on the ground—solid ground. 'I particularly like the way you've portrayed your hair as though it is blowing in the wind, not the neat cut Matt had sketched for you. That's how I remember you at the House of Pan, having just walked through a forest. Do you remember? Or is it too long ago?'

'O, I remember.'

'You should wear it down now.' His fingers moved to the two combs in her hair and it fell lose about her shoulders just as Sue came into the baptistery.

'Gracious, you're not about to do a Paul are you?' She glowered from Greg to her hostess.

'Good, you've come just in time, Sue.' Francesca smiled at her. 'It's Greg's turn to place his figure on the wall and I think you and I will make a good audience. We were just reminiscing about our student days.'

'Oh, I'd forgotten you were part of his fan club,' and Sue mimicked surprise, 'then there were lots of things I didn't understand when I put you on your train home, your belly already swollen, and nausea writ large on your face.'

SEVENTEEN

ANNA

To know it had not become her prison she had only to walk away down the track; once her feet trod the loose stones she'd feel free. A sharp bend and steep drop, and Francesca's castello was gone, left behind, trapped in its own claustrophobic world. Ahead, an empty landscape of trees and fields patch-worked the view. It was a happy interaction of olives, vineyards, fallow fields, and stands of cypress and pines. God was definitely Italian. A gnarled apple tree overhung the path and its fruit lay in random falls, bright shiny yellow. Perfect. Only of course it wasn't. Anna stooped to help herself from the fallen harvest; the fruit grub-pitted and no longer able to cling to its branch. Grovelling, she found one less marked than the rest, and as there was no one around to see, she spat out the diseased bite. Ugh, she aimed the offending morsel into the undergrowth lying thick about the path.

The sound of rejection sluiced the silence. The returning quiet so welcome that for a moment she stopped walking so that even her soft footfall would not pollute the morning. The Garden of Eden must surely have been like this before Eve ate of the apple, and nothing was quite the same again.

The day was hot, the sky azure blue, unmarked by cloud. An expectant hush, a perfect stillness, not even the chirp of a sparrow, the nightingales and blackbirds had long since welcomed the dawn.

She had heard the tawny owls hooting long into the night. Now they would be off amongst the cool foliage of the oak wood, not treading the arid path she walked. It would be quite a climb on her return. She resisted the temptation to look back, for now it was all downhill. Sinuous lines of hills like giant prehistoric monsters coiled away into the unknown. That distance offered a welcome new perspective. It could be somewhere else for her to go? Perhaps she'd ask Matt to take her there, though he seemed unusually tetchy, and not only with her. On the other hand it might be more politic to spend some time with Fabio. Increasingly resentful of her, he was frequently absent from the castello. She was seeing him full-faced at last.

Enough of niggling thoughts. She was free to enjoy the morning. She looked about her. In spring wild flowers would carpet the way, fields aflame with poppies, now autumn was nudging summer, there was an absence of colour. Eryngium pockmarked the verge, their brittle spikes an early pointer to season decay. The fields overflowed with sunflowers but she was not blinded by a thousand suns; instead, heads hung crestfallen and dejected, their brittle dried faces shadowing the brown earth.

The sudden sound was strident, like metal on metal; a sword scything the morning. Harvest of the sunflowers was deafening.

'You can hardly tolerate the noise they make, can you? It's like some science fiction horror scene. They say it's even worse on the tractor. It sounds like continuous gunfire and it's almost as bloody. The fragmenting stalks are like shrapnel.' Matt was in the minibus on the track behind her. His shouted words added to the decibels as he blasted the horn. She was clearly in his way.

'Where are you off to, Anna?'

'I don't know.'

'That seems to be your permanent state.'

'That's my concern not yours.'

'True.' He shrugged and neither spoke as the tractor drew alongside them and words became superfluous. Matt sat drumming his fingers on the steering wheel.

She made to walk on. 'Don't let me keep you.'

'You won't. Can I give you a lift to nowhere in particular?'

Anna grinned and climbed onto the seat beside him. 'I thought I needed the wider world. But that blast of grating reality has shown me Francesca's castello isn't such a bad place after all.'

'Bad place?' He sounded startled.

'Of course I don't mean that really. It's incredible.'

'Two different viewpoints in one sentence.'

'You know me.' She laughed.

'Yes.'

'I love it.'

'Do you really mean that, or are you regretting coming?' She waited for the '*I told you so*'.

But it didn't come and she knew he wasn't like that. She strove to sound positive.

'It's great being included in the fresco painting, but—I'm not sure about being shown as the Madonna. You certainly didn't see me in that role in the Accademia in Venice. You said so.'

He grinned at her. 'That was when you were white and thin—a bit like a slice of cut loaf. Now look at you since Rita got her hands on you, not to mention the Tuscan sun.'

'So I've become more a crusty wholemeal chunk then?' Anna laughed. 'I'm taking it as a compliment, though thousands wouldn't.'

'It's meant as one.'

She said, 'It's great being included in the fresco painting. I mean...'

'Why the hesitation?'

'Well, I'm thrilled to be one of the artists. But so prominent a figure in the mural?' Her niggling worry was out.

'That's what Francesca wanted.'

'I know.'

'That's all that matters isn't it?'

'I worry about Fabio.'

'Ah.'

'What do you mean, 'ah'?'

'You seem to be a bit in and out with him, going out of your way to annoy him when you did your self-portrait. Now you are concerned about his feelings. Is he back being the flavour of the month? A bit inconsistent aren't you?' She needn't have turned Matt into a saint quite so soon. He wasn't one. 'I did tell you not to play games, there's always a looser.'

'Perhaps, but it doesn't have to be me.' She didn't bother to waste his and her time protesting that she didn't know what he was talking about. Instead, she pushed her luck a bit further.

'You told me not to come. Why?'

'A number of reasons.' It was his turn not to dissemble, and

179

it annoyed her.

'Don't bother to enumerate them all. Basically, you didn't want me at the castello.'

'That's right.' At the moment she reached for the car door handle he started up the engine. With a most unlike Matt piece of driving, he sped down the last few yards of the track, startling a goat tethered by the bridge and sending a shower of gravel and dead vegetation on to the village road. The sunflower harvesters continued to sever the protesting crop in an orgy of noise that shut out her protestation.

She carried the discordant noise of harvest and her unquiet thoughts in the silence of the minibus. Matt was not up for any further confrontation. No need to question their destination from the signposts and the diminishing miles, she could see they were heading for the wider world.

Siena, and like the castello, it's claustrophobic, ancient walls shut in the modern confusion in a contortion of ancient streets, narrow and dark. Buildings like rock faces rose sheer and un-scalable on either side. And far below the red roofline, the throng scurried as ant-like creatures.

People jostled, a vast crowd scene in a Renaissance picture. She had seen these figures in the Uffuzzi and the Accademia but on canvas they were without body odour and deafening noise. It was engulfing; there was no sense, no direction, she was being swept along in a vast surge of anonymity. Panicking, she thrust out her hand to grab hold of Matt's arm just as he disappeared into a group of voluble girls. 'Matt,' she shouted his name, knowing the futility of the action.

'Anna, I'm here.' His head appeared above the crowd.

'Oh, thank goodness.' She seized his hand and together they were swept along the street and out into the vast main piazza.

There was space to breathe in the Campo though it was still enclosed; mansions and shops rose in towers, colourful terracotta and burnt sienna. At the far side stood the Cathedral; a confection of white marble inlaid with black.

Still there were hordes of people, noisy, involved, happy. At the taverna, their table was hemmed in by others. The waiters twisted like coiled springs, knowing that somehow they'd get back to the kitchen from where they'd started. Matt ordered them a long cool drink and a paninni. He hadn't asked what she wanted, but when the boy threaded his way to their table, she devoured the sandwich, savouring every mouthful. She had missed breakfast, not wanting to face the others, still perturbed by the bouquet of dead roses. Who had left it? What did it mean? The food made her feel instantly better.

'I panicked back there in the throng. I'm sorry. It was silly.' The noise in the square was deafening and she mouthed her apology. Matt shook his head and then turned back to his sandwich, conversation impossible. Bang, crash, clatter, workmen were hard at it, building a stage for an evening rock concert; the adverts everywhere for the local bands. A scream of noise blasted above them. They were testing the amplifying system.

'We could probably stand on the castello terrace tonight and hear the whole concert,' Anna suggested in a brief lull in the activity.

'We could come if you like.' So Matt was a saint, or just food had restored his good humour.

She shook her head and laughed. 'I don't think I like crowds, you saw how I panicked when I thought I'd lost you.'

'Hardly surprising when you might have been left stranded without a Euro in your pocket.'

'Help, I hadn't thought of that. I'd have had to resort to pavement-art to earn my return fare. Though come to think of it, I haven't got my pastels with me. Anyway, I'm fed up with painting portraits. I really fancy painting the castello. This morning I wanted to get away from it as far as possible, now I can hardly wait to get--'

'Life is never boring when you're around, Anna.'

'Thank you, another compliment.' She grinned. 'Matt, do you feel the castello is a bit like an Italian Mamma, controlling and manipulating your every thought and action?'

'Is that how you feel?' His dark eyes pierced hers.

'I do.' She shivered, 'I know it's irrational, even for me, yet somehow I think my mobile phone will ring, even though I don't have it on me, and my absence questioned. We have stayed away long enough and it's time to return to the fold. It's a queer feeling. I can't really explain it properly, especially as I usually need to be mothered.'

Her words echoed in the quietened square where work had momentarily come to a halt. She knew she was digging herself into a big pit as far as Matt was concerned. Oh how wrong he was. Life was totally boring when she was around, always desperately predictable in her neediness.

'Francesca would be delighted if she could hear you say that. You should tell her. She needs to be loved as well.' The loud speaker system was uncannily quiet. 'Yes, the castello can engulf you if you're not very careful. I know that. But, at the grand old age of thirty next birthday, I'm one of its grownup children. I can resist its power to suffocate.'

'Are you telling me to grow up?' She pouted.

'O, no, Anna, I hope you never do. That is part of your charm.' He took hold of her hand, raised it to his lips and raised his eyebrows, all in one deft movement. 'Now we must go. I made my escape from the castello for an all-important reason.'

'Oh, you mean you weren't following me?'

'No, not you, but your figure in the mural. I want to get a more vivid blue for your dress in the painting, to match the one you wore last night. It was rather stunning.'

Her words of pleasure were lost in the scrape of his chair on the tiles and his retreating back. She jumped up. She had no wish to be lost in the maze of Siena that lay between them and the minibus.

The art shop window was an orgy of colour, an abandonment of reason and restraint. They stood together gazing at the pigments, like children at a sweetie shop. Vibrant, strident, blatant, the grains of colour vied for attention, each trying to outdo the other; jazzy, eclectic reds, blues, yellows, purples, merged, mixed and matched with no hint of bad taste. She wanted to scoop up the lot and transfer them back to Francesca's castello. He saw immediately what he wanted and held his purchase up against her eyes. 'Perfect,' and then lowered it with a self-conscious shrug.

'Perfect,' he repeated, pleased with his purchase. 'So now you know where to come to if you ever need to earn your artistic keep in Siena.'

'It's breathtaking. The shop is a veritable shade card, of colour, colour and more colour.'

The blue pigment was in his pocket, yet they loitered. Anna sighed. 'I'm reluctant to return to the true world.' She took a last look at the packed shelves. 'Look at this purple. I think Francesca must be buying her clothes with a colour guide from this shop, I swear her new skirt yesterday was that very shade.' She pointed to a pigment that stood out even above the rest. 'So what do you think she'll be wearing tonight? She seems to have given up on the black-anonymous.'

'She's changed in the last day or so.' Matt nodded.

'Ah, that's it.' Anna stopped in front of a spectacular turquoise.

'If you're right, we'll need dark glasses. Be careful to wear something that doesn't clash; you'll be sitting next to her again no doubt.'

'What about black?' She held up a stick of deep night against her face.

'Yes, very grown up.'

'You're laughing at me again. Don't do it. I don't like being laughed at.'

'Something you share with the spoilt Fabio then. He laughs only when he has started the joke.'

'Spoilt! Surely you mean charming.' She watched Matt's face change, then, as she replaced the black pigment on to the shelf, she said, 'Fabio favours black. I suppose because it suits his dark hair.'

'So you go for the Latin types do you?' He smiled patronizingly.

'I was really thinking about his birthday present to Francesca.' She sought to extricate herself from her apparent partisan thoughts on Fabio. 'It is very black.'

'Not very appropriate for a birthday present.'

'I hope Francesca likes it.'

'Won't she?'

'It's Etruscan ware, a really lovely artefact and found near the castello. But it's grave goods all the same.'

'So where did he get hold of that?'

'I don't know; it's a joint present from Paul and Fabio. They offered—'

'Don't touch anything that those two suggest giving you. Come on.' He seized hold of her hand. 'We are wasting valuable time.'

She did not demur, once more the throng was close and confusing and the mass of humanity threatened to separate them. His grasp was achingly tight. It was a good thing she was going voluntarily, she thought. It almost felt as though she was being returned home like some truanting child.

The castello awaited them, aloof on its hill, ready to chastise and bang its great wooden gate closed behind them. She grinned to herself, they could be characters in a fairy story, where artists confined in a dark castle were doomed to paint forever. There were worse fates.

The shop pigments coloured her thoughts as they sped through the countryside. She thought of the blue chosen especially by Matt for her mural figure. It had always been her favourite colour. Of sea and sky, it was now to be her raiment amongst the purple and red of a group in which more and more she felt an intrinsic part. She stole a glance at her companion. How dedicated to art he was.

The castello was dark, silhouetted against the skyline. Was she glad to be back? How foolish was that? They would climb the tortuous way up to its gate as inevitably as, come a new season, the sunflowers would bloom vivid yellow in the fields below. Matt slowed the car, the turning narrow and restricted over the ancient bridge that crossed a summer-low stream, its stone castello colour, timeless, mellow.

They both saw the goat at the same instance. Matt stuck his foot on the brakes as Anna let out a shriek, and they shuddered to a halt. But there there was nothing to be done. The animal now hung limp on its chain over the parapet of the bridge. It was lifeless. The scream of the machine at work cutting off the sunflower heads followed them up the track.

EIGHTEEN
FRANCESCA

She would spend her morning in the baptistery with Greg and his art. She could only guess how his style had developed over the intervening years, just as she has glimpsed how the man himself had changed. Shut away in her retreat from the world, it had been Sue who had told her of his popularity with corporate business and banks; many of his large canvases covering pension funds. To have Greg Pearson work on her wall would be a coup for next year's brochure. To art lovers it wouldn't matter whether it was Etruscan or Christian art. Convincing herself was another matter. Then why should she care, except to have the bare baptistery wall covered in a painting that was both a work of art and a labour of love.

Greg was mixing the pigment, Sue had established herself on one of the dining chairs, having pulled it out to get a better view of the prepared wall. Francesca placed herself in the exact spot where Greg and she had stood together. Yes, the mural would be a labour of love, created by people who cared. It was a wonder indeed, that she was suddenly surrounded by a group of intimates when, but a few days ago, she'd been a sad recluse. Looking at Greg's back, intent on the job in hand, she pondered the wasted years; and wondered whether it was too late.

There were only the three of them in the baptistery. Sue looked set for the morning, choosing to sit in the subdued church-like building on such a beautiful day; the Tuscan morning had no allure for her. She was quite a sight in herself; a smart skirt, shorts not deemed correct for these surroundings, and the top matched perfectly, a striking blue that clashed with her hostess's turquoise dress. Francesca's shift had not seen the light of day for years and it had noticeably lost colour. She had tried to jazz it up with a scarf of bright blues, though she feared the coupling had made the dress look washed out and the scarf garish. But beside both of these women, Greg looked positively scruffy.

'See you've got your work clothes on, Greg,' Sue said.

'Yes, I've dressed with care this morning.' He made no effort to hide his amusement. 'I thought you'd be the first to notice, Sue, but you see, my old painting trousers will be just right on a jobbing gardener.'

'Gardener? Isn't it your turn to paint this morning; not thinking of taking your turn in Fran's cabbage patch are you?'

'Indeed both, I'm going to depict myself as Francesca's gardener in the mural and I might even put in an application for the post in real life. Any chance, Francesca?'

Francesca smiled, 'You might have to be under-gardener. I think Riccardo rather likes his job. But I shall look kindly on your application.'

'Good-o.' Greg seized his shirt and pulled it off over his head. 'For the uninitiated I should explain, the wonderful Riccardo only ever works in trousers.'

'Some bare flesh on this side of the picture will balance Paul's on the right.' Francesca applauded. 'And, as my gardener,

188

you shall stand on my side of the picture. Sue and Paul can be on the other one.' Francesca pointed to where she wanted him. 'I'm sure Matteo won't mind us changing the figures around, and besides, it's a good excuse to include my beloved garden.' She looked happy. 'Bare back one side and Paul's behind on the other. What more can I want?'

'Fran, how you've changed,' Sue said. 'Not the shy convent girl you once were. I seem to remember Greg and I used to laugh about your innocence. Do you remember, Greg?'

Greg didn't bother to reply and carried on working, his bare shoulders resolute and determined both in reality and depiction. The two women watched the movement of his hands, his working muscles, the tightening of his thorax as he bent to scoop up more of the sienna brown.

'As the gardener, I need to give myself a good tan. Artistic licence of course. I would need to stay here a long time to get the enviable colour of Riccardo.'

'At least until the end of summer. I'd like that—and of course so would Catarina. She finds it very boring just looking after me.' Francesca flushed, but her eyes flashed encouragement.

Sue said pointedly, 'Don't forget we are due at my sisters' at the end of the month.'

At that moment, Fabio chose to walk across the threshold and Francesca waved at him. 'I was just saying how bored Catarina gets with just me around. I never asked you, why the last time you were in the region you didn't come and see us in the castello?'

Fabio sounded pained. 'Francesca, how can I put it? There

are younger ladies than you in the village and—'

Greg laughed. 'That sounds healthy. Mother figures have their places, but come on Francesca...'

Fabio frowned. 'Francesca, you know I'm in your debt and always will be.'

He'd got enough sense publically to acknowledge his reliance on her. What harm to voice her reliance on him? She said, 'And I never cease to be grateful to the young Tuscan boy, already made for me by fate.'

Sue chipped in, 'Add to that a pretty blonde girl who appeared at the castello, and already grown up?'

'To whom do you refer, Sue? Surely not—' Fabio frowned.

'Anna of course. Who else?' Sue had centre stage. 'O come on, why the surprise, Francesca? We must all have guessed Anna is your lost daughter.'

'No-o—' The protestation was an inaudible denial, but they all heard Francesca's strangled words.

Sue laughed; it was brittle. 'Your belly was big and getting bigger when you left college. You never let on who the father was. Hence the speculation. So what did happen to that child? Why couldn't it be Anna?'

'Y-you've taken leave of your senses, Sue,' Francesca said grimly.

Fabio looked from one to the other. 'And Anna made her portrait to look like you?' The young Italian moved subconsciously to Sue's side in an unlikely pairing. 'She is not here by accident. It was she who picked me up in Venice. Her intention was obvious—

to get to you through me.'

Greg said casually, as though it was time he made some contribution, 'She paints like you.'

'Anyone can copy any artist's style.' Francesca's reasoning was lame.

'So you gave up your art college?' Fabio questioned. 'It must have been a compelling reason, for you to throw everything away.'

She said quietly, 'There is no child. I had a miscarriage.' The lie came easily. She'd had years to perfect it.

The silence was profound. Sue looked startled.

Greg said, 'Look here, what are you all getting so steamed up about? It's no big deal now, not after all these years.' Only later did she contemplate, *his no big deal.*

'So, my dear Fabio, you need have no fear, the castello will be yours.' Francesca's tone was bitter and Fabio had the grace to flush. She'd touched his raw nerve. His obvious fear was for his inheritance from this pathetic childless old maid. Because that was how everyone saw her.

'Anna is such a sweet girl. I am sure we would all like her for a daughter.' Chameleon Sue had found her voice, and now it was sugary. 'Though not you of course, Fabio.' She sneered, 'Why don't you marry her, that was always the way to settle dynastic rivalries, wasn't it?' A born stirrer, Sue was agitating the situation as only she could.

Greg had had enough; he put down his brush, stooped to find a rag to wipe his hands, and for someone who let everything wash over him, looked decidedly ruffled. 'Why the hell don't you all go away, you're spoiling my concentration?' A few vehement sweeps of the cloth again and he had wiped away his annoyance. And in that time Francesca had recovered.

Greg said, 'Anyway, don't forget it's Paul's turn on the mural this afternoon, so give the baptistery a wide berth.'

Sue said emphatically, 'I shall be here. Remember I'm down to paint Paul, whilst he paints me.'

Greg smiled, 'That should be interesting. So, Sue, don't forget to stay on your right side. No creeping over to us, eh, Francesca?'

'Definitely not! My gardener and I have work to discuss.' Francesca gave him a friendly pat on his bare arm, 'And don't worry, we'll put sweat on your back, that's what you get when you work for me.'

'I've already decided I shall plant a cypress in the mural, if that's alright with you, Nymph Pytis? Ah, here come the others to admire my artistic work if a bit premature for my horticultural labour.' Anna and Matt came through the door.

'So where have you two been?' Sue, sensing her exclusion from the conversation, welcomed the newcomers. 'So what's the master been teaching his pupil? Oh—'Sue stopped when she saw Anna's face. 'Or shouldn't I ask?'

But the flustered girl ran past her to Francesca and caught hold of her hand. 'Francesca, is it your goat, the one at the end of the track, the one by the bridge?'

'Why, yes, we have a number. Rita makes cheese from their

192

milk. They keep down the vegetation. Gracious, he hasn't eaten your painting has he?' The others laughed at Francesca's sham horror.

'No, and from now on he won't be eating anything else, either.' Matt grimaced. 'He's been too greedy, went after something over the bridge parapet and hanged himself. The goat is dead.'

Anna, still visibly shaken, said, with a catch in her voice, 'That dreadful sound of the dead sunflowers being harvested must have driven him demented.'

Fabio was gleeful. 'Well, whatever the true cause of the wretched animal's death, our Paul will have it down as an Etruscan omen portending doom.' He looked mock impressed. 'Sue, I definitely wouldn't put myself into a room with a naked man this afternoon if I were you. You know what the gods can get up to when they take on human form?'

'No, Fabio, I don't know. Tell me, what will the gods do?'

NINETEEN

ANNA

Francesca suggested they all take coffee in the garden. This was unusual for the norm had been for the others to drink it on the terrace, whilst Francesca made herself scarce. It was as though she wanted to keep them with her for as long as possible, reluctant to let them go their separate ways. Their hostess appeared surprisingly light-hearted and Anna couldn't make up her mind whether it was real or put on. She had appeared flustered in the baptistery, even before they had told her about the goat. Perhaps the woman really was not bothered by the animal's death. She would not see it as Anna saw it, the extinction of the vulnerable chimera goat by the stalking lion and insidious snake. Anna struggled to dash the thought from her mind. But the sight of the dead animal still clouded her vision, when all she really wanted to think about was the rainbow-coloured morning she had spent with Matt.

Sue strode towards the bench under the walnut tree and made space beside her. Anna had no choice other than to join her. The others dragged the wooden garden seats unnecessarily to the shaded area beside them, purely out of habit she noted, because the sun had gone, midday haze taking its place. Catarina handed round the coffee, her usual bubbly self, and a colourful substitute for the lack of sunlight. Did anything ever rattle her? In her red dress she was like a pepper from her garden, vivid, piquant and adding zest to life. She pressed macaroons on them and Anna took two. Sue shook her head.

Sue asked about the morning trip to Siena. And Anna found herself eulogizing about the art shop and complementing her companion on her blue outfit, which she said paled the shop pigments into insignificance. Sue stared back at her, as though it was too trivial a compliment to note, and pursed her lips.

Their antipathy was mutual. Strange to think it was because of Sue Simpson that Anna had come to Chiesa a Castello. But now it was Francesca's world that intrigued Anna as she became drawn more and more to her troubled hostess. She could feel Matt eyeing her from a distance and she turned her back on him. Fabio had disappeared yet again.

It was a lovely summer scene with the feel of a childhood picnic that was going to last forever. Francesca had a strange smile of satisfaction hovering around her lips. Sue was unsmiling, displeasure just below the surface. There was an uneasy silence.

'So tell me, Anna, about yourself. Tell me about your family; where do you live?' Sue questioned half-heartedly.

'Bromley.' Was that amorphous enough for her?

'Ah, we have a connection with Kent. I come from Sevenoaks.'

'I read somewhere that's where the most eligible men are to be found.'

Sue laughed, 'Well, I can't think where they all are, not that I am looking.' She'd looked straight at Greg as she'd said it, but he was too engrossed in conversation with Francesca to have heard. 'It isn't a relationship that appears to occupy you at the moment, my dear. Francesca has told me about you wanting to find your—'

'O, did she?' Anna was nonplussed, Francesca had appeared to be a listener not a gossip.

'So do you have any clues about your real mother? There isn't a locket with a photograph that would reveal all?' Sue laughed.

'How did you guess?' Anna smiled and rose from her seat. Just then, the absent Fabio reappeared, striding purposefully across the grass to the group under the tree. All conversation ceased as if on cue, followed by a stunned silence.

In his hands Fabio was carrying a knife and from it red blood dripped to the ground.

Matt jumped to his feet. 'What the hell are you up to, Fabio?'

'So, live theatre has come to our garden, or perhaps I should say dead...' Sue's ready wit was never far away, whatever the circumstance.

Paul laughed, 'What the hell indeed?' He eyed the bloodied instrument with glee. 'So, a real life divination. What a splendid idea, only wish I had thought of it, Fabio, then you always were the opportunist.'

'What on earth are you up to, Fabio?' Francesca was clearly irritated at the interruption.

But Paul was animated. 'So, you've been butchering the goat, so kindly delivered to us by the gods.'

Fabio nodded, his face expressionless. 'We cannot ignore the chance to use Etruscan *Hepatoscopy* to show us what the future holds, 'and as he spoke he opened his hands to reveal a bloody shape. It was an animal's liver.

'Glad to see you have it in your left hand. The Etruscan protocol was specific on that count.' Paul was in his element. 'But wait, Fabio, we must do the divination as they intended. Hang on, I shall be back.'

Was it just good manners, post-prandial idleness or a grudging interest in the macabre scene taking place in the hillside hollow that made them keep their seats? For Anna it was the latter and glancing at Francesca she saw that the woman looked surprisingly involved.

They waited, expectant, and there was a loud gasp of amusement when Paul reappeared. At least he was fully dressed. He was enveloped in a large cloak, or what was obviously the sheet from his bed, fastened at the breast with a pin.

'The priest's costume was decreed, but my shorts must suffice for the short tunic, and apologies to the owner of this hat.' He pointed to Francesca's straw hat that he had tied on with her scarf. 'Their hats were coned shaped, it's the best I can do.'

He peered at Fabio, standing at the edge of the group. 'You were right, Fabio Renaldi, to take the death of the goat as highly propitious. As the great Roman philosopher Senecca said: "The Etruscans believed not that things have significance because they have occurred, but they have occurred because they have significance".'

They all groaned loudly and Anna waited for Matt to express impatience. But he sat impassive. And Fabio? He was surprisingly content to let Paul hold centre stage, in this harmless fun. For that was surely what it was, thought Anna, just like childhood charades getting everyone involved in a silly situation. She had always loved playacting, other people's answers to life so much better than her own.

Paul was lead performer. 'It's important to keep to the script, and luckily there's a depiction of such a ceremony on an Etruscan mirror.'

Slowly, Paul walked away from them to a boulder at the edge of the path, carefully placed his left foot onto the stone, put his right foot at right angles to it with exaggerated precision, and then positioned the sole of the foot flat on the ground. 'This then, folks, is the accepted ritual posture for reading omens from the entrails of animals.' He pronounced the procedure as though it was an everyday occurrence. 'Now, Fabio, hand me the liver.' He added, 'The liver is the command post of the body.'

Fabio, his face inscrutable, placed the bloodied object onto the palm of Paul's left hand. Paul slowly moved his right hand over the surface of the liver, loudly intoning 'I seek for imperfection'.

And still they watched. Fabio said laconically, 'The ritual usually took place in a sacred grove in the early morning, so that the slanting rays of the sun could show up any blemish. Sorry to say our sun is over head, and look at the cloud. I don't think we'll get much of a reading today.' He was as knowledgeable as Paul in all things Etruscan.

At his words, they all looked up obediently into the overhanging branches of the tree, but the sky was hidden by dense foliage as well as cloud. Perhaps all of them were waiting to witness Paul's comeuppance.

The little man's voice had become hypnotic. 'The liver is divided into four quarters, and they become the microcosms of the universe. The kindly gods are to be found in the south and east, the unkindly ones in the north and west.'

'So then, where is the imperfection in this sacrificed animal?' Fabio was still playing along with the joke.

'O, for goodness sake. The wretched animal was not sacrificed. Anna and I can both testify to the fact that it met its death by accident. It was just unfortunate it hanged itself over the parapet of the bridge.' Matt's impatience had surfaced at last.

'But, Matteo, it has never happened before.' Francesca interrupted his disbelief, her eyes still fixed on the animal liver in Paul's hand. Suddenly, the branches rustled above their heads and they all looked up. Later, they would dismiss it as just a midday current of air when the leaves began to part and a great beam of sunlight fell through the gloom, shining directly on to Paul's hand and the dripping organ. They craned forward.

'Ah, as I thought, the left-hand side and the evil west.' Paul, visibly shocked, staggered backwards and fell to the ground. Fabio's face showed his confusion. Francesca stood open-mouthed. Anna gulped. Surely no one could have been unaffected.

No one except for Matt, that was, who looked meaningfully at his watch. 'I don't want to break up the happy scene, but some of us have got better things to do. Like Sue and Paul for instance.' His words tipped them back into reality and Anna frowned at his

199

spoiling of the moment.

But Sue readily agreed. 'You're quite right, Matt. Come on, Paul. That's enough of your little tricks, we have to be in the baptistery, like now.' She seized both his hands and dragged a reluctant Paul to his feet. Then, without another word, Paul's audience dispersed.

Anna watched the others drift away, still contemplating the bizarre ritual under the tree. Paul had been at his most over-the-top, and yet it had been Fabio who had instigated the scene. And then Paul had hijacked Fabio's original joke and had turned it into a memorable matinee pantomime. What had been Fabio's original motive? Why had he gone to the length of cutting out the animal's liver, only for it to end up in a pagan ritual that they had all been forced to witness? Forced? Could any of them have walked away? And Fabio, surely he must have known what Paul's reaction would be. Again, Anna felt the castello's lengthening shadows. The morning interlude in Siena with uncomplicated Matt had been but a brief respite.

The deep darkness of the wood positively welcomed her. The path through was wide and well worn, long trodden by pilgrims on the old route to Rome. It was a comforting reminder that there was a world out there beyond the castello. The trees were dense. There would be no rays of sunshine slanting or otherwise to reveal a message from the gods.

So who, if anyone, was trying to usurp Francesca's celebrations? What had their hostess made of all that nonsense? Yet she had been the one to suggest they take their coffee outside.

Perhaps she had known what was coming? Anna stopped abruptly and laughed out loud. How they had been hoodwinked. That scene just witnessed was probably re-enacted religiously for every Etruscan visitor week held at the castello. Francesca, Fabio and Paul had all been in it together. Even Catarina, smilingly carrying out the coffee cups. It had seemed like a charade and that was exactly what it had been. Traditional entertainment whenever a group of visitors got together. Why look for any other reason but a visual aid, thoughtfully conjured for the themed week?

Yet even Francesca could not have summoned up the breeze and the shaft of sunlight. So in truth had they seen only what they'd expected to see?

She followed animal tracks through the wood and thought of the poor goat, its liver a prop in a modern farce thought up to entertain Francesca's guests. If it really was a regular weekly enactment, then the local goat population must be diminishing at an alarming rate.

TWENTY

FRANCESCA

Francesca watched the group break up, Fabio off to clean his bloodied hands, his little mischief usurped by Paul; Catarina to the kitchen, Matteo to his interminable sketching, perhaps that would help improve his temper; Anna keen to make a quick get-away, Paul to the mural, and of course, inevitably, Sue with him. That woman faced a whole afternoon with the resident fanatic. Good luck to her, she if anyone would bring him down to earth.

Dappled sunlight lay all around. In this part of the garden the trees were well spread and beams of soft light danced and played games through the wide branches. Who cared from which direction it came, north, south, east or west the gods were smiling down on her. Greg was waiting for her, and even more amazing, he was thinking of staying on after the others had dispersed to all parts of the continent. As under gardener. That was a good ploy, one guaranteed to appeal to his hostess.

A pool of light fell on to his head and snaked down his back like a spotlight; it was just a few simple steps for Francesca to cross the clearing to join him. It no longer seemed a chasm.

'Thank you for this.' He indicated her world in a lazy sweep of his arm. 'It's good for body and soul, Fran. Perhaps I should really now call you Francesca?'

'Yes.' She paused and then added, 'I answer to both. I

started out with 'Frances' but now—' She didn't add Francesca was her new persona built up painfully, stone by stone.

'And while you've been busy here, Fran, I've spent half a lifetime painting, turning ideas into reality. I haven't spent enough time sitting around in the sun, letting fate take over.' She had no reply. He smiled,' I hasten to add, of course, not Paul's reading of fate.' And they laughed together. 'A strange chap. Can't say I take to him very much.'

Silence, and Greg scuffed his feet. 'You really have made a marvellous job of the castello, Fran. You must be delighted.'

'O, yes I am.'

'Your life has been rather different from most of us. Out of the norm, out of the rat race. Didn't you want—'

'A normal life?' She questioned and he grinned.

'Sorry, I don't mean to be rude. It's just surprising you have never married. Had chil... Everything I thought you would do.'

'The castello took their place. I can assure you it has been just as fulfilling.'

Silence again. 'So what about you?' She struggled to sound neutral.

He shuffled his feet again. 'I let you down, didn't I? Led you on. And Sue. It was callous when I had no intention—'

'No intention?'

'There was a reason.' He looked her straight in the eye. 'I vowed when I was nine years old that I would never get married, never have children.'

She laughed. 'Never thought you had monk-like leanings.

That's a new one on me. I've seen you look at Anna.'

'There's no harm in looking.' He flushed, his pristine hairline made jagged by the dark infusion of colour. Discomforted, he said tersely, 'Didn't want to continue my genes, it's as simple as that.' Silence. 'So how about giving me a guided tour? I'd love to see your tower, according to Sue not open to everyone. How about making me the exception?'

Involuntarily, she looked up to her solitary sanctuary, but did not move.

To fill her silence he said, 'It's been rather strange meeting up with Sue after all these years. You know I had quite a shine for her when we were students. Passion of youth I suppose. Though, as I've said, I had no plans then and I haven't any now. Funny how twenty years can pass and nothing changes.'

She said quietly, 'I think everything has changed.'

'Perhaps.'

'Well, I've matured with the castello, Greg. Chiesa a Castello wouldn't be here now if it wasn't for me and what I've become.' She was pleased with the certainty in her voice.

'Yes,' Greg nodded. 'Total dedication and no distractions. You've shown no ruin is beyond restoration. Perhaps, after all, you and I could make a go of it,' and he paused. 'Come on we had better get back.'

They saw Sue standing in the shade of the south wall, beside the passion fruit, her striking blue resonating with the vivid orange. A Van Gogh scene, reality painted with a disturbed hand. Francesca rubbed her eyes, her vision distorted. Sue was gazing straight at them and then she waved, a long, obvious greeting until they both waved back.

Greg let go Francesca's arm. It fell to her side and Francesca laughed, a brittle sound like cracking twigs on a strewn path. Did she really want to upset the calm of this garden of Eden when Sue could still be the viper in their midst? And with a thrill of excitement she knew the answer was yes. But patience, she was good at that.

'Look, Greg, I promise to show you the tower, but another time. I think we should go seek the others.' She said over her shoulder, 'I don't think Sue has changed one little bit since College days.'

'I think she has. She is even more determined.' He sounded wary.

Only four figures awaited Catarina's afternoon tea ritual, chatting about anything or nothing; anything except the bizarre scene under the walnut tree. So what had the group thought of the after-lunch entertainment? From the general good humour Francesca guessed it hadn't been taken seriously. So what had been Fabio's motive for setting up the scene? He would have known that Paul would not fail to react?

Fabio and the girl were chatting amicably, sitting on the terrace wall. Anna was swinging her legs in a gentle rhythmic movement, back and forwards as she listened to what he had to say and then she laughed loudly. Youthful *joi de vivre* had a lot to recommend it. No wonder Greg looked at the girl.

'Where are Sue and Paul?' she enquired of Matt, lounging apart from the other two youngsters.

'I presume holed up in the baptistery where they have been all afternoon. Do you want me to go and tell them tea is served?' His offer was half-hearted.

'No, leave them. I'm sure they are enjoying themselves.' Francesca was emphatic and Greg was openly amused at the prospect. Everyone joined in the joke.

'Let's hope they are getting on with the mural. We only have another day or so if it's to be finished by Francesca's birthday.' Matt frowned, 'Sorry, Francesca, your present isn't going to be a surprise. It certainly won't be gift-wrapped.'

'Don't worry, Francesca will get a few surprises.' Fabio patted his nose, the figure of intrigue.

'Hope they're all ones she wants.' Matt raised his eyebrows.

'That would be telling. 'Fabio put his cup down on the tray as Catarina collected the empties. 'Come on, who's coming to see the artists at work?' His expression was much like the one he'd worn at his entrance carrying the goat's liver. Were they about to witness another of his games?

'It depends whether you girls feel strong enough to see Paul in his painting gear.' Matt was prepared to be amused.

'Why not? Then we can use turps on him to remove any stray paint.' Anna joined in the fun.

Francesca frowned, 'You are all being cruel, especially when they've put in a hard afternoon's work. Catarina, you come too, you'll like what you see.' Arm in arm, Francesca and Catarina joined the exodus.

Catarina's gasp was loud even though she was aware that

Paul painted without a stitch of clothing. He was there as expected, his slim, taut buttocks towards them and now replicated on the wall above. Sue had done a good job. The others thought so too.

'Well done, Sue,' said Greg. 'You could have a new career painting nudes. Though I'm not going to offer to sit.' He moved to her side. Francesca fixed her eyes on the mural, though it was real life that held her interest.

'What the hell has happened?' It was Matt who joined Catarina's exclamation of surprise, and with it they all homed in on the central figure in the painting: the Madonna in her beautiful blue gown. For just the briefest of moments Francesca's eyes saw only what they expected to see, and then she let out a sharp cry of protest. The gentle face of Anna should have been staring down at them, smooth soft young skin, blonde silky curls. Instead it was an older lined face, with dark straight hair. It was Francesca. Anna's master class painting now adorned the wall.

TWENTY ONE

ANNA

The chimera stood on the sill, a beam of light highlighting the horns of the goat, caught in dilemma between lion and serpent. After the accident to the real animal Anna had moved the bronze so it wasn't the first thing she saw when she woke. But sometime during the day it had been put back, presumably when the room was cleaned. She didn't bother to alter it again, for she was feeling nothing but relief.

Relief that Francesca had taken her rightful place in the fresco. No longer would Anna be the focus of resentment from any of the others. Now the bouquet of dead roses could no longer have any significance.

Her reaction at seeing the mural change had not been reflected on the faces of the others. Francesca had made no effort to hide her outrage, a deep, florid crimson covering her neck and cheeks as she struggled to keep her composure. All eyes had instinctively moved from the virgin in her vivid blue gown to the dark-haired woman standing in her pale faded dress, so much the diminished replica.

Matt had taken it upon himself to express her fury. 'What on earth do you mean by it?' He fixed accusing eyes on Paul and Sue.

She tossed her head.' How do you know it was us?'

'Well, you've been here all afternoon.'

'How do you know? I left the baptistery for some time. In

fact, Greg and Fran saw me. So perhaps you should just be looking at Paul as the culprit. Here,' Sue threw Paul's robe to him, 'you might be better able to deflect their criticism if you have some clothes on.'

Paul eased it on and slowly tied the belt. 'I also left the baptistery during the afternoon.' There was disbelief amongst his audience; someone had worked quickly and efficiently, as all of them knew that was how fresco painting was done. There could be no dawdling when plaster and paint were involved.

Matt moved to the mural, his critical gaze levelled at the brush strokes on the figure. 'I'll be able to see who did it by the style. The painter will have left his signature as surely as if he had signed his name.'

Paul said resignedly, 'We both decided to make the change. Though Sue now sees it is as prudent to deny all knowledge.'

'God in heaven!' Matt exploded, and small wonder. All of them had altered his original sketch but this violation was the final straw.

Paul shrugged in a curiously childish gesture. 'It was Sue who suggested it as a way to placate the gods. You saw this morning their displeasure.' The small man, caught in a corner, was extricating himself in the only way possible, accusing someone else of the deed.

Sue left them in no doubt why she had mooted the change. 'Why all this pussy-footing, anyway? Why not Fran the mother figure?' She laughed. 'Fran left art college because she was pregnant. She was not the sweet little nymph you wanted to believe.'

She looked straight at Greg.

'How dare you?' Francesca's voice was brittle. 'You bitch.'

Sue was unflinching. 'Just think, my dear, if you had actually chosen an Etruscan painting, you could have been portrayed lying with your man on the couch; whoever he was.'

'The soul grows gradually out of chaos only to disappear back into chaos.' Paul, the pedant, was milking the scene as only he could. 'The Etruscans knew that only too well.'

'You don't know what you are talking about, you silly little man.' Catarina, mute up to this point, entered the fray. 'How dare you, you violate both the present and the past by abusing the Signora.' She lifted a hand as if to strike him.

'Don't, Catarina. He's not worth it.' Matt shook his head at her.

'Now I think we should all go away and calm down.'

He turned to the silent figure beside him. 'Sorry, Anna, for this.'

'But I've always thought it should be Francesca. Blonde Madonnas just don't look right.' Her laugh was genuine. 'This figure of Francesca reminds me of the St. Galgano Madonna, dark, aloof and regal. I like it.' She pointed to the mural. 'Paul's painting is lovely.' She turned to Paul. 'Whether you know it or not you have found your old faith and painted a medieval virgin, whom all can venerate.'

'It's like the St Galgano fresco alright, right down to the addition of the serpent.' Fabio was gleeful. Coiled around the virgin's cloak, clinging to her shoulders, they had painted a snake. Originally decorating Eve in the church depiction, it now reclined on

Christ's mother. The others look bemused but Francesca's hands flew to her face in horror, then blindly she ran from the room.

'So who's coming to the group therapy meeting tonight?' Fabio was sarcastic. 'It would seem politic for someone not to show up. And it all points to Paul, not the flavour of the month I think.'

By now Fabio didn't need to explain his reasoning. Yet, everyone was well aware that even if seven seated themselves for the communal meal it would make little difference to the degenerating mood.

Anna walked alone, oblivious of her surroundings, wondering how to salvage the situation so that Francesca would have the happy time they all wished for her. Then, not everyone could be included in that sentiment. She considered Fabio's suggestion that not everyone was welcome at the birthday feast. Sue and Paul must surely be on the list. And what of Anna herself, someone in the castello thought she had outstayed her welcome.

Out in the garden, no chaos here except chaos of profusion as tiny vine tomatoes cascaded like bunches of grapes, and the grapes themselves, dark mauve, hung like wisteria about the wall. So nothing was as it seemed, it was a fantasy, an illusion, a chimera. The heady basil and rosemary invaded her head. She stooped to pick some grapes. Only a day or so and the vine harvest would begin. Not the brittle noise of sunflower gathering but the quiet dropping of fruit into baskets. It heralded the start of September and Francesca's celebration. She prayed for fruitful results for both events.

The perfume of the herbs lingered, her legs must have brushed against the bushes and she carried the aroma with her along a new path she had not trod before. A stately stand of Cypress pines beckoned and she aimed for it. A cool glade was what she wanted, and surely it was where everyone could head to cool down. Of course, why hadn't she thought of it before, the evening meal could be al fresco? Out in the open there would be no mural to dominate their thoughts. No restricting walls would threaten limit to the size of the group. Anna could feel a burden lift from her shoulders.

She reached the trees with quickened step and was surprised to see they screened a squat, stone building; its purpose unmistakable. Gravestones littered the ground; a mausoleum that once was heavily involved in the life and death at the castello.

Rusty railings surrounded the forgotten building, once vertical they now lay in a horizontal trellis of unconnected metal. The gate hung limply from a solitary hinge and creaked a loud protest as she squeezed through. Late afternoon sunshine speckled the old stones, giving an air of resignation. Here everyone knew their place, she acknowledged with a rueful grin: the deep-etched letters on the stones named the past, but now no longer had any meaning for the present. They could belong to the last century or prehistoric times.

But there was life here. Tomb-shaped hives clustered about the building for the dead and the bees hummed. Theirs was the gentle murmur of pleasure, as comforting as the bunches of grapes and the clusters of tomatoes ready for harvest back in the garden.

Harvest? She thought of how she had wasted her time there; she'd done nothing, painted neither landscapes nor profiles. She had explained to Matt, in what seemed an eternity ago, that it was the prospect of landscapes that had brought her to Tuscany. But what of the profiles that surrounded her? What better subjects than her fellow guests at the castello? She had seen them all full face and began to think she knew what made them tick. The trick would be to try to reveal them side faced. She felt a thrill of pleasure. The challenge of this disparate group could turn her portfolio from Italy into something more than just a zealously recorded gallery of unknowns.

Handsome Fabio would be as she first saw him, no reason to think he was other than the strong-jawed striking figure on the vaporetta. Or was he? For good or bad, Chiesa a Castello controlled what he was. Her early glimpse of Francesca had shown a rather insignificant plain woman, but now she knew differently and had seen her change in just a few days. Greg was charming with a roving eye, but he was weak. Sue, with her cold eyes and put-you-downs, pert and clear cut; Paul she would show sympathetically. Even now he needed consideration; Catarina's face had perfect proportion; attractive to look at, as was her personality. Matt? She stopped to consider him, calm, reasonable but—

Yes, to her it was Matt who had changed the most. She remembered in the Venice trattoria she had considered him not worth the paint, but now— And what about herself, in this confined world? She was beginning to see herself as Paul saw her: the troubled rebel ready at last to step out of her past fetters.

The bees were busy, coming and going. They seemed remarkably free and yet she knew they led heavily controlled, short lives. For now they buzzed cheerfully in their corner, not knowing what tomorrow would bring; the mausoleum held only yesterdays. She tried the door and it opened easily.

Fabio looked up in surprise as she entered. 'Anna. I knew you would discover this place sooner or later. So you have found my little workshop.'

'Workshop?' She glanced around, no tools or machines, just a number of objects lying atop the stones.

'Well, let's just say it's the wash house. This has just been through the dish washer, so to speak.'

A rectangular stone chest lay covered in water droplets. It looked like any garden-centre planter but even to her unpractised eye it was obviously ancient.

'What's that?'

'An ash chest. Used by the Etruscans in their burial rites. The ashes were placed inside the chest and then a stone on top kept you nice and snug; away from the rats and serpents.'

'You make it sound very cosy.' She smiled at him. 'Is this the lid?'

'Yes, carved during the lifetime of the occupant, that way you got a pretty good likeness of the deceased. Only after death did others work on the box, because it was only then that they knew how the end had come about.'

'Very efficient.' Intrigued, she studied the lid. 'So I'm looking at a genuine Etruscan?'

'Indeed.'

The head carved upon it was small and well defined; eyes wide apart, mouth and nose merging. Was there something mean about the mouth or was it just a hesitant smirk? Did he tease his viewers? Fabio's sunglasses lay beside the chest. Playfully, she picked them up and placed them on the sculpted head, and then burst out laughing.

'Look, Fabio, our friend here looks just like Paul. He could be his double. Do you think he also went round naked?'

Fabio smiled lazily. 'And so that appeals to you, Anna? Few clothes mean less inhibition, wouldn't you agree?' He moved towards her. 'Don't tell me the cold Englander has become hotter under the Tuscan sun?' He ran his hand down her arm. 'So much life in you I think, if the manner of it can be found.' His lips pressed hard on hers. His hands were cold on her arms.

'Get off me.' She was furious, but equally surprised that his delayed attentions were so unwanted by her. A few days ago, and she would have welcomed them. He stopped, his face reflecting his amazement at the rebuff. Slowly, he retrieved his sunglasses from the funereal lid and said sarcastically, 'Still the little frigid Anna I see.'

'Fabio, I— You surprised me, this isn't the—'She indicated the mausoleum. 'This isn't the place.'

'So tell me, where is the right place?'

'Well, not here.' She shivered, but already she knew she would never welcome his advances.

'No, the castello is no longer the place for you. You and I see that now.'

Angrily, he picked up his glasses that Anna had placed on the burial lid. 'How clever of you to see the resemblance of Paul to the carving, I shall take great pleasure in showing the insufferable little man his awaiting casket.'

'O, come on, Fabio. I only said I saw a likeness.'

'Indeed, as will he.'

'You couldn't be so cruel.' Desperately, she wanted to end this encounter, but hesitated, not wanting to leave soured relations between them.

'Why not?'

'Well, for a start, Paul isn't a hunter.' She sought to diffuse Fabio's threat. 'It looks like a hunting scene.'

'So is he the hunter or hunted?' Fabio queried. 'Yes, it's a winter wild boar hunt, when feasts for the dead were held.'

'So,' she gulped, 'that makes our summer party safe.' With a sense of relief she traced her fingers over the hunted animal on the lid, smooth and plump and waiting to be caught.

'Perhaps.' He surveyed the artefacts strewn about them. 'But there are plenty more beside that one. The chests were two a penny, made of terracotta and of no intrinsic value.'

'But now they must be worth quite a bit?' She strove to humour him.

'Yes, so let's look for a lid for you, Anna.' He caught hold of her hand. 'Let us play your game of fit a carving to a castello inmate.'

'O come on, Fabio. Stop.'

'You started it.' Fabio bent over a chest. 'The sculpture is badly worn but I can see a brush, and as the figure is definitely a woman it must be a female artist.' He was making it up as he went along. 'Now, that is intriguing, is it not? We have a choice of three candidates within the group, you, Sue or Francesca. The figure is slim so that rules out Francesca. It is young so that rules out Sue. That only leaves you, my dear Anna.'

TWENTY TWO

FRANCESCA

The tower had always been her refuge. The best preserved part of the castle, even on that first day as she'd scrambled up its crumbling steps, pushed open a protesting door and entered its shadowy interior, she had felt its protection wrap itself around her. And when she opened the sagging shutters, looked out of the glassless windows and saw Fabio among his goats, she knew she had found her home.

Sanctuary had never been more needed than now. How well had she hidden her distress from the others, of the mural change of the Madonna? She closed the door behind her and lent against the solid chestnut. Bracing her back ramrod straight like the door, some sort of composure returned to her frame. She would be equal with her bastion walls; there would be no crumbling. Sue had wrung bitter tears, but that belonged to the past. She would not let her succeed again.

Tapping sounded on the door, just one inch away, on the other side of the wood. Who could it be? No one climbed those steps other than her. The knocking came again. This time it was more resolute. Anna stood on the threshold, an uncertain smile about her lips. She was right to wonder at her reception.

The girl was agitated and did not wait for an invitation but walked past her hostess, into the room. Then she turned and put her arms around Francesca in a long embrace. And Francesca felt the girl's need.

'Francesca, I've wanted to do that all afternoon.' She was engagingly eager.

'Thank you, Anna,' Francesca said stiffly, squashing the thought that a daughter would do what the girl was doing now, just showing natural family concern. Francesca said, 'We have missed so much: you a mother, me a daughter.'

'Yes, you'd have been better than the real one.'

'I—I thought you didn't know her—'

'O, I know who my real mother is. I've always known.'

The disappointment was a nonsense.

Anna said, looking about her, 'How lovely this room is. No wonder you like it so much. And look at that view.' Together they gazed out. The courtyard with its cell bedrooms slumbered in lethargy, and beyond, the immediate fields were green and purple. A line of Cypress trees rose as fingers into the late afternoon haze; one to five, like a green gloved hand pointing the way. The girl had it in her sights.

'I've been to the mausoleum.'

'Yes, it's reassuring to know I shall end up there.'

Anna said, 'Fabio has your sense of humour.' There was a quizzical look on her face.

'I'm not joking, I mean it. Could you really want a nicer corner?'

'After a good life span.' Anna was quick to qualify the sentiment.

'That goes without saying.' Francesca was dismissive.' So

what do you make of Fabio? What further tricks has he been up to, nothing I hope to compare with the performance from Sue?'

Anna sighed, 'No. That would be hard to beat. But Fabio and Paul, they seem to be heavily involved with all things...'

'Etruscan?' Francesca smiled, 'very necessary in the early days when we needed credibility, anything to catch the punters' imagination. What better ploy than to magnify the small pieces of foundation dating back to those times as something significant? Everybody knows about the Romans, not many can tell you anything about their predecessors.'

'Surely Paul and Fabio don't perform the *haroscopy* every week.' Anna was disbelieving.

'O, gracious no. I've never seen that little enactment before. It must have been put on for the entertainment of you, my special guests. Don't worry, I'm sure Fabio and Paul weren't serious. I must say I didn't find it as disturbing as—'

'Please don't be upset by the changing of the Madonna. I don't know why they did it, but I truly believe you are the mother figure of the Castello, and it is that I came to tell you.'

'O, Anna.' The tears Francesca had been determined not to shed pricked her eyes; momentarily her vision became the afternoon haze lying about the hills. 'That is the nicest thing anyone has ever said. You are a dear girl.'

There was sound on the steps outside and another knock on the door. Catarina entered at the summons and then stopped, amazed to see another figure in the hideaway. Her concern was immediate.

'Are you alright, Signora?'

'Yes, Catarina, of course I am.'

She had a parcel in her hand and she thrust it forward. 'Your birthday presents arrive already. The Lucia family delivered this.'

'How kind. Put it down there, Catarina, I shall not open it until tomorrow.'

Anna still hovered. 'What's this, Francesca, it's lovely?' She picked up a paper pad from a small table under the window.

'It's not really meant for other eyes. I've sketched an imaginary Etruscan scene.'

Anna laughed nervously. 'The Etruscans are taking over. There are even ash chests in the mausoleum, waiting for occupants, or so Fabio wants me to believe.'

'Gracious, what do you mean by that?' Catarina still stood, reluctant perhaps to leave the girl in the sanctuary. Well, soon she would have to accept change. What would have been her reaction if Greg had been the tower intruder?

The uninvited visitors lingered, both staring at her drawing. Francesca said, hurriedly, 'You should be painting, Anna?' It was a nudge for the girl to disappear, though Francesca felt torn. The girl looked so vulnerable, her fair hair a halo of innocence. 'You look so young when your hair hangs loose.'

Anna tossed her head. 'I like long hair. Lots of possibilities.'

Francesca laughed. 'So we await a new hairstyle for my birthday banquet, Anna. Perhaps you should go and practice in front of a mirror.' Another gentle hint she would like her to go.

'Fran—Francesca, I—I think the time has come for me to leave.'

'That's what I've been suggesting, my dear, there's still enough of the day for you to—'

'Oh, no, I mean leave the castello.'

'What? Before my birthday celebration?' Francesca looked stricken. 'You can't mean that.'

'Yes, I do. I've been the gatecrasher for long enough.' Then, as Anna saw her hostess's expression, 'Well, the day after the birthday, then. No later.'

Francesca sighed, 'So you've tired of us?'

'I've taken enough of your hospitality, that's what I mean.' Anna was close to tears. 'I take Paul's warnings seriously, even if no one else does. When we are seated in the baptistery, all I feel is the one not invited to the feast.' She shivered, then, 'Look, why don't we have a picnic tonight? Then perhaps I won't feel quite the intruder.' Her face lit up. 'We can all help carry it,' she added as she noted Catarina's hesitation. 'What about under the cypress trees? It would be ideal there. And a picnic would mean no one has to sit next to anyone they don't want to.'

Sceptical, Francesca looked to Catarina. The housekeeper was definitely not a picnic person. Her loving introduction to each bottle of wine might appear somewhat contrived outdoors.

But Catarina nodded, 'The menu would be suitable.'

'So that's settled then. It's a Solomon idea. Spread the news, Anna. It might make folk change their idea about what to wear— informal, you are right, no place settings, no eight people sitting around the table when there should only be—' With a shock Francesca realised she was repeating Paul's mantra.

Catarina crossed herself. 'Signora, do you think we are slipping into chaos?'

Shocked, Francesca shook her head. 'Definitely not. How could we when you are in control. You know how I depend on you.'

As if to verify her employer's belief, Catarina took hold of Anna's arm and they moved to the door. Francesca heard them descending the ancient stone steps and watched them walk their separate ways. She glanced down at the small table and her sketchpad. This was her own masterpiece in the making, Etruscan tactile man and woman in a wild feasting of dancing and loving.

The sketch showed the man and woman mirroring one another; bent and extended limbs intertwined, making them one. They followed convention: the female with pale skin, the man in red. The woman was slim and graceful, in delicate clothes, the bare-chested man sturdy. Shoulders and torso were viewed from the front, whilst feet, legs and heads were seen from the side. The woman was dark haired, the man was fair. The woman wore earrings, and Francesca had added a beautiful necklace. The castanets held by the woman added music to the dance that would lead them to Eternity.

Even now, in its unfinished state, the sketch moved her. She wanted to touch the bronzed flesh, feel the warmth of the man's skin. Every stroke of the brush was hers. She smiled indulgently, relieved she had put no facial features onto the figures. Neither Catarina nor Anna could tell who were the dancers. She stared at the figure of the man. Did he really merit his role in the dance?

Her sigh was loud and long; and there in her sanctuary, she considered for the first time the possibility that her partner would have to earn his place. She picked up a pencil, but did not make a mark. The man's features were left undrawn.

She showered, and on impulse put on the simple cream dress she had planned to wear the next day for her birthday banquet. The baptistery was confining, just as the fresco being painted on its wall.

TWENTY THREE

ANNA

They were a noisy carefree lot that trooped through the garden, down to the glade by the cypress trees. Everyone had got the message about the change of venue. All except Paul, though Anna had slipped a note under his door, so he would know where to find them.

It was a much under-dressed group that assembled in the courtyard at the usual time. They'd all taken advantage of the proposed informal gathering, their hostess the most dressed. But her outfit was lovely, and flowed naturally with the movement of her body as she negotiated the path. She had a grace that Anna hadn't noticed before. Sue as usual was immaculate, her dress plain and simple. She looked elegant, though not out of place, and Catarina followed a similar code. Greg and Matt wore just beige cotton trousers. Anna was surprised at the extent of Matt's informality and her eyes were drawn to the muscular back that moved in front of her. He was looking rather dishy and she felt a sudden shyness at her reaction. She would miss him. His broad shoulders looked supportive from any angle, his arm about her an attractive thought. Fabio's playful bullying, if that's what it was, had upset her equilibrium? Fabio had made little effort. From his appearance it would seem he had hardly washed his face, let alone changed his gear. In contrast, Anna had taken some time to choose what she was going to wear, a summer dress hardly manageable sitting crossed legged on the grass. At the end it was back to trousers and top, though she had managed to come up with something other than jeans. Her linen Naples yellow cut-off trousers provided a bright focus in the single file.

They were all beasts of burden, everyone helping to transport the essentials plus goodies. She wondered how much Catarina had considered to be picnic-essential. Had she fought with herself to stop ordering table and chairs, even of the garden variety, to be carried down to the spot? But there was none to be seen, just a crate of wine placed under the trees. No doubt Riccardo had been roped in to be beast of burden for that.

Anna carried two of the rugs, Matt the other two, and they spread them out randomly. Each would hold a couple, the occupants reluctant or happy to partner their companion. If not, they had the choice of leaning against a tree or just wandering off to sit amongst the cypress, though at this time of day shade was irrelevant. In the south-eastern corner of the grounds the lowering sun was trapped behind the resolute walls of the castle. Neither Greg nor Matt would add much to their skin colour.

Everyone was soon on hands and knees, setting up the picnic. Carefree chat interspersed with laughter showed that the unpleasantness of earlier in the day had been forgotten. Francesca could still have a happy birthday on the following day, now they'd found the propitious corner.

Anna felt a rising of her spirits. She loved picnics, her happier memories of childhood were of going en famille up to

Greenwich Park and standing astride the meridian line, holding a ham sandwich in the west, and a tomato clutched in her other hand in the east. Of course, then she hadn't known that the tomato would have been the food of the gods. She smiled to herself. What a good thing she hadn't been aware of such things then. She would have been an even more obnoxious child than she had been.

It was no ham sandwich, Battenburg cake and banana picnic here. Rita had prepared an al fresco feast and Catarina was coping as though she presided over an outdoor meal every day of her life. Deftly, she uncovered the dishes and set them in the middle of the rugs, silver knives and forks wrapped in thick napkins awaited takers, and the salt and pepper cruet would have graced any table. It could never be said they were slumming it. Crystal glasses had come with the wine bottles. No plastic was within sight.

Understated elegant life wherever it was lived at the castello, and very soon it would all come to an end. For her an unknown period of her life stretched ahead, another week or so in Italy and then what? Painting suburbia's children and pets? She had not coped well with her own childhood, the thought of other little dears was too awful to contemplate. She looked toward Sue. She had always been someone to emulate; a successful artist, doing her own thing for those out there willing to pay high prices. She could be useful to her in her own future. Gracious, she came to with a jolt. The Shangri la of Francesca's home was having a detrimental effect on her objectivity.

In response to her selfish thoughts, Anna jumped to her feet. 'I volunteer to be waiter this evening.' So saying, she seized the

227

plates from Catarina and went to where Francesca and Greg were seated on one of the rugs. In turn she served the rest, though there was still no sign of Paul. Sue was lounging alone. There was also a space beside Matt. Job complete, Anna chose to sit beside him.

'Hi, Anna.' He was already involved with his salmon pâté and offered no other word, but looked pleased to see her. From the first mouthful she could see why.

'Wow, Catarina, this is one of the best things I've ever tasted.'

'A family secret recipe, but I am happy to give it to you, Anna. It is just a mix of salmon and mascarpone with extras.'

'What gives it the slight bitterness? Whatever it is just makes it.'

Catarina smiled. 'Artichoke hearts.'

'Something to try when I get home, though my artichokes will have to come out of a tin. I hope the special taste isn't because these are grown in the Garden of Eden here.'

Matt finished eating, took her plate with his and rose to his feet. She wanted him to come back, then remembered he was usurping her job anyway, grabbed at his leg and he subsided without a struggle. 'Okay, I'll let you do it, Anna, if you promise to return. I'll keep the place for you.' His words reflected her thoughts exactly.

'Has anyone seen Paul?' Anna espied an unused plate and a set of cutlery.

'When I saw him, he seemed rather out of sorts.' Francesca threw in her unhelpful comment, and no one else bothered to reply.

228

Anna collected the empty plates and went round with the wine bottle. It seemed to take an age, people moving around, spreading out, but Matt did as he had promised. She collapsed down beside him, and without speaking, both listened to the bees buzzing their contentment.

'I presume, if you know about butterflies, you must know about birds and bees as well.' Anna was being flippant.

'Yes. Does that surprise you?'

'No, tell me more, I'm very innocent.'

'You'll soon wish you hadn't got me on to my favourite subject.' He cleared his throat as though he was about to start a lecture.

Anna laughed, 'Oh, well, I asked for it.'

'You did! So here goes—folk wisdom had it that bumblebees shouldn't be able to fly with such heavy bodies and simple wings. They look as improbable as Jumbo jets taking off. But it's all to do with heat control. They actually shiver to get their muscles to the right temperature for lift off.' He paused.

'Oh, Matt, you can't stop there.'

He grinned,' No such luck, but you'll have to wait. That's enough for this instalment. I can't hog you all evening, and you have your waitress duties.' He helped her to her feet, and when she looked to return, Francesca had taken her place.

They cleared away the aftermath of the picnic. Willing hands stacked away the residue, though they clung to their glasses and Anna did the rounds with the bottle again. People were standing, now wanting to stretch their legs, leaning against the trees. The heavy scent of the pines was soporific.

But Francesca had no intention of letting proceedings come to an early conclusion. From nowhere she produced castanets. She moved to the paved area in front of the mausoleum, and slowly she began to dance, her fingers and her feet following the vibrant music. It was a sharp staccato crack of noise. She twisted and turned, her simple cream dress in rhythm, clinging to her body. She danced a figure of eight, in, out and round the other way, in perfect time with the evocative sound. The others watched, fascinated. Tonight their hostess had moved outside her character.

Matt, standing beside Anna, whispered, 'Folklore always said bumblebees should not be able to fly. She has taken off.' Anna bit her lip to stop herself laughing out loud. It was unkind and not like him. But no one else could hear. The castanets were raucous, like the metallic sound of dead sunflower seeds being cut from their stems. Yet that image did not belong to the magic of this night.

The sound of the music faded, and slowly Francesca uncoiled out of the movement. She stopped before Greg. He needed no invitation. Falteringly and then with increased confidence, he danced with her. They watched the pale woman dancing with the bare chested man. His body glowed red with sweat in the deepening gloom. The scene stirred primeval memory, ritual dance with hidden meaning. Francesca was lost to the music and the moment, and Greg followed, obeying her every move. They danced until Greg spluttered for breath and fell beside the nearest tree for support. Francesca laughed; it cracked into the dark, unsympathetic and dismissive. She stopped in front of Matt.

She was not finished yet. Her breath came deep and fast. She was triumphant. She held out her hand and Matt took it. The two figures stood, momentarily still. Then castanets began again, slowly, harsh and discordant. They had no melody, yet Matt was immediately into the dance, showing none of the first unsure steps of Greg. He was a natural, his movement unconscious. Matt and Francesca danced as equals. They moved together, apart, and then as if drawn by some hidden note, moved together again. The older woman hugged him to her when they finished and he kissed her lightly on the cheek as he extricated himself.

He came, breathless, to stand in front of Anna and she said with a pout, 'Quite a performance.'

He was roused. 'Something I share with the bees.' And seizing both her hands, they began to move, even though Francesca had ceased her music. 'Bees always dance a figure of eight when they return to the hive. Their waggle dance shows the rest of the group the direction of the best pollen and nectar.'

Deep into the dark, all sound of the others melted away. There was silence. Their movements were as old as time and so were his embrace and kiss.

The moon had risen and it showed the retreating figures. 'We should go.' His reluctance held her.

'Should we?' But she knew he was right. They followed towards the dark shape of the castello, looming large and solid in the pale light, resolute, always there. For a brief time the picnic had transported them away from its constraint, but now, obediently, they returned like bees to their hive. Anna waggled her behind. Matt's hand stilled the movement and suddenly Anna was immeasurably happy.

They caught up with the others loitering in the courtyard, and not knowing why, she counted them. One to seven, tonight they had been the magic number. No number eight to spoil the proceedings. Surely Paul had got her note?

'O, at last, there's Paul.' Sue interrupted Anna's concern, for climbing up the steps into the courtyard was the missing artist.

'Paul, how could we possibly miss you?' He had followed them from the direction of the mausoleum. His eyes behind his glasses blinked in the unexpected light.

'Where have you been, Paul?' Francesca questioned her guest.

'You missed a good picnic.' Catarina sounded personally aggrieved, yet neither she nor anyone else had commented on his absence. Only Anna had missed him. Was it because of his non-attendance that the picnic had been such a success? Anna found herself thinking the unthinkable, that the Etruscan number seven influenced even the twenty first century.

And immediately, with the old grouping, there was tension. The earlier good humour was melting away, back down into the bee glade with the addition of Paul. But their usual numbering of eight was short lived; in the shadows there was another figure. Anna was not the only one to jump in surprise and Francesca exclaimed, 'Why, it is Giu…Giuseppe,' as the man moved from the shadows. A tired looking Catarina scowled as he moved to her side. Instinctively, Anna guessed he must be her unknown husband.

'You are too early.' Catarina's tone was far from pleased, but his boyish grin lit his swarthy face in the otherwise camouflaged figure.

'I cannot go to bed. It is always thus on the eve of September. Not many men around here will sleep this night.' His accent was thick. Without a word, Catarina turned on her heel. Giuseppe followed, meekly for such a large man, like a dog with its tail between its legs. For some reason they all found it funny. Anna giggled with the rest, glad the evening was ending in laughter.

Matt whispered to her, 'Birthday celebrations will get in our way, but then— Promise me you'll stay.'

TWENTY FOUR
FRANCESCA

Francesca's birthday dawned with firecrackers. They resonated about the castello, a juddering salvo of noise, so loud they could have woken the dead. Francesca jumped out of bed and ran to the window, almost expecting to see some giant weaving Chinese dragon prancing below, in a ritual dance of celebration. There was nothing, but the sound came again and with it she was fully awake. Of course, it was September the first, and she recognised the noise. It shuddered again in a splintered rasp of sound, a morning bugle call targeting the shirkers. But then many like Giuseppe would not even have slept in their beds.

The hunting season had returned and there would be no tardy answer to the summons. Any man worth his calling would be ready, eagerly anticipating this day since the end of the previous season. She found herself hoping the wood pigeons were in hiding. The target for today, in a fortnight it would be the pheasants. As September progressed, no birds or beasts would be safe in this part of the world. She peered out but the hunters were deep in the wood.

She was wide awake, like a child eager for its birthday treats. Today was her day. Everyone would be on their best behaviour, perhaps even Sue. Francesca smiled with satisfaction; that would be something to milk. She gazed down into the courtyard, empty now, but the stage was set for her birthday pageant. They would come from the wings out onto the stage, and she would direct them in what to do and what to say. Yes, Francesca, no, Francesca, whatever you say, Francesca.

Her nonsense thoughts occupied her dressing, so bizarre they were only worthy of a hangover. She'd drunk a considerable amount of wine at the picnic. How otherwise could she have made such a spectacle of herself. They didn't know she could dance like that. Sue had made no protest when she chose Greg as partner, and she had tamed him. He was glad to stop. Then on to dear Matteo; bare chest indeed, so out of character. Only Paul had not been there to see her abandoned dance, and of course Fabio had known to stay out of her reach.

Paul should have been dancing attendance if nothing else. She'd had enough of Paul, he was wearing thin, very thin. How dare he ruin this time for her. He'd been shocked at her summons to see him and even more shocked at the bad news. Enough to skip the picnic. Well, served him right. He was arrogant, self-opinionated and not at all grateful that he owed his income to her. He needed teaching a lesson.

Breakfast on the terrace awaited. It was only when she reached the bottom of the tower steps that she remembered it was far too early for the first meal of the day. Even the faithful Catarina would probably still be in her bed, lying doggo, like the rest of the group. Only the hunters would be abroad, seeking the early bird. A shudder of firing broke the morning peace. But it was spasmodic, muffled by the surrounding wood. In contrast, a heavy stillness hung over her home, and she stood, indecisive, by the pots of geraniums.

235

The distant firing came again; safety lay confined in the small world of her castello. Out beyond its secure walls, the earth would be sullied.

She was not the only prompt riser. Anna swung round as Francesca opened the door to the baptistery. 'O, you're an early bird.' Both women blinked at each other.

'Definitely not the thing to be today,' Francesca laughed and gesticulated to the wider world beyond as another burst of firing sounded nearer to home.

Anna shuddered, 'It sounds an orgy of killing. I shouldn't think anything is safe today.'

'Certainly not if you're a pigeon. But where ever you are, take care if you leave the castello. The hunters have been inactive too long. Anything that moves will be a target.'

'Oh, but no one will think of leaving the castello. Not on a day like today. Francesca, I haven't wished you Happy Birthday.' Anna grinned and gave her an affectionate hug followed by a peck on the cheek. Francesca returned the embrace, somewhat stiffly, and then they both stared at each other, suddenly embarrassed. Francesca looked beyond the girl and saw she had interrupted Anna as artist at work.

'My personal birthday present to you, Francesca: I've removed the viper.'

Francesca smiled for the first time that morning, her birthday. She was surprisingly tense.

'Thank you.' The gratitude was brief and Anna looked disappointed.

236

'The change isn't perfect but the new thicker line of the cloak is passable; no one will notice the difference.' Anna smiled to see the sudden relief on Francesca's face. 'I don't think either of us care for reptiles very much.'

'No,' Francesca frowned, 'especially the local horned viper. Here we have the longest snake in Europe. You should ask Matt, he knows about such things.'

'I will next time I've got half an hour to spare.' They both laughed and Anna asked, 'Are the local ones venomous?'

'Yes, lethal.'

'Oh well, it took just a few brush strokes to get rid of it, not so easy in real life.' Solemnly, Anna turned to her. 'Francesca, tell me who is the viper here?'

'What do you mean?'

'I think you know.' The girl put her hand into her pocket to retrieve a small metal object. The Chimera rested in the palm of her hand, and she smoothed the goat. 'I know it's ridiculous, but this bronze has got to me. It's followed me from Venice.'

'You're not still thinking about the dead animal are you? It probably deserved all it got.'

'No, I know that. It's this Etruscan goat that intrigues me. It's fanciful of course, but Paul likened me to the creature, and I almost feel as though I've become it. Unhappily, caught between viper and lion.' Anna laughed apologetically. Then, 'You haven't answered my question. Who is the viper at Chiesa a Castello?'

Francesca looked at her long and hard. 'Don't you know?'

They clapped as she descended the final step on to the shady area that ran along the south wall. They were expecting her, packages piled beside the croissants and the soda bread. Catarina still hovered. Then, there would be nothing usual about today.

'Many happy returns, Signora.' Catarina pushed a package from the pile into her hand. So began the day's theatre as she dutifully opened her presents. Did not one of them know her sufficiently well enough to realise she didn't want this fuss? Not even Catarina. So she opened Catarina's present first. It was a box of her special biscuits, made from a family recipe.

'Thank you, Catarina. You know what will please me.'

'Prego, Signora.'

She picked another package from the pile. It was Anna's turn to look concerned, though it had Fabio and Paul's cards attached.

'It is rather delicate, Francesca. Take care,' the girl warned.

'Gracious, where on earth did you get this?'

Fabio noted her change of voice. 'What's the matter, Francesca, don't you like it? It's highly collectable.'

'The Bucchero Sottile of Etruscan Funeral banquets, not your everyday ware. I shall have to keep it for a very special occasion, and not one I care to dwell on today.' She turned the shiny black cup, with its dark grey inner core, over in her hand, questioning their motives. 'I'm desperate for something to drink, but not in this.' Immediately, a flurry of hands sought the coffee pot and cup. She took a long gulp of the reviving liquid.

I've never drunk coffee from Bucchero, but I expect you

238

have, Paul?'

She sounded belligerent, and as she spoke she wondered if anyone in the group could take him to task. Just tell him to cool it on the Etruscan thing. 'Come on, why don't you fill it up, Paul, or will I desecrate it?' She held out the Etruscan vessel, but it was Matt who filled up her china one. She took another long drink. Paul stood silent beside her.

'Thank you, my dear Matteo, that's just what I need; certainly no food, the killing about us has put me off,' she said as Matt offered the plate of croissants. Above her comment they heard the hunters.

'That was close. It will be slaughter all day. You chose the wrong birthday, Francesca.' Fabio admonished as a loud bang reverberated, this time just below the castello.

Matt frowned. 'Anyone planning to venture forth this morning should take great care.'

'Indeed, Fran, don't you go lurking in the woods. We wouldn't want our birthday girl as target.' Sue picked at her croissant. 'Don't let Greg lead you up the garden path.'

'Look, the hunters have built a new hide just beyond the garden.' They followed Anna's pointing finger to the large open field. In its very centre, a makeshift hide had appeared overnight.

Fabio laughed, 'Giuseppe must have built himself a comfortable little billet. Catarina, did you force him to sleep there last night?'

The housekeeper chose to ignore him.

Anna questioned,' What is it? It's shaped like a beehive,

239

and-or an Etruscan tomb.' But Paul remained silent, his usual willingness to instruct not forthcoming. Was he towing the line on this, Francesca's name day, or had he really taken her decision to heart?

Greg stood up and stretched. 'Well, I don't know about you lot, but I'm staying put within the castello walls. Preferably, some place with uninterrupted sun. Not much more time to feel the beneficial ultra violet rays before we leave tomorrow.' His comment dropped like a bombshell.

'Tomorrow?' Francesca did not hide her surprise.

'Oh, hasn't Sue told you? Sorry. She wants a couple of days in Pisa before we go home?'

'Who's thinking of tomorrow when we have all of today to look forward to?' Matt interrupted. 'Francesca, I've booked a table for two at La Fenice for lunch. The others have things to do,' he added meaningfully.

Francesca struggled to take in his words, her mind filled with Greg's treachery. 'I—I can't think of anything better. It's a lovely idea.' So they wanted her out of the place, and it was Matt who had drawn the short straw. She left them to finish their last dregs of coffee. Francesca knew their eyes followed her steps. She felt exposed, as if she were out in that open field, trying to reach the safety of the temporary hide. Watching eyes and silence. There was no birdsong, then how could there be on such a day.

TWENTYFIVE
ANNA

'That was a bit unnecessary, wasn't it?' Anna could hardly wait for Francesca to be out of earshot before she turned on Greg. 'It sounded as though you're desperate to get away.' She was surprised by how furious she was with the man. It was obvious to anyone, Francesca's feelings for him. He looked surprised, as she was, at her tone of voice.

'Little and fierce aren't you ? Sorry, I didn't think.'

Anna didn't reply, she guessed that was the story of Greg's life. Hardly an excuse. She had felt the intense disappointment of Francesca, though the woman had hidden it well. She'd changed so much over the few short days. What a shame to remind her on this day of all days that soon she would be alone; left once more in her solitary lifestyle.

'We should all be on our best behaviour today.' Anna was still addressing Greg, and he was taking it on the chin.

'You're right, Anna. It was stupid. I am not the most diplomatic person around.' He looked chastened.

Matt said, 'She's on edge. Only natural I suppose. There are birthdays and birthdays. I don't suppose I'll be too thrilled to reach thirty, let alone forty for that matter.'

'You will never notice, Matt, you'll be far too busy watching wildlife, oblivious of the more fascinating human antics around you. You'll be behind a bush, half way up a mountainside, spying on the lesser crested bogwarbler.'

Yet again, Sue had defused the situation with her insightful sarcasm. Anna joined in the amusement. The woman kept them from becoming totally introspective. But her intention to leave in the morning, and Greg's compliance, had thrown the cat amongst the pigeons. Especially when Anna herself had hinted to Francesca that she had thoughts of leaving.

'Actually, Matt, too bad you're otherwise engaged this morning, I had hoped to persuade you half way up a hillside to photograph wildlife. You seem to attract it to you. Have you seen any more rare butterflies?' Sue was clearly eager to find something to do other than birthday plans.

Greg interrupted. 'Don't take her, Matt. Sue can't sit still. In fact, all the females of the species are edgy at the moment.'

Anna didn't rise to the bait, surprised Greg was that observant. Sue was indignant.

'Hey, come on, I can sit still for hours if necessary, and as for Anna—' The older woman had turned to face the girl, but stopped in mid-sentence and looked at her as though she was seeing her for the first time. She said reflectively, 'Anna is a past master of watching and waiting. You should get her to tell you about her misspent youth some time.'

'What do you mean by that, I—I—'

Matt said, hastily, 'No, I haven't seen a single butterfly, Sue, not since the Blue Tailed Pasha. If it hadn't been for Anna, I wouldn't have seen it then. Anyway, count me in on any butterfly

242

watch, though not today when Giuseppe and his mates have got their blood up.'

He looked round the room to check Catarina had followed her employer and said, 'Catarina is certainly a bit het up. Then, this day is almost more important to her than it is to Francesca. She is the party animal.'

Fabio said languidly, 'Catarina is Tuscan! Her feast for a funeral banquet would be as big as for any wedding.'

'Hope you're not tempting fate. Do stop mentioning them in the same breath. Catarina would be crossing herself if she could hear.' Anna shivered, the terrace was shaded at this time of day, and though it would be hot by noon, there was a morning chill. She had dressed in scruffy jeans and t-shirt to do the painting, had got heated whilst she worked, now she needed sun or something extra on. What a mess she must have looked. Who indeed was she to chide other folk at the birthday breakfast? She reflected on her state of dress, and her earlier conversation with Francesca in the baptistery. It had hardly been a laugh a minute, talking of her obsession with the chimera and the local deadly snakes. She got to her feet.

'Where are you off to?' Sue was watching her.

'I've just remembered how untidy I am. I'd better go and do something about it.'

'Your waif and stray look suits you, doesn't it, Matt?' Sue's tone of voice gave no indication whether it was meant as a compliment or not.

Anna grimaced, 'I bet, Sue, you look scruffy sometimes?'

'If you mean do I get messy when I paint, of course I do,

who doesn't?'

'Oh well, you usually look glam. I remember a time at the Tate Gallery.' Anna tried to smile.

'Tate Gallery?' The woman was surprised, but Anna already knew the cogs of memory were oiled. 'Anna, have we met before?'

Oh, she knew alright.

'Sorry, I can't remember...' Sue sounded convincing.

Anna said, 'You were wearing a lime green suit. I thought it the most stylish thing I had ever seen. And I told you so.' Eleven years old and she had been seeing colour for the first time, and it had been on Sue Simpson.

'Why, I do remember that outfit, but honestly, I can't remember any conversation with...' Now she looked from Anna's face to her stained jeans. 'Anyway, what have you been up to this morning, Anna? You look as though you've been in at the kill.' It brought all eyes to her legs. There was a wide red stain above the left knee.

Fabio reached out to touch the offending spot. 'Is it blood?'

'No, I've added roses to the mural.'

'Shit—Great, of course. Well done, Anna. So that's it, finished on time. I must admit, after the debacle yesterday, I couldn't go near the mural. I'd had enough.' Matt looked apologetic.

'So that's that then.' Sue sounded bored. 'Everyone recorded for posterity, even Catarina, and she is only staff.'

'Hardly.' Fabio looked bemused. 'If you really think that, then how do you consider me?'

'Well now, Fabio, how do I think of you? There's an

invitation to be brutally frank. To be honest, I think you're rather a parasite.'

Fabio didn't react as expected, instead he looked smug.

'That's where you are wrong, Sue. And if you want to stay biological, I would say my relationship with Francesca is—'

Sue burst out laughing. 'O, surely not, Fabio—'

'If you would let me finish, I was going to use the term symbiotic.' His pomposity never far away, he curtly emphasized each word, 'Francesca is less than altruistic, as well you know. Always, she assesses what she can get out of the situation. Your move, then my trump, that's her way of getting through life.'

'Don't you think it's time we stopped discussing our hostess behind her back?' Anna was getting heated. 'She certainly gets nothing in return from me. If we are looking for a parasite, then I clearly fit the bill.'

Fabio regarded Anna with open amusement. 'That's nonsense, Anna, and you know it. You are the child substitute for now. She likes to play at mothers and fathers, well, perhaps not fathers. But there always has to be someone in the nest, and you fit the bill. It was a young French girl last year.' He laughed, though without mirth. 'It's my job to supply the play things. Of course, sometimes, as with all children, she gets a little too fond of her favourite toy. Then I have to think up ways of getting rid of the opposition.'

'Quite a dilemma, Fabio. You have a task on here, I think.' Sue puckered her brow. 'How about, why don't you go out into the wood, Anna, on this lovely September morning?' By now she was grinning.

'I've already thought up some fool errand for her.'

Matt said emphatically, 'Take no notice, Anna. We all know Fabio's warped sense of humour. Actually, I was here last year when Marie-Jeanne left at the end of last season, to go back to University. Anyway, enough of all that, does everyone know what they're doing, whilst I've got Francesca out of the way this morning? Anna?'

'I'm going with Fabio to the market to get the flowers.' She forced a grin.

'O, dear. Watch him.' Sue was amused. 'Anyway, that sounds much more exciting than my morning. I've already painted the dinner name cards. Think I might do a seating plan. It would be good to add some spice to the event.'

Anna said casually, 'You're all witnesses to what's just been said about accidents.'

'Don't worry, Anna, your fate has already been fixed, so there is nothing you can do about it.' Paul spoke quietly; he'd been taciturn up to that point. 'I've already told you, that's why the Romans found the Etruscans such a pushover.'

'Ah, Bradley. Just the man to tell Anna if today is an auspicious day. Or would it have been safer to stay in bed?' Pointedly, Fabio put a protective arm round Anna, much to everyone's amusement, and together they headed for the courtyard steps. Matt followed close behind. Paul brought up the rear, for once ignoring Fabio's leading remark.

Back in the courtyard, they fanned out in all directions. Matt caught hold of Anna's hand as she sought her room. 'Take care.'

She nodded abstractedly. The day already was a minefield.

Her room was overnight stuffy. She lifted the latch to the window and it swung open effortlessly. Voices drifted up from the terrace. Sue had stayed behind and someone must have returned to the terrace. Anna peered down. Francesca was back and Catarina was clearing away breakfast. The kitchen girl must have been busy on some other task. Then Catarina was nothing if not adaptable.

The Italian was listening to Sue, her head bowed and to one side, as though she did not want to miss a word. Those words floated up and into the cell, light as the air they rode yet in reality as heavy as an anchor.

'Well, Catarina, what do you make of us all? What a group of misfits we are. I've remembered all about that girl.'

'What girl? Who do you mean. Are you referring to Anna?' Francesca was genuinely surprised.

'Yes, that girl Anna. You missed my earlier conversation with her. You had already gone. We were talking about this and that and she let slip she had seen me before.'

Francesca sounded mystified. 'So why shouldn't she have seen you somewhere else? You have quite a name in the art world, and after all, Anna is an artist.'

Sue brushed the obvious explanation aside. 'It was a long time ago, and she has changed. A scrawny little adolescent has become the pretty young woman. Anyway, all I wanted to do then was forget her.' Sue was defensive. 'She made my life a misery with her pestering.'

'Pestering? I can't imagine Anna pestering anyone.' Francesca was cross. 'You must be mixing her up with someone else.'

'Of course not. No, I remember the girl's name was Anne…Anna… It hardly matters. Anyway, Francesca, I should warn you she means trouble.'

'What sort of trouble?' Catarina's voice was low.

'Sue, forget it. Tomorrow, if you still think some shaky memory is worth repeating, then come and get it off your chest.' Francesca was close to losing her temper. 'O, I'd almost forgotten, you're leaving tomorrow.' Her voice was heavy with sarcasm. 'If that is the case then you can forget it. Anna isn't going. In fact, I am going to ask her to remain. I'll still have her here when there's just a cloud of dust to show your speedy getaway down the track.'

Out of sight Anna stood very still. How she hated Sue. Then she had hated her for a long time.

She could feel fury flooding her whole body. Now Sue's open animosity joined with Fabio's threatening behaviour towards her, and Anna knew growing disquiet. She breathed deeply.

She'd not go with Fabio to the market to buy the birthday flowers. His facetious words drummed in her ears, almost loud enough to drown out the shotguns of the hunters. Matt's warning words had been 'stay out of harm's way'. Then he'd been warning them all. He'd not just been targeting her.

She sought the fresh air, the garden could hold no terrors. Certainly the gardener didn't look as though he suspected lurking danger. Riccardo was picking grapes. The harvest had begun, in harmony with the September slaughter of birds. Continuity was reassuring.

The thought brought a faint smile to her face. There had been another girl in her place last year, and Fabio had hinted—what? Matt had been quick to reassure. So there's nothing wrong with continuity. The path she trod she had trodden yesterday, someone else was there the day before and someone else the day before that. How long had feet followed this path, how long had the beehives murmured their contentment beside the mausoleum? But the bees were destined, like the Etruscans in their doomed world. Again she felt disquiet.

Fabio's words had been openly hostile, warning her, scaring her; how dare he? How dare Sue spread her venom? She would not be intimidated. What nonsense to let the place get to her. She wouldn't let it. Thank goodness for Matt; his the only sane voice. She thought of their dance under the trees; it had been a kind of madness. Pointedly, he had chosen her, somehow freed from the constraint of tutor/pupil relationship, roused surely by the exotic dancing of Francesca. Anna, in his arms, had felt his latent excitement, buttoned-up Matt still visibly wounded by his failed marriage. It was her hostess she had to thank for freeing him.

And Francesca's bee dance had shown them all a very different side, a woman now visibly at peace with herself and her surroundings. How long could it last?

The mausoleum was locked. The stout door flouted her resolve. She picked up a rock half hidden in the grass and brought it down on the corroded lock with a bang as loud as rifle fire. It

249

reverberated in the stillness, but the only answer was an echo, reluctant to escape the hollow. The door opened without a creak. The tell-tale trickle down the chestnut door showing it had been recently oiled. Someone, namely Fabio, would have to fit a new lock against her vandalism, oil no longer the panacea.

As before, the small building was a jumble of stones lying in confusion, waiting for some hand to give it order. The two ash-chests stood upon their plinths, lookalike Paul still recognizable. Had he been carved by friend or foe? How therapeutic to be able to carve the death head of your enemy.

There was a slab of tufa rock lying beside the ash-chest, sent by the gods? It would be easy to sculpt the friable rock. Eyes, nose, mouth would take shape and she had no problem whose head to choose. A knife lay beside the stone. She couldn't believe her luck. She worked as one possessed.

'Are you thinking of taking up carving?'

'O, Paul.' She was relieved. 'You've come just in time to stop me making a fool of myself.'

'How's that?'

Anna didn't answer, embarrassed by her project of the last hour. Instead, she pointed to the ash-chests lying open, and giggled.

'I can imagine them in a car-boot-sale, can't you, just right for someone's conservatory plants.'

'Only to end up years later on telly in the Antiques Roadshow,' Paul joined in the banter. 'And then the astonishment on the owners face at their value. Only, of course, they're not interested in that, and they'll continue to grow their geraniums in the pots.'

Paul put on a pompous pundit's voice. 'So how did you come by them?' Then shrill soprano. 'Well, my family were part of the great English invasion of Tuscany in the Twentieth Century. They always took their car and filled it up with wine and any other mementoes they could get their hands on, terracotta pots, parmesan cheese by the kilo, not to mention Etruscan artefacts.'

'Genuine or fake?' Anna pursed her lips. 'Fabio told me these ones here are the ubiquitous ash-chests.'

'Yes, they held human remains, not garden soil.'

'Collectors' items then.'

Paul nodded, 'Of course they were only for the hoi polloi. The Aristocrats were laid out in their tombs, as we saw. But whatever their funerary habits, all of them were only sleeping, just waiting to wake up and enjoy the afterlife. The yellow-haired courtesans weren't just there for decoration.'

'I can imagine.'

'Will you wear your hair in an Etruscan coil at Francesca's Banquet, just to please an old man.' Paul smiled and then, 'Tell me, Anna, when I came in, you really looked as though you had it in for someone. Why, if my eyes don't deceive me, this is Sue.' He picked up Anna's carving. 'Do you see her as an occupant in one of the boxes?'

Anna didn't reply.

'She's easy to recognise with her supercilious look. I wonder if she ever loses it?' Paul looked reflective.

'I doubt it, she has no fears like we lesser mortals. She knows exactly what she wants out of life.' Anna sounded envious.

'It was her great confidence that attracted me to her in the first place, all those years ago.'

'So you did know her before you came to the castello?'

'There's that question again. The past links us all in one way or another, doesn't it?' Anna stared at him. 'Yes, I did know her before, not that she wishes to remember. Not that I really want her to, if I'm honest. It reflects rather badly on me. My only excuse: I was immature.'

Paul peered at her through his thick lenses. 'Why don't you tell me, my dear.' He was here in his Catholic priest role.

'I stalked Sue. Can you imagine that? Made her life a misery. I even truanted from school.' She paused. 'Then you know all about obsession; it made a silly, mixed-up little girl fix herself on to a successful artist.' Paul nodded encouragement and falteringly she continued. 'I first saw the poster in the local library. It was a self-portrait of Sue, announcing an exhibition of her work. She looked at me with her-confident smile, and I knew I wanted to be like her. I didn't own brush or paints, but I knew I wanted to be an artist, just like her.'

'So that's how it all started.' Paul was smiling, sitting comfortably in the confessional box.

'I told my friends that famous Sue was my real mother. Why not? And in time, I believed it.' Anna could feel tears welling. 'As you can see, I'm still the unsure pimply, little waif.'

'She should have been proud you had chosen her. What a shame you didn't pick someone more worthy of your adulation. And do not sully it by saying it was stalking.'

252

'But, Paul, I'm still the stalker. I came to the castello because of Sue.' How easy it was to admit the truth to Paul. She could not have admitted it to anyone else. 'It was a silly whim when Fabio told me Sue would be here at Chiesa a Castello. I came because I wanted to prove to myself that I had finally grown up. It's hard to find I still have some way to go.'

'My dear, I understand why you want to fashion her head for the ash chest. I would do the same.'

'Thank you.' She pointed to the other chest lid to distract him from her immature behaviour. 'I promise I didn't fashion that head.'

'Ah, that's the one I have come to see.' They both gazed at the old carving.

'And this is my designated ash chest?' Paul had visibly paled under his tan.

'No, of course not, Paul. Somebody else has already had use of it.'

'It's my head.'

'So, Paul, you look Etruscan. That should please you. Just think, one of your ancestors could have carved it. No need to look further where your artistic talents come from.' It was her turn to be the agony aunt.

'The lid is mine. Fabio told me the chest was waiting a body.'

'Oh, come on, Paul, let's get out of here. It's far too gloomy' She was talking to herself. Paul had gone.

TWENTY SIX

FRANCESCA

The group stood straight along the terrace wall. Like a line of beaters at a corporate shoot waiting to cock up the victim. Late afternoon and soon the hunters would gather there before disbanding. Francesca had explained it was a colourful sight, and all except Paul waited expectantly.

An impatient Anna peered out across the prolific garden and beyond to the makeshift hide that had appeared overnight, and turned to Francesca. 'Do they build that every year?'

It was Catarina who replied, 'No, I've never seen one before.'

'Well, it can't have come there by chance.' Anna laughed, 'The rounded staves mimic an Etruscan tomb. Where is Paul when he's wanted?' She looked along the terrace for the one likely to explain the intrusion in the stubble field. He was nowhere to be seen.

Francesca said, 'Paul is probably sulking.'

'Sulking? What do you mean?' Matt was surprised.

Sue interrupted, 'He was certainly upset when I saw him.'

'Upset, what about?' Fabio joined the discussion, his words moving along the line like Chinese whispers. Only no one lowered their voice.

Sue's clear voice rang out, she obviously meant business. 'Hardly surprising, when Francesca has told him there will be no more Etruscan themed weeks.'

'What?' Fabio could not hide his disbelief. 'Is that true?'

'Yes, I've decided to end them at the end of the season. I told Paul so last night, before the picnic.' Her voice was defiant. Paul had been devastated. Francesca looked to Catarina. She's surprised too, then why should she object? It would be less work for her. She might even be able to see more of her husband.

Fabio persisted, 'But why?'

Francesca did not reply, but said, 'I was going to tell you, but Paul managed to get it out of me when he came to see me.'

'Did he really believe you?' Matt joined the questioning.

'I left him in no doubt,' she said calmly.

'So how do you intend funding your restoration?' Fabio was still frowning.

'It is almost finished,' Francesca said firmly.

'What about the restoration of the church?' Now it was Catarina's turn to be agitated.

'It will be left as it is. It's no longer a Christian building with a modern use. It makes a rather fine ruin. Customs come, customs go. Remember, as Paul never ceases to remind us, we started life as an Etruscan Temple.' No one answered.

It was Anna who saw Paul first. 'Oh there's Paul, what on earth is he doing?' She pointed beyond the cared-for garden to the open country and the overnight hide. There were gasps and then raucous amusement as they caught sight of him striding towards the bird hide. He was naked. Did he know they were there? He stopped, looked back toward the terrace, then crouched down into the hide.

'So where are his brushes and paints?' Fabio frowned. Paul

had been empty handed. 'I thought nudity and painting went hand in hand with him. Today he looks more like he's aping primeval man.'

'I'm really going to miss Paul when I leave. He's the most normal one amongst us.' Sue's comment brought surprising assent.

'I think so too,' said Anna, 'I've become quite fond of him. He is so...' The rest of her words were drowned by the arrival of the hunters.

They were a noisy intrusion below the terrace. The sportsmen, exhilarated by the blood-let, wiped damp hands over weary brows as they prepared to disband. They clapped each other on the back, shook hands, and then took aim as the final salvo rang out across the field to mark the end of their day. With shouts of satisfaction they turned and headed for home. The carnage was over. The smell of cordite hung heavy on the air.

A figure staggered from the hide, stood looking toward the castello, then fell to the earth, face down. It did not move.

The huntsmen had gone. There was no gundog to retrieve the spoil. Francesca's guests stood seven in a line, toes flush to the wall, backs erect, searching for movement. There was none. The frieze lasted but a few seconds. It seemed a lifetime. Matt came to himself, in a gasp of horror. The small sound returned them all to their senses and the line broke. Matt was first over the wall and running across the field, Fabio following in quick pursuit. Anna was crumpled to the ground, sobbing.

Francesca turned to Catarina's teapot, newly arrived, and began to pour. The hot brown liquid spilt into the cold white porcelain. She handed cups to those remaining; pieces of lemon floated expectantly on the surface. Catarina took the proffered tea, shock cancelling any word of thanks. There were three cups without takers: Matt and Fabio would find their drink cold when they returned. Paul's would go un-drunk. Francesca picked up Paul's cup and methodically emptied the contents over the wall. It left hardly a trace on the brown earth. The only sound was heartbroken Anna.

'That was waiting to happen. It was madness? Matt told us not to go out.' Sue said what they were all thinking.

Anna's voice trembled hysterically. 'But, he was under cover. He should have been safe in the hide.'

'It's the custom for them all to fire at a single target at the end of a day's shoot, to show their solidarity.' Catarina's arm was about the girl's shoulders. 'They wouldn't know Paul was in the hide.'

'So unlucky!' Anna's voice rose. She sounded very young. 'Just chance then? How desperately ironic.'

Catarina said softly, 'He was quiet this morning. So unlike himself.' She moved to stand beside the tray. Briskly, she undid the lid on the thermos flask and emptied the steaming hot water into the teapot. How easy, another round of comfort. No one refused; watching the cups being filled, lifting them to their lips, drinking, it was positive action. Otherwise they were helpless.

Catarina had begun to get back her colour; the white face and brilliant red dress reminded Francesca of the bleeding heart on one of her Catholic pictures. That one had always disturbed Francesca.

'He was so unlike himself,' Catarina repeated herself. 'How

257

strange he chose to go to the hide—'The Catholic ritual sign of the cross was slow and precise. But her hand trembled. Their world had become slow motion, with every movement lasting forever.

Greg scraped his chair on the stone floor and stood. 'I feel a bit superfluous here. I'll go and see if I can do anything.'

He was superfluous. They were all superfluous. There was nothing anyone could do. With a shock Francesca remembered her birthday. Catarina began to gather up the empties. She looked toward her employer, an unspoken question on her lips.

Francesca nodded. 'Yes, you must go ahead with the arrangements, Catarina, as planned.'

Catarina said, 'But first I will make more tea. It looks as though it is needed. 'They watched as figures crossed the field back towards the castello.

Anna let out another deep sob. 'Anna, my dear, you mustn't—' But any words of comfort Francesca might have said to the stricken girl were forestalled by the arrival of Fabio and Matt and two men. One of them was Giuseppe. He looked toward Catarina and she flickered him a smile.

It was the other man who spoke. 'Buona sera, Signora.' He knew immediately to turn to her. The local police chief was dressed in hunter's garb, dark clothing that camouflaged both his corpulent form and his calling. Today the local criminals would be safe. He had very different prey on his mind. His off duty pastime had been rudely interrupted. He struggled with his chagrin. 'Signora. I must say how sorry I am for this unfortunate occurrence. It is truly dreadful.' He looked around the group, his eyes darting from one to the other. His breath came in short gasps, his fingers played in agitated movement with his hunter's weapon. He saw Francesca's gaze and shook his head. 'It is cruel indeed, that we hunters this day have killed a man.' Again he shook his head as he placed his gun beside the wall, together with the brace of pigeons tight in his grasp. They brushed plump and warm against Francesca's leg. It was the first calm gesture he had made. She realised, with a rush of remorse, the man was upset. And he had not even known Paul.

Something was worrying the policeman. 'The victim was unclothed, why was that?'

'He was artistic and rather eccentric.' For the down to earth hunter Francesca's explanation was enough.

A few more questions. But no one knew the answers. Then the police chief and his companion left. Francesca's guests sat on, withdrawn ever further into their tight little circle.

'It appears to be a most unlikely accident.' Matt's voice was trying to sound level. But he added, 'If so, it has to be a chance in a million.'

'There is no such thing as chance. Paul himself told us that.' Fabio's voice was strange.

Sue exploded. 'O, you're not still peddling that, Fabio. I thought we might have lost all that nonsense with Paul gone.'

'But he's still lying out there in the field,' Anna reacted to her heartless words.

Sue saw her mistake. She tossed her head. 'You know I wouldn't have wished any harm to Paul, but his endless harping on about Etruscan myths did get on one's nerves. You do have to admit that.' She looked around the group for support. It would be hard to come by just then.

But Greg was back in spaniel role. 'I agree it was a bit much, but they were his passion and an awful lot was tongue in cheek I think. He had rather a nice sense of humour.'

'He had no sense of humour.' Francesca's contradiction was immediate. Matt raised his eyebrows but made no comment. 'I mean, he did take it all incredibly seriously.'

Sue's voice was flippant. 'How spooky. Paul is no longer needed and he makes a conveniently timed exit. The gods are truly in tune with your needs, Fran. The rest of us had better be careful. Don't make yourself surplus to requirements, anybody.' Catarina made a loud noise of disapproval at the woman's words. 'Anyway, Catarina, you are okay. She can't do without you.'

Matt was concerned. 'Sue, you should be careful what you say outside these walls. It could be misconstrued. Remember, the police chief seems to think it is a terrible accident, however bizarre.'

Anna whispered, 'It was a firing squad. No one knows who shot the lethal bullet. But all of us are equally to blame.'

Her words impacted the room.

'Anna.' Matt moved to her side and put his arm round her. 'I know how you feel, but you mustn't--.'

Anna raised her voice. 'His time had come and he knew it.'

Matt scoffed, 'Anna, you are shocked, you don't know what you are saying.'

Fabio said quietly, 'The powers of earth take life as they give life. The Etruscans knew that very well. We all have our ordained end.'

'And after the death the manner of it is carved on the ash-chest.' It was as though the rest of them did not exist, Anna accepting Fabio's every word.

'There is a chest with a fishtailed sea god. They think the man met his death by drowning.' Fabio was working hard to convince his audience. He was more than half way there with Anna.

'Paul already had his ash chest. I have seen it.' The girl's voice was matter of fact. 'Don't you remember, Fabio, the one with the hunt scene? It was worn and not easy to read. You interpreted it as a boar hunt and you said it was winter. I think Paul came to the mausoleum to change it. To alter it to summer.' Anna had convinced herself. 'Because I was there he couldn't do it. Yes, he would have carved a pigeon on it.'

'Anna, please stop.' Matt grabbed her arm. But the girl pulled away.

'The head on the chest was Paul,.' Anna laughed mirthlessly, 'I put glasses on him to show Fabio the resemblance.' White faced under her tan, she walked unsteadily to the small wall dividing the terrace from the garden. 'I was intrigued when I saw the hide. It looked so out of place. I couldn't see its significance. Paul did, he realised in there lay his nemesis.'

'Truly,' Fabio rose to his feet. 'So then, Signora, your birthday celebration will be Paul's funeral banquet.'

When they entered the courtyard, it was filled with flowers. Every September bloom was there, every possible source had been decimated to achieve the birthday show. From scented bower it had become a funeral parlour.

TWENTY SEVEN

ANNA

When would the carabinieri come to interrogate her? Anna guessed she had been the last person to speak to Paul. She imagined his state of mind during that scene in the mausoleum. But on the surface he had appeared totally normal. He had been more concerned about her.

She was filled with guilt at her role in the tragedy. She replayed in her mind every word and action in her dialogue with Paul. Of course Fabio had been as deeply involved in her little joke. But it was she who had suggested Paul's name for the ash-chest, fitted him into his final resting place. It had been just a bit of fun. Had the gods laughed? Had they known what was to come?

The thought made her shudder although it was warm late afternoon, muggy and oppressive. Surely it felt like thunder. Was there to be another storm with the deities showing their displeasure, but also their glee? It would come from the west and their target would be her.

A concerned Matt had followed her from the terrace, but she pleaded she needed to be alone and reluctantly he watched her until she disappeared into the trees. There was something she had to do before it was too late and the gods claimed another victim.

Her chagrin was a tangible weight slowing her steps as she took the familiar way to the mausoleum. How stupid she had been, how brainless had been her actions. Not content with putting the curse on Paul she had done the same to Sue in a childish fit of pique. Deeply chagrined at Sue's remembrance of Anna's youthful infatuation she had feared it would threaten Francesca's good opinion of her.

As usual, Anna had overreacted. To get it out of her system she had fashioned the famous artist's head and it stood now on its funerary urn. She must destroy it before anyone saw it—least of all the avenging gods. Paul had witnessed its making. And Paul was dead. She trembled at the memory.

When he'd left the mausoleum, his mind would have been filled with the image of his intended ash chest and lid. And then Francesca had told him his beloved Etruscan weeks were to be no more. He saw then his ordained forecast end. Yes, of that she was now quite certain. It seemed a lifetime since Francesca had opened her birthday presents. The hunters' presence had provided a noisy backdrop. But Paul had been lethally quiet.

Moisture hung in the air, it was oppressive, today there was no relief to be had in the open air. The light like her mood was low, sunset not far away, and shadows kept her company down the steep path. The mausoleum looked dreary. Francesca's last night's dancing image was a long shadow already receding. Yet it hovered, the vibrant figure that had entranced them all. So Francesca had changed and they had seen it happen. A week ago they would not have witnessed her dance two partners into the ground. Poor Greg, he ended up gasping for breath and Francesca showed her disdain. Only Matt had been her match. She'd responded to their spontaneous applause. But Anna hadn't joined in.

The lock still hung broken against the mausoleum door. Access was easy, though the gloom inside made it difficult to find her fashioned headstone. At last, her hands found the two chests, their lids propped beside them. Where was the head, Sue's head? She had to destroy it if there was not to be yet another tragedy. Anna had never wished the woman harm in all the years she had played her game.

Hers eyes accustomed to the poor light; her carving must be somewhere.

'Is this what you're looking for?' Sue was standing in the darkest recess, holding the image. She moved forward, and Anna recoiled with a sharp intake of breath. Sue was unfazed. 'This is an amazing likeness. You have quite a talent, my dear. I would have recognised myself, even if Paul hadn't told me.'

'Oh!' Anna felt the betrayal. So Paul had sought out Sue specifically to accuse Anna of what—practicing witchcraft?

She was close to tears as Sue's cold eyes studied her face—looking for contrition? Anna braced herself and stared back at her accuser. A rogue shaft of light, like a hidden spotlight, reflected every detail of Sue, full-faced and just inches away from her. She'd changed little since the day in the art gallery when Anna had come face to face with her role model. Her vivid green dress had been stunning. Fleetingly, Anna wondered if it would be Sue's choice of colour that night. Strange what thoughts filled the mind in the weirdest situation. Yes, she would wear green when black would be more fitting. Did anything impact Sue Simpson?

'You must have bad feelings about me.' Sue looked at the

worked head and then at the girl. 'It is a death head, isn't it?' Her expression showed only annoyance.

Feebly, Anna shook her head. 'Well, I cannot imagine you made this because you are fond of me.' Sue's laugh grated. 'Why don't you like me then, if hate is too strong a word?'

Hate, love, indifference, suddenly Anna felt desperately sad. How could such words ever have connected her with this superficial woman? With a laugh she seized the carved head from Sue's outstretched hand, and with cold deliberation, threw it to the ground and stamped on it. Eyes, nose and supercilious mouth blunted into nothing. Anna enjoyed the demolition as much as she had the making.

Sue laughed, a mirthless sound. 'Not the way I would choose to go, but then we are not usually consulted, are we? Certainly poor Paul was not given the choice, or was he?' Her voice faded, 'Anyway, that's water under the bridge, I'm more interested in the here and now. Tell me, what have I done to you to warrant this?'

Anna said slowly, 'I was ten. My substitute mother cared nothing for the fact that all I wanted to do was paint. I secretly went to your Exhibition. And suddenly you were everything I wanted to be.' Her explanation sounded pathetic and she dug herself a bigger hole. 'I went to all your exhibitions, read about you in the newspapers, bought your postcards and even a print. I couldn't possibly afford a painting, though I started to steal money to do that, until I was discovered.' Her words brought back her obsession. 'When others screamed at pop stars, I followed you like a puppy dog. You could do no wrong.'

'Well, obviously I did eventually.' Sue hesitated. 'So what happened?' she questioned but Anna knew she remembered.

'You told me to get lost!' A childish explanation to end her adolescent crush, brutally annihilating the make-believe world she had created for herself. An illusion that had grown and grown in the telling, and finally told to her friends as truth. Sue Simpson the famous artist was her real mother.

Rejected at birth by her actual parent, young Anna had chosen one she could revere and look up to. Inevitably, in the end Sue had left the disillusioned child sobbing in the foyer of the Tate Gallery.

Anna gained her room without further encounter and for that she was thankful. Matt's door was open and she could hear movement inside, but he did not appear. Closing her door behind her, she sat on her bed, gazing into space, knowing somehow the next few hours were to be got through. The thought of Francesca's birthday banquet filled her with dread.

It would take a miracle to make her appear even half presentable. But she still had time to shower and wash her hair and then perhaps she'd feel better able to face the ordeal. She sat in front of the mirror, lost in thought, her hair falling wet about her shoulders. A peremptory knock at the door and it was Francesca who entered. Dismayed, Anna remembered Sue's vindictive words to their hostess on the terrace. Was that her reason for coming to seek her out now?'

Francesca studied her through the mirror, her face inscrutable, then wordlessly she picked up Anna's hair brush and began to brush her hair; firm precise strokes, up and down, up and down. Anna closed her eyes. Deft hands piled her hair high upon her head, pins gently but firmly pushed into place. When she opened her eyes and looked in the mirror, she saw she had been transformed. The resulting coil was intricately stunning.

Bemused, Anna watched through the mirror as Francesca placed a necklace about her neck and then added matching earrings. Jewelled grape clusters sparkled against her skin; spectacular ancient gems in a breathtaking display of wealth. She gasped with amazement and Francesca looked pleased. Then into the frame another figure, Sue, came uninvited to join the hairdressing session. She said, 'You look amazing, Anna. I wonder if to complete the picture you will wear this?' Sue held up a vivid green dress. 'I think we are a similar size and it is your colour.'

Anna was engulfed by a huge feeling of relief. Surely, her past had been well and truly left behind.

Francesca and Sue left, but still she did not move. On the windowsill the chimera was spectator and she averted her gaze. She did not need its eyes to destroy her newly-gained calm. The physical act of brushing hair had swept away her angst. Her reflection in the mirror told it all, her hair in its thick complicated coil was just as Paul had wished, and the dress fitted as though it were made for her. She was ready for the birthday banquet, which was now to be funeral feast. Paul had been right. Everything was written whether one was seventy or forty nine or twenty one.

She almost grinned at the chimera bronze. Did it grin back? She picked it up and felt its reassuring solidity. Familiarity had lessened her dread of the love-hate image, one of many that rightly or wrongly had dominated her life until her coming of age.

Her fingers caressed the smooth metal. She knew every line, every contour, every fold of skin. It was different. The serpent had gone, only the goat and lion remained.

TWENTYEIGHT

FRANCESCA

Paul was dead. Francesca's guests gathered in the courtyard with their pre-dinner drinks. 'Italian' champagne flowed. The loud retort as cork left bottle brought momentary silence before a buzz of conversation halted any lurking unpleasant memory. Dear Matteo raised his glass into the evening air and Anna followed his lead. It was amusing, Francesca thought, to see how easily she could be led. How keen the girl had been to placate the older women in the ritual dressing. Tonight she was trying to put on a brave face. She had a hidden radiance shimmering below the surface, as if she knew it would be a night to remember.

Catarina stood beckoning at the Baptistery door. Flickering candlelight illumined the courtyard and Francesca led the way, stopping before the new mural, as they would all expect her to do. The others crowded about her, the painted figures grouped both on and off the scene. It was a group photo, but unlike a photograph that caught the moment, the painting showed their history for the future to see. The models were looking in a mirror, only it was no mirror image, for one of the group was missing. He stood only on the wall, his bare back to them, looking inward and away from them. A heartfelt sigh emanated from Anna, and Francesca put a comforting hand on her arm.

Sue said appreciatively, 'That is just how Paul will like to be remembered..' No one disagreed.

'Not to mention the really fine piece of painting from him. His last was one of his best.' Matt pointed to the central figure in the fresco. The Madonna sat in her beautiful blue dress, a timeless ageless figure, the face fixed in time. She, Francesca Green, restorer of Chiesa a Castello, looked out on the world, aloof, withdrawn. Her expression was enigmatic. Her hands held a child. Paul had captured the diffidence of the woman. She looked bemused, unsure like any maiden aunt. The child sat, neither easy nor content. There was no comfort cradling here. Then Paul knew her well and he had shared his knowledge with the world.

Francesca turned to Matt, reached up and kissed him on the cheek. 'Thank you, dear Matteo. The fresco is very fine.' They stood admiring the finished work of art. How long must she admire the addition to the baptistery? The Christian scene. Did the others see it as fitting? Then how would they interpret the other mural? The one they would never see. It would be the fate of her masterpiece ever to go unpraised.

The table and its feast awaited. Francesca went to the head. This evening she did not hesitate. 'Oh,' she stopped, 'I see there are place names, so where is mine? She moved along the table until she came to her name; beautifully italicized. 'So, everything is different about tonight.' She did not demur. Greg, who had been following her, was placed at the other end. He had given Francesca his arm to enter the baptistery and she had taken it willingly enough. But someone had chosen for him not to be her dinner companion. Again Francesca made no comment. Fabio was at the head of the table; that

271

should please him. When Anna took her seat beside her, Francesca put her hand on that of the girl and smiled. Anna, in her Etruscan jewellery, was her beautiful creation.

One place setting had been removed, now they were seven about the table. As usual, it was set with the pristine white porcelain, and the silver sparkled in the diffuse candle light. There had been no lessening of detail in the table preparation, though the usual brilliant colour of garden flowers bedecking the virgin cloth had given way to dark ivy. Catarina had protested, but Francesca had insisted. It was apt. Ivy was of Bacchus and the underworld and befitted the trappings of an Etruscan Funeral Feast.

The ivy trailed between two incense burners standing erect and splendid at either end of the table, their delicate perfume wafting amongst her guests. *Thymiaterum*, or incense burners, always graced Etruscan Banquets and these ones were particularly fine. The bronze base was a fashioned human leg and up it a cat stalked a mouse. The detail was exquisite. Beside them, a large bronze pail held the wine; there would be no bottles that night. Two ladles and a strainer completed the service. The others eyed the additions to the table, intrigued, unsure. They had seen nothing like it before, only in museums. They admired in silence. And what did they make of the dazzling girl beside her? Good old, solid Matt appeared less than impressed by her transformation, and rightly hovered by the birthday celebrant. And now Paul had usurped her day.

Francesca said petulantly, 'So tonight is Etruscan. I am forty nine not fifty. We were eight, one too many. But now the gods have been placated. The portents are good. Our banquet is a banquet for both the living and the dead. So we shall eat wild boar and drink Chianti il Paradiso and celebrate life within death, for it is fitting that I share my celebration with Paul.' Her words were greeted with silence.

She looked along the table at her troubled guests. Faint smiles hovered about their lips. They listened to her statement, playing with their damask napkins, corners twisted and creased. Anna sat very still, her hands clasped in her lap. Francesca felt her empathy, in tune with her hostess. Both of them like the ancients filled with wonder, fear, but also acceptance. Then the girl's childlike persona had appealed to her at their very first meeting.

'Like the Etruscans, use your senses not your intellect,' Francesca spoke into the silence and they all turned to her. 'Life is much more bearable then. Do not mourn Paul. It was his time. Paul knew that, accepted it. Death is a journey not a final ending, and it is right to start him on his way.' She raised her glass, the dark Chianti was blood red. She knew that a few more glasses and they would cease to question, as the incense crept into their awareness. She turned to Anna. 'Anna, is it your senses or intellect that dominate you?'

The girl smiled, 'When I get back to Kent it will be bread and butter art for me.'

'What a waste. You must stay on at the castello and transform the rest of these walls. The subject matter can be entirely your own choice.' Francesca gestured around the room. Anna's eyes lit up and a slight flush darkened her cheeks.

Matt interrupted, his eyes drawn to the girl. 'Remember

273

your Scholarship urged a broad picture of the country you chose. Naples would give you a rather different perspective from here.' His words offered an abrupt return to the normal world.

'You could be right, but—' Her tone was doubtful. 'Hell, I don't know.'

Francesca said lightly, 'You could stay here as well, Matteo. Give Anna some free advice when she needs it, and you could do some painting yourself. There is really no need to go off to Naples or anywhere else for that matter.'

The girl brightened at that suggestion.

Greg backed his hostess. 'My idea of hell is painting in an urban environment. All noise and confusion; yes, literally hell.'

Fabio said languidly from the end of the table, 'Real hell was Etruscan.' He raised his glass. 'We should start Paul on his journey into Paradise. Damnation in the underworld is to be avoided.'

Catarina crossed herself. 'He must not go to hell.'

'No,' Francesca nodded. 'Etruscan hell was permanent and not very nice.'

Greg laughed. 'You surprise me.'

'Hell was overseen by the monster Charun who had the head of a wolf with great flaming eyes, but he had the body of a man. He carried a huge mallet to crush the skull of the newly deceased.' The wine was already talking in Fabio making him sound more and more like Paul.

Francesca interrupted, 'They had good gods as well, for example, the Etruscan Aplu who we know as Apollo.'

Slowly, Catarina began to sing.

'Aplu, Aplu, Aplu.

'Thou who art so good and wise,

'so learned and so talented,

'I pray thee give me fortune and talent.'

Heartfelt supplication in the voice, only her faith's praying hands were not to be seen. There was spontaneous applause.

Fabio laughed. 'Good old Catarina, always ready to hedge her bets, Christian or mythological, whichever is right at the time.'

'Amen to that.' Greg raised his glass.

'I'll drink to that.' Sue looked contrite. 'Paul should have been more adaptable, then he still might…'

Matt murmured, 'So, Sue, are you saying expediency in life is always the best bet. If Paul had followed his early Catholic beliefs he would be alive today?'

'Something like that.'

Matt raised his eyebrows, but said nothing. He had ignored Francesca's suggestion to stay on when the others have gone. He'd change his mind. Anna would be swayed by his decision.

Francesca smiled reassuringly, 'So, Anna, the general drift of our conversation is expediency, it is better to stay on at the castello than go to Naples.'

Fabio played devil's advocate. 'Remember, Anna, you'd be in the hands of goddess Turan and she was their wicked witch.'

'Are you implying I am Turan?' Francesca was rattled.

Greg looked smug as he winked at the others. 'So if that's the case, what plans does the wicked Turan have for me?' She didn't reply, thinking: I shall wave him goodbye tomorrow and that will be it. A youthful dream that had lasted half a lifetime had become nothing. Pointedly, she turned away from him. Attentive Matt filled her glass and she put her hand on his arm and lightly rested it there as the plates were gathered.

'That was truly delicious.' Francesca had turned to Catarina with her appreciation. So much effort had been put into her celebration meal and it had been hardly noticed. The talk had been intense, the conversation a thin veneer hiding everyone's inner deliberations. Their unspoken thoughts, was it really birthday celebration or funeral banquet? Damn Paul for his inconvenience. His unseen presence dominated still.

Fabio from the other end of the table raised his voice again. 'Let me bring you back to why we are her, Francesca. You talk only of the future. What of Paul? Some would say he has only a past, but he thought differently. Do you think even now Paul is lying on his couch, larger than life, his slaves small and insignificant waiting on his every whim?'

'Oh, I do hope so.' Anna raised her glass. 'You weren't there at the tomb, Fabio, but that is what he asked for, do you remember…' Her voice trailed as the others in the group all recalled the conversation.

'He specifically pleaded for a beautiful girl to be his companion on the couch.' Greg grinned, 'Paul could get some things right.'

'He was right about a lot of things. 'Fabio touched the incense burner. 'He forecast his end. Then it was his seventieth birthday yesterday.'

That silenced them, Anna was dumb.

'Getting back to a beautiful companion,' Fabio looked straight at Anna, 'do you think he had anyone in mind to go with him into eternity?' His fingers traced the cat climbing the incense burner, the mouse always just out of reach.

'Oh, lay off, Fabio, can't you?' The girl was irritated. 'Just because Francesca wants me to— And there's your problem I think.'

'I warned you in Venice, didn't I?' Matt had 'I told you so' written all over his face.

'Yes you did, Matt, but when Fabio gave me that chimera I didn't realize—'

Matt wasn't amused. 'That damned thing, Fabio Renaldi, will probably haunt Anna for the rest of her days.'

'But you're wrong, Matt.' The girl voiced her relief as she bent to her purse, opened it and placed something triumphantly on the table. 'The serpent has gone. Look.' She held it up for them all to see. Matt seized the bronze from her hand, his face a mask as he looked at it from all angles.

'Anna, you can't possibly believe this is the same bronze.' He could hardly hide his scorn.

'Of course not, but this new animal is an omen, a good omen this time.'

'O, Anna.' Matt was speechless.

Francesca raised her glass. 'So let's drink to good omens.' A loud crack of thunder resounded above their heads. Anna jumped. All conversation stopped. Paul wasn't far away.

277

'Don't worry, the storm is in the east. The portent is good.' Francesca was reassuring.

'Remember the effects of lightning were always harmful, destroying the status quo.' Fabio, unconvinced was speaking for the absent Paul.

'No, that's where you are wrong, only the Fulmen Peremptorium were harmful,' and now Catarina had surprising authority in her voice. Had Paul chosen to speak through her?

The wine was clouding Francesca's reality. She said sharply, 'Yes, where lightning struck , the ground became sacred.'

'Wow, Paul was an incredibly good teacher. Just listen to you all,' and Anna looked positively happy.

'So, if the baptistery gets a direct hit, it could become even more of a tourist attraction. Mural rent asunder.' Matt lifted his gaze to their painting. 'The final plaster hardly dry and the group could be split right down the middle.'

'Oh well, as long as Francesca and I are on the same side.' Greg's hard-done-by tone of voice made his hostess smile.

'O, Greg, how pleasant you make that sound.' Francesca leaned towards him. 'Sadly, it can't happen. Well, only in the mural plaster.'

He pulled a face. 'Oh well, I'll just have to live for the moment, this food is divine.' And he turned his attention to the dessert.

Before them were ramekin dishes, faintly warm, holding a delightful mix of ricotta cheese, creme fraiche, cinnamon, and peaches. 'Tuscan pudding of course, we couldn't have had anything else.' Catarina smiled across at Francesca.

'Hold on a minute, it could have been English trifle. Fran hasn't always been Francesca you know.' Sue made her contribution.

Catarina chose to ignore it. 'Rita makes the creme fraiche herself by stirring cultured buttermilk into double cream and refrigerating it overnight.'

'And Tuscans have probably been doing that for centuries, though not the refrigerator bit.' Sue smiled, breathing in deeply as the incense wafted across the table.

Mollified, Catarina replenished the glasses, wielding the wine ladle as though she used it every day. 'Before we leave the feast, there is a toast to be drunk.' Catarina had lifted a small cauldron to the table.' This is a drink mentioned in the Illiad, wine with goat's cheese grated into it and a white barley sprinkled on top.'

Everyone rose to their feet, waiting, unsure whether Francesca or Paul the name to toast.

'To Paul.' Catarina's voice was tremulous.

'He must be lying on his couch by now.' Anna grimaced, her voice echoing her regret and affection for their absent companion. They all raised their glasses.

'And getting all the earthly pleasures he enjoyed.' Greg placed his hands on his stomach. 'He would have loved this meal, Francesca. This has been a night to remember.'

'It isn't over yet.' Francesca held his gaze across the table. He was the first to look away, and she said, raising her voice, 'besides Greg, you won't be leaving in the morning.'

He looked startled. 'What do you mean?'

'I mean the chief of police phoned this evening to say no one is to leave. He wants to question us further.' Their sudden unease hung heavy in the wafting incense.

She went on, 'It was only through Catarina's pleading that he didn't force this evening's celebration to be postponed. Thankfully, my banquet—our banquet—has been a time for us all to regain our confidence and composure.' Her words sounded hollow, her news exposing how thin was their self-belief.

The meal finished with granita, the timing perfect, though how many of them appreciated or even noted the Tuscan dish which had to be served quickly; lemons, sugar and cold water frozen and stirred, the resulting lemon slush a perfect way to end. It left a bitter taste.

The storm was grumbling but there had been no rain. The gods indeed were smiling down on them. Francesca beamed, 'Signors, Signorinas, fireworks will conclude our evening. See you in half an hour on the terrace.' The party broke up in silence. Paul had begun his journey, of that they'd been left in no doubt by Fabio and Catarina. Fireworks were Francesca's added dimension. The Etruscans did not have rockets.

Francesca climbed the tower steps, her happiness a mixture of Chianti Il Paradiso and anticipation. Though no one, she reflected darkly, had drunk her health, Paul uppermost in their minds. At the top of the steps she stopped to take a final look over the castle roof. To the east, the gods rumbled benignly. Below, she watched Anna and Matt walk towards their separate cells. Almost at their doors, Anna stopped abruptly then turned, and ran back across the courtyard. Matt hesitated then he was close behind her as she reached the baptistery door. And together they disappeared inside.

What game did Anna play now? Intrigued, Francesca stood in the shadows above them, watchful, senses alert. What now? Eavesdropper. It was a role Francesca had filled many times in her tower that knew all secrets.

The medieval squint, even now, her hidden spy hole. It's all seeing eye had kept watch on castello intrigues over the centuries. High above the adjoining baptistery, a narrow line between it and the tower gave sight and sound of those blissfully unaware below. It was as good as any modern surveillance camera. Anna and Matt were within her sight and sound. Her role was once more to be hidden voyeur.

TWENTY NINE

ANNA

'Butterflies carry the souls of the dead, so at night it must be moths,' Anna called out in wonder as something brushed against her face and she stifled a cry, almost colliding with Matt. Together, they watched the moth, drawn by the ray of light from the baptistery, and Anna closed the door behind them.

The creature fluttered straight to the light, high in the roof, its wings in a frantic drumming. Anna could feel its agitation.

'I'll put out the light, then he will calm.' Her fingers found the switch as Matt came into contact with the table.

He exclaimed loudly before saying breathlessly, 'Here, give me your hand.' They made contact as their eyes became accustomed to the dark, and pale moonlight broke the shadows. The moth's frantic beatings ceased, and it fluttered gently downwards, coming to rest on Paul's naked backside. There it stayed.

'I knew it was Paul. I'm so glad we let him in.' Matt did not laugh, instead he squeezed her hand. They stood, hand in hand, looking at the moth. Its paper thin wings were tightly shut without volume or form. Anna said, 'I saw flashes of purple-grey, yellow— but now it's colourless, without identity. Even so, we know who it is, don't we?'

'Well, it looks as though Paul has chosen an Emperor Moth. We get them at home. It lays its eggs on sloes and hornbeams.

There's one growing down by the Mausoleum. This moth is particularly interesting because it transmits pheromones.'

'So, tell me what that means exactly.'

She imagined his grin in the dark.

'Well, they're chemical substances that actually influence the behaviour of others.'

'Fascinating.'

'Are you laughing at me, Anna?'

'Of course not, go on.' It was her turn to squeeze his hand.

'An Emperor female moth secretes the chemical into the air to attract a male. He will heed the call from a long way off.'

'So Paul is keeping up his earthly pleasures.' She laughed, happy to keep up this pretence; anything to keep from replaying the morning horror and its awful reality. She said, 'If he did come in here seeking a female, I wonder who it would be?'

'He had quite a shine for Francesca, you know. He kept coming back here on and off throughout the year.'

'I didn't realise that.'

Matt laughed. 'Quite the little innocent, aren't you?' He put his arm about her. 'You know Francesca secretes pheromones.'

'What on earth do you mean by that?'

'Precisely what I say. She's a female Emperor moth.'

'So, if I try hard enough, I'll see our hostess with purple wings and yellow eyes.'

Matt murmured, 'Yes, of course.' His voice changed. 'In fact, that's it, and I've never realised it before. She's unremarkable as a lone individual, but as a social insect in a group she becomes part of a complex chemical communication. She secretes pheromones in large amounts to influence others.'

Anna remonstrated, 'That sounds just too weird.'

'No, not really.' He sounded intrigued. 'But as a mere male I was very aware of something over lunch today—perhaps there were pheromones flying around..'

'Did she proposition you?' Anna's eyes widened.

'O, come on, Anna.'

'I did wonder if she was flirting with you over dinner, "dear Matteo".' Anna giggled.

'She'd enjoyed her wine.' Matt was rueful.

There was silence. Anna said quietly, 'I'm disappointed in you, Matt Grant, you make a really rotten Emperor moth. You can't smell a pheromone when it's right under your very nose.'

'What do you mean by that?' and he was disbelieving.

'What do you think I mean?' She raised her face to his and, standing on tiptoe, she kissed him.

'Oh, Anna.' Exploding fireworks. They clung together. 'Oh, Anna, why didn't you do that a long time ago? I've known for a long time I wanted to,' Matt whispered.

His hands moved to her hair and her Etruscan coil. 'I've wanted to get rid of that all evening. It's not you. You look highly sophisticated like that, but I prefer it down.'

She clung to him, wanting the moment to last forever. Destiny had brought her to Chiesa a Castello. It was her turn to whisper a prayer of thanks to the gods.

At last, Matt pulled away and looked at her. He murmured,

'Anna, you'd better do a few running repairs before we join the others. I don't think Francesca would be too pleased to see her little protégé in disarray.'

They were back in the real world. Matt's words filled the void, echoing up into the rafters, bouncing back down from the ancient stones.

She put her hands up to her hair. 'How do I look?'

'Beautiful.'

'You can't see.'

'Well, it's part imagination, part intuition, part glimpse. It shows how much I'm on your wavelength, Anna.' He kissed her again. 'Come on, it will be noted if we truant.'

In the shadowy courtyard cascading lights fell through the sky, down to earth and reality. How much of the fireworks display had they missed?

The others were all on the terrace, watching the show, and Anna left Matt to explain their late arrival. She could not trust herself, she had no right to sound happy on such a day. He said just the right thing. 'Anna has been her usual scatterbrain self, lost her earring in the baptistery. I've been helping her to look for it.'

Sue looked sceptical. 'It must be catching, Fran has only just beaten you to it. She said she had lost her watch. Anyway, Anna, you're here now. We must remember to swap addresses before we split up.' She was thinking beyond the next day even though the police chief had other ideas. 'I shall want to keep up with your career.'

Anna wanted to laugh aloud. Now it was turning into the

fond farewell stage of a holiday group, names written in address books only to be forgotten. So much wasted ink. Yet the very name she had sought and schemed and striven for was being offered on a plate. She could hear Paul somewhere in the soft evening breeze saying emphatically 'You know there is no such thing as chance'; surely everything was falling into place.

Fireworks screamed up into the night sky. Matt was as far away from her as possible, and it was Francesca who came to stand on her other side from Sue. Like the afternoon dressing, Anna was hemmed in between the two women. Their hostess put her arm about Anna's shoulders. It rested just lightly, but Anna, surprised, sensed just a little added pressure would make her the goat, twisted between the lion and serpent. Foolish, for now the viper no longer existed, and anyway, her slayer of dragons, or butterfly collector, stood only feet away. She need no longer be threatened by irrational fears.

Francesca said, 'Dear Anna, so many exciting things are happening to you. Perhaps next time we all meet it will be at your exhibition.'

'I hope so, I'm going to miss you.'

'Well, one thing's for certain. Your show will have to be here. The baptistery walls will be very much your paintings' final resting place.'

'Francesca, I don't...' Anna's words were drowned by the great swish and swoop of rockets as, in the garden, Riccardo lit the touch papers.

No more questions or decisions. They exclaimed and admired and feigned fear as great arcs of light flared the night sky.

The storm that threatened had subsided, like a damp squib. All eyes were on the cascading lights.

It was a warm balmy night and, judging from the mood of her fellow guests, the night was young. All Anna wanted was to be alone with Matt.

The fireworks spluttered and died. Fabio moved around the group with wine.

Anna protested, 'I should put my hand over my glass, but I'm not going to.'

'Of course not. The night has only just started. We owe it to Francesca to make it a night to remember.'

Anna smiled, 'It has already been a memorable evening.'

Fabio smiled down at her. He looked very much the handsome young Italian at home on the terrace of his big house. He bowed stiffly, acknowledging her praise. 'Yes, but there is plenty still to come.' He looked over to Francesca who momentarily stood alone, silently watching from the shadows. Her cheeks were flushed, as though she had already been dancing. She was swaying now, it wouldn't take much to get her moving.

Francesca said peremptorily, 'I shall dance now.'

'There's room here on the terrace if we move the tables and chairs.' Matt threw Anna a hasty glance, and then moved to where Francesca waited. He took her hands. She laughed up into his face. Anna saw the swaying wasn't reaction to imagined music. Francesca had had rather a lot to drink.

Fabio was amused. Matt looked a little out of his depth. If there was to be any dancing, it would have to be the slow and close-encounter kind. Not the wild abandoned peasant dance that had entranced them all the night before. Matt and Francesca stood close together, her arm round his waist.

'Perhaps we can move back the furniture so we can all dance.' Anna caught Fabio's arm.

Francesca said loudly, 'O, no, how can you suggest dancing on such a sad day. Anna, how heartless you are. You cannot have forgotten about Paul already?'

Anna moved into the shadows to hide her discomfort. Yes, she had momentarily forgotten. How could she be so heartless? Francesca's words of reproof were the sharp crack of a gun, and they achieved almost physical contact on the intended target.

'O, Francesca, forgive me. I—'

'Well, *you* seem to be enjoying yourself, Fran.' Sue's words hit another target and at once they released Anna from her guilt.

Francesca's voice was peevish. 'My decision to end the Etruscan Holidays had nothing to do with Paul's death. Perhaps Anna was right when she suggested that we are all to blame for his end.' Her words were greeted with a heavy silence. 'We are all to blame if you think about it.' Her speech was blurred. Annoyance had turned to accusation and she punctured the discomfort of her audience. She said, 'Anna could have been resentful that he painted her out of the mural.'

From the dark someone said, 'Francesca, stop.'

'Fabio had certainly quarrelled with him, I heard them arguing. Business partners always fall out, and Greg—Well, he was jealous of the naked Paul with Sue, and as for Catarina—'

Now they were laughing, though with a note of exasperation and disbelief.

'Francesca!' Fabio moved to her side.

'Don't fuss, Fabio. I play only Devil's Advocate for the police interview tomorrow.'

Fabio's voice cut across the reminder. 'Francesca, it is time.' He was close beside her now, an authoritative note to his voice. 'We have reached the climax of your birthday, and on such a night you must agree the ritual is apt.' He ended on a defiant note.

'On such a night we must placate the Gods.' Francesca finally let go of Matt and Anna had to stop herself taking her place. 'The Gods await the Ritual.'

Sue was bored. 'Ritual must mean it happens every year. That's what rituals are all about, aren't they?'

'It has happened every year since the Signora came to the castello.' Catarina's voice emerged from the shadows, excited to be back on familiar territory. 'It is time now for us to placate the gods.' She was repeating Francesca's words, though they were strange coming from her lips.

Matt was amused. 'So which god, Catarina, do you refer to?' Anna remembered the first morning and Catarina crossing herself at the mention of the evil eye.

'You took the words right out of my mouth. I can't believe you've joined the Etruscan fan club, Catarina.' Greg was equally bemused.

She had no words of denial, but in the dark night it was easy to feel closer to the mythical Gods, the Christian Chiesa strangely remote. The spirits of the underworld seemed just a fingertip away. As if to make their presence felt, a rumble of thunder echoed behind them from beyond the castello. The night was oppressive, and the air movement had changed direction; it was coming from the west. Francesca had a look of triumph on her face. 'Paul is here. He is telling us to pacify the gods.'

'Yes.' Catarina was excited. 'It is time.'

The group had been split by some unseen hand; on one side, Sue, Greg, Matt had looks of resignation on their faces; on the other, Francesca, Catarina and Fabio, the initiated, their faces animated.

A night jar screeched, and answer came from far away in the silent wood. Then a low haunting wail of music filled the air. Against the skyline, Fabio stood silhouetted, dark defined, the double pipes distorting his profile. Catarina moved to his side and briefly they became the figures on a tomb wall.

Tonight Catarina was wearing a deeper shade of red, the Tarquinia flesh colour of the tomb fresco. Anna's thoughts exploded into the dark night like fireworks. Who was the figure on the couch? Had Paul seen himself there? Though he had pointed out he was the wrong size. If it was Paul reclining at the feast, then who were the painted ladies, dark haired and blonde?

A hand touched her head. It was Francesca. She had worked the hairstyle just a few hours ago, now Anna could feel fingers releasing the pins, allowing her hair to fall heavily about her shoulders.

'What are you doing, Francesca?'

'You must look the innocent, my dear. In our procession the

sacrificial goat must be docile and demure. Only then will the gods accept our submission.'

At that moment Catarina joined the grouping, a white garment draped over her arm. 'Anna, you must wear this chiton.'

'O come on, that's enough!' Matt's voice was loud and indignant. 'Just leave Anna out of your little fantasies.'

'Fantasy?' Francesca's voice was cold.

'Just go along with it, guys,' Greg tried to sooth as Catarina slipped the garment over Anna's head. 'Remember, it is Francesca's Birthday.'

Sue was intrigued in spite of herself. 'So who normally fits the bill? Anna wasn't here last year. Don't say you slaughtered a real goat.' Her choice of words rankled.

'Always a girl brought by Fabio.' Catarina's tone was matter of fact, and her words rang in Anna's ears as they all moved downhill, snaking along the narrow path in the strange procession, part birthday celebration, part funeral cortege. Could this procession be the cold reality of Fabio's invitation to the castello? Francesca in her cell, preparing her for the night and its rituals, and Anna felt a tight band of apprehension. She thought to protest but no sound came. She walked, hearing Paul's voice. Everything in the Etruscan world was meant.

THIRTY

FRANCESCA

The girl is beautiful. Her fair hair gleams in the torchlight, making her look young and vulnerable, compliant even. But not too young, she would have been the animal chosen by the gods, an adult with second teeth, always the one taken for sacrifice. She could feel the girl's unease.

The others were silent, but Francesca cared nothing for their thoughts. They would do as she wanted. It was Signora Francesca who called the tune now. Sue and Greg had become little figures in her landscape, no longer figuring in her calculations. Matt was close to his hostess. Anna walked ahead, the two of them separated now. Not the comfortable little duo of just a few hours ago, locked in an embrace that she had longed to pull apart by brute force. Her plans had been for Anna and Fabio, not Anna and Matt. She had had to listen to them laughing at her and her eccentricity. How dare they? The tower spy hole had well and truly revealed their ingratitude, their treachery.

Now Catarina had the girl by the hand whilst Fabio played plaintively upon the pipes. They had become a procession on an Etruscan vase, silhouette figures, locked into their eternal round.

A loud crack of thunder rolled almost overhead. Sue let out a cry of surprise and then she was on the ground and gasping with pain. They stopped in confusion and for a split moment Francesca wondered if the gods had chosen their own victim. But Sue was at once vociferous. 'My ankle—I think I've sprained it in this fool errand.'

Greg tried to help her, but she had fallen awkwardly and made heavy weather of getting back on her feet. 'Francesca, I think I'd better take Sue back to the castello. I don't think it would be a good idea for her to continue.'

Matt offered support. 'It might be a good idea if we all—'

'You can't go back now,' Francesca said, 'we are nearly there. Greg, you take Sue back to the castello. But the rest of you humour me just a little longer.' She had used just the right words. They could not decently rush back to the comfort of Rita's kitchen.

They left Sue and Greg behind. Matt increased his pace, to just inches behind Anna as they walked on into the night.

'How much further, Francesca?' Matt was less than amused.

'You know where we are heading.'

'Haven't a bloody clue.' He had lost his usual good manners.

As if to make up for him, Anna answered, 'The mausoleum.'

The girl had empathy. A few more steps and they came to a halt as the familiar shape broke the dark.

They stood in silence. Francesca said, 'Close your eyes and think of it in Etruscan times.'

In the torchlight the girl and Matt exchanged glances. Their eyes stayed open, resisting her.

She went on, 'Remove its roof and you have an Etruscan

Temple; orientated toward the southeast, fronted by a sacred area and altar. Everything here has its origins in the past.'

'Yes,' Anna agreed.

'The poignancy of perfect things, long forgotten. D. H. Lawrence understood.' Francesca's voice floated about them.

'That world was hardly perfect?' Matt scowled.

'They knew a state of perfection before fate brought about their inevitable chaos.' Catarina's voice was confrontational, her everyday persona nowhere to be seen. Francesca was close enough to Anna to see the girl note the change.

Catarina was now openly excited. 'Tonight is significant. The Signora's life is at a crossroads and with that transition comes dangers. It is necessary she appease the gods.'

Francesca heard Matt's exclamation, but Catarina was oblivious. 'Paul could not escape his destiny; he knew only too well the impact of every seventh year. His seventieth birthday was profoundly significant.' The girl's sighs rose audibly above the soft wailing of the pipes.

As she spoke, Catarina moved to the raised area at the front of the mausoleum. The grass covering had been moved, and the ancient altar stones lay revealed in the light of their torches. Fabio joined her and Francesca raised her voice. 'He carries the Lituus, the priest's stick, smooth and unblemished. There can be no twists or knots in the ritual rod.'

Catarina lifted her hand for silence. 'We must listen now for auguries and signs. Anything out of the ordinary can be significant.' Matt snorted his contempt and Francesca saw Anna place a hand on his arm. Francesca closed her eyes against that touch, and at once the dark comfort of oblivion hid the present. Only the past lay within reach.

-- -

She can see the boy-cum-half goat, in the castello ruins, as old as the stones, as young as the frisking kids that, bemused by his pipe music, gambol in the heat. Together with the animals, she listens to the easy rise and fall of the notes, as natural as day and night, and her impromptu tears fall onto the jumbled stones. Blindly, she picks up the splintered rock and smothers it in the dew-coated grass beside it. She begins to fashion a crude ball of plaster. She has no model, but without hesitation, her fingers sculpt a tiny form. The boy and the goats watch with knowing eyes.

When she's finished, the goatherd takes her hand and leads her out of the ruins, down the hillside, to an isolated building. Like the rest of the place, it suffers time, four walls enclose space. The boy stoops and picks up a stick, and with a small knife from his tattered trouser pocket, she watches as he whittles away the blemishes. His fingers test and try. At last, satisfied, he moves to stand before a shape of stones and she sees it to be an altar.

Solemnly, he points and she places the small graven image on the sacred slab then instinctively bows her head. Nodding, he lifts the staff above the inert form. A bird screeches in the far wood and sunlight filters on to the altar. Gently, he places the fashioned child into the opening between two stones and her precious figure is safe in the ancient womb. Her young companion nods, satisfied, and bends to the ground. He lifts a tiny protesting kid that kicks and

flails its legs in a helpless gesture of terror. The knife flashes in the
sunlight and the mother goat cries its concern. The boy turns and
smiles at her, and taking her hands, they dance a wild abandoned
gig. Why not? It is her birthday and the gods will listen to the pleas
of a barren woman.

- - -

So long ago. Francesca was back in the present. The boy, now man,
stood on the plinth, the Lituus in his hands. Fabio, his face
inscrutable, scraped aside the grass on the altar. As the first stone
was revealed, Matt reached for Anna's hand.

Fabio found the cavity retrieved the Etruscan shape from its
hiding place and cradled it on the stone. Francesca lifted the votive
uterus, moulded by pleading hands millennia past and Anna craned
forward pondering the strange bulbous shape with the slit opening.
Francesca breathed heavily, moved that even now it held her crudely
shaped child, the womb pierced with her unborn child. She
remembered other Septembers and the girls Fabio had found, young,
pretty would-be daughters. This year he had brought her Anna. She
above them all had empathy with the past.

And here she was. Young, pretty, caring, breathing deeply a
mixture of emotions. Sympathy, fear made her immobile. Slowly,
Fabio raised his hand and as he did so the girl let out a loud piercing
cry of horror. Francesca laughed, a strident triumphant sound. Matt's
arms were about the hysterical girl.

Francesca said, 'How clever you are, Anna, knowing it was
only the docile sacrificial animal that was killed. If it protested it
was reprieved for another day.'

296

Matt swore loudly.

'And so, for the libations.' On cue, Catarina moved forward and placed the season's first grapes onto the altar. Close behind, Francesca poured new wine onto the sward. It flowed like sacrificial blood, back into the earth. Fabio took Francesca's hands and slowly they began to dance. There was no music but the steps were known. They danced to the rhythm of time; pulsating and primeval.

As they climbed the hill, the first streak of light hit the castello facade. The tufa stone soft in the morning haze welcomed their return and Francesca felt heady emotion as they stood before the ancient walls. Here in reality was her true offspring.

The smell of coffee on Rita's early morning stove was the scent trail to follow. The kitchen was like returning to the womb, warm and enclosing. The dawn air had cooled those still attired in evening garb, and they looked out of place in a room already allotted its morning function. Rita was pleased to see them and clucked around like a mother hen. The hot liquid revitalised. Recovery was instant. Their tired faces glowed in the warmth of the stove.

Sue had had time to regain her composure. The others were surprised to see her and Greg still in the kitchen. Sue was seated by the stove, her leg raised in front of her. Greg got up as the others entered, then almost instantly fell back onto his stool, as though they played musical chairs and he was afraid he'd be left standing. He need not have feared. There was a seat for everyone. They all found a perch and sat. It had been a long night, but no one knew quite how to break up the party. It was too early for auld-lang-syne and the letting-go of hands.

Francesca saw the colour return to Anna's cheeks. Though there was a seat for her the girl had chosen to sit on the floor by Matt's feet. She leaned unashamedly against his long legs, sipping her coffee. He looked happy and relieved and— He could hardly keep his hands from her. Francesca closed her eyes, but she could still hear Matt and the girl down in the baptistery becoming a couple and laughing at her. How dare they? Their words and actions beside the mural stabbed Francesca's drugged state. How dare they? She moved to the couple and crouched down on the floor beside Anna. She said, 'Dear Matteo, have you told Anna about all the processions you have walked with Fabio and me? Every September the first, the ritual ceremony down at the mausoleum, and with a new girl each time. How pretty they have all been, as now you find Anna.'

Matt frowned. Anna sat bolt upright, looking from one to the other in undisguised surprise. 'No, I didn't know that.' She shuddered. 'And, Matt, you let me go through all that. You might have warned me.' She struggled to her feet.

'Anna, I knew you would not come to any harm. It's just one big charade, as everything is here.'

Francesca said, 'Is that what you've come to think, Matthew?' She got to her feet. Anna had already moved to the other side of the kitchen, where normality was Rita's preparation of breakfast.

Thick slices of ham and soft yellow eggs appeared as if by magic. They ate as though they had fasted for days, followed by more coffee and hot rolls from the bread oven. No food had ever tasted better. It was nectar from the gods. She saw Anna accept another helping, Matt just picked at his.

The gatehouse bell shattered the feast. It resounded through the kitchen, a great awakening clang that echoed long after it had ceased to sound, striking their world like a thunder bolt of Fulmen Peremptorium. And they all knew now that where that struck it destroyed. Francesca flashed surprise, concern, then slow dawning realisation that it was already tomorrow. It had come and it was the day of reckoning.

Today the local chief of police was not wearing his huntsman's gear. He was out of his play clothes. This was work. He refused the coffee, as though the self-inflicted abstinence was his hair shirt. Rita looked chastened. A subdued Matt smiled at her and held his mug under the lip of her jug. He'd not be the one to refuse.

'Signora,' and the policeman took Francesca's hand. 'Signor Bradley, Signor Paul Bradley, he died.' There was a long silence. They waited. 'The signor—It was an accident. He was killed by a huntsman's bullet, yes. We have the shotgun. A sad accident,' and he shook his head. 'It was not meant. It was unlucky chance.'

Anna cried out, 'It cannot be. Paul said there is no such thing as chance.'

The inspector ignored her. 'Some of you will know it is our custom to let off a final volley at the end of the shoot. Signor Bradley was indeed unlucky to be in the wrong place at the wrong time. He would not know the field-hide had been chosen to be the target for our final round this year.'

'A firing squad. He knew alright.' Anna let out a long, low moan.

The party was over. The final notes of the auld-lang-syne and they had dropped hands, become individuals again, already thinking of departure. There would be no leisurely leave-taking. Indecent haste would cause a stampede over the stone portal and through the stout wooden gate, out into the outside world.

Sue was first. 'Fran, please could you ask Riccardo to have the car ready for nine o'clock. Greg and I would like to make an early start.'

Even Catarina was anxious to go. 'Signora. Do you need me around today?'

Matt stretched his stiffened legs, evidence of his need to get away. 'Francesca, would you mind if I make use of the car as well? It's the last day I can see a colleague in Pisa who I promised to visit whilst I'm in Italy.' He looked over towards Anna and raised his voice. 'Come with me, Anna, we can go see the art gallery?'

Ah, Francesca thought, the girl has an excuse. But would she go now with Matt?

Fabio rose to his feet. 'Come with me, Anna. You haven't met any of the young locals yet.'

'Anna,' Francesca turned to the girl, 'you will stay with me, won't you? You can't all desert me.'

Anna smiled at her, 'Of course. I'll see you later, Francesca. I've got some serious landscapes to start getting down on canvas.'

THIRTY ONE

ANNA

Anna eyed her chosen view: mellow walls, hazy background, Mediterranean vegetation in its dense profusion. It would make a good picture, if she could only focus. The plan had always been for her to paint landscapes; one of the original reasons for her coming to Chiesa a Castello in the first place. Now she had the tools of her trade about her feet, sketchpad and pencil on her knee, but her hands were idle.

The party was truly over, the guests had gone. A heavy silence hung over the place and Anna heard Paul's absence loud about her. The brassy geraniums had paled, now trite and insignificant, no longer part of the obsessed man's imaginings. The basil and rosemary were indistinct, losing their flavour in the castello's cauldron world. It was a soup without taste or aroma and Francesca's unseen hand stirred only the dregs. She stirred in vain. None remained to taste the feast.

A noisy, relaxed group had gathered in front of the great portal to say goodbye, a fitting backdrop for the group photo. Francesca had not joined the smiles, she would not figure in Sue's goodbye snapshot. They awaited their hostess to come down from her tower. But she did not appear.

Renowned artist Sue Simpson thrust her smart address card into Anna's hand and in return the girl scribbled her address onto a piece of paper torn from her sketchpad. The woman was pressing in her hope to meet, once Anna was home.

Matt interrupted the cosy leave-taking, anxious to speak to Anna. She had avoided him. 'Can I make you change your mind about coming to Pisa? You would love it.'

'I'm sorry, I just can't leave Francesca in the lurch, especially today.'

'My meeting won't take long.' His look of exasperation said everything.

'You, if anyone, should understand my obligation to Francesca. You've obviously been under her thrall for some long time.'

'Look, Anna, I don't want the same thing to happen to you, can't you understand that? I was only eight or nine years old that night at the House of Pan.'

'House of Pan? What are you talking about? Anyway, it's all water under the bridge. I obviously share with you an oversized sense of duty. Though mine is a relic of being adopted, rightly or wrongly I feel my obligation to Francesca.' She sighed. 'I can understand why Paul clung to his dormant Catholic faith. Though, in the end, it was his obsession with the ancients that triumphed.' Her voice trembled.

Anna stood stiffly beside Matt, fiddling with her floppy old t-shirt, her painting gear for the day shabby beside the sophisticated travellers about to go back into the real world.

She said, unable to stop her herself, 'Matt do you believe Paul knew about the hunters' final volley?'

302

'Of course not!' Matt lowered his voice, anxious for them not to be overheard.

'But he was a good Catholic, so suicide was out.' She was unconvinced. 'So the next best thing was surely to get someone else to fire the fatal bullet, like I said, a firing squad and no one person to blame; hey, fellas, I'm here and such good target practice.' Her words were tremulous. 'It was his chosen way out as soon as he reached seventy, irrevocably caught in the clutch of not just one belief but two. Even the Bible says three score years and ten.'

'Anna, for God's sake, forget it.' Matt grabbed her shoulders and shook her. 'Come on, come with me to Pisa. It will give you something else to think about. I'm not suggesting you leave for good, just for today. We can be back by evening.' But he was clutching at straws and he knew it.

'But it's the next few hours that are important. Francesca will be a pricked balloon when Paul's death finally hits home. I owe it to her not to leave her by herself, and besides, I still have to pay my debt for board and lodging. What better way than to paint her walls. The sooner I start the better.'

Matt raised his eyebrows in a look of resignation. 'Okay, but take care. I'll be back tonight.'

'Don't rush on my account.'

He climbed into the mini bus and Anna watched them disappear down the track. Her eyes were on the tall spare frame in the back seat, until he was out of sight. Silently, Francesca joined Anna, her arms stiff by her sides, a tight smile about her lips. Anna knew she was right to stay behind.

303

The two women walked back together into the castello. Anna watched Francesca climb the tower steps whilst she hovered at the base, rebuffed by a long cold stare from an already distracted Francesca. There was no invitation to follow. So much for her offer of support! Anna felt the dismissal. It seemed a lifetime since her arrival with Fabio, when she'd watched the lone figure descend into the courtyard to greet them. She wondered, did she know Francesca any better now than on that first evening when she had clearly sensed the woman's need? But through the past week she had changed from moody recluse to an active member of the group of artists.

Anna sat; she was in no mood to paint, yet she knew introspection would be counter-productive. Like Francesca, she was a bubble waiting to burst, every sense heightened. But underlying everything was an intense feeling of fatigue that threatened to engulf her. She stayed trancelike, giving into the sensation, Matt uppermost in her mind. She had glowed in her awakened feelings for Matt, hardly able to believe her luck. Chance or destiny had led her to him. And then had come the charade of last night and Francesca's birthday ritual.

It was becoming the perfect day, early mist evaporating, the scene suddenly distinct. She could see beyond the castello, out into the distance. How much longer should she stay with Francesca? Matt had been volubly against her finishing her Italian trip here in the confined world of the castello. She had found herself contemplating a heavenly return to Venice with Matt. That would not be.

Certainly heaven was not in this place, she reflected, where owner and home ruins were patched but could never be made entirely whole. The Christian church would never be refurbished. The disturbed Francesca had chosen to remain in the very distant past, suffused by Paul and his Etruscan knowledge; encouraged by Fabio and Catarina, both of the modern world, but rooted in the past.

With a start Anna remembered the Etruscan Exhibition in Venice that had so obsessed Fabio. Now, in its last few days, there was still time to see the ancient artefacts housed where they should be, locked within the walls of a museum. There they were powerless to have any influence on the present or future.

The thought brought her down to earth with a jolt. She laughed out loud, the first time that day. She'd had more than enough of all things Etruscan: enough to last her a lifetime. In her mind she retraced the ritual procession, knowing she had been downright scared. When Sue and Greg had returned to the castello, she'd had to fight the impulse to run after their vanishing torchlight. With one of the torches gone, the path had been difficult and she had wanted desperately to hold on to Matt. But Francesca walked between them. On purpose? She had sensed the woman's mood. It had changed since the Banquet. Why? Anna sensed a new hostility.

Standing before the altar, Anna had recognised the heart of the Etruscan site; here was the forgotten temple and the destination for Francesca in her bizarre birthday procession. Supported ardently by her fellow believers.

And with that thought had come the fear that had made Anna shiver in that dark strange place. The chimera bronze flashed

305

before her eyes and she saw herself the sacrificial goat chosen to appease the malignant presence within Francesca's castello. How foolish had that been? And then Francesca's amused comment, that only docile ritual animals met their fate. Then she had never been docile.

And now, to add to that horror, had come the new doubt. Matt's long term connivance with the ritual. However much she brushed it aside, it was still there. Later, the coffee on Rita's stove had smelt of normality. And sitting close to Matt her foolish terror had seemed a world away; the familiar Catarina was back in her kitchen beside the cook and her natural workmate; Fabio stifling yawns and attacking a bottle of Prosecco. How could she have feared their intent?

In broad daylight she could see how childish it had all been. Always too melodramatic, too paranoid! Everything about Chiesa a Castello was blissful. The sun warmed her back, highlighting the beautifully preserved medieval building and its garden. She could almost see the fruit ripening. Catarina had gone, but Rita, any time soon, would emerge from the bowels of her kitchen to harvest their lunch.

Surely here was arcadia? And yet? Even now there were niggles. The mausoleum was eerie. And disturbingly compulsive; the timeless site of death but then also of rebirth, hummed about by the ever-present living bees. At the picnic, Francesca had danced before its facade and Matt had said that bees dance to reveal to others the source of nectar. Slowly, as through the clearing morning mist, she began to understand Francesca's fascination with the place.

She'd thought it had been her own clever suggestion for picnic spot. But had she been the one influenced? But, by whom? Their steps had led surely and inevitably through the courtyard, past the walnut tree and the passion fruit bower, beckoned on by the cypress fingers to the ancient ritual site. How much choice had been there, how much manipulation? She scribbled a note to Francesca to say where she had gone and left it on top of one of the geranium pots.

The morning path was trod deep into the earth, tinder dry. No footprints marked the progress of the previous night's dark procession. The sky was plain blue. On such a morning the castello hypnotized. Anna's irrational fears seemed shamefully grotesque. She had considered staying on here with Matt? But now she saw this would displease Francesca. Their coupling would emphasise the woman's solitary existence, Anna reflected sadly. Well, now that wasn't going to happen. Had it been her and Matt's sudden obvious fascination with each other that had tipped Francesca's fragile state of wellbeing? She thought back to their tryst in the baptistery, their discovery of each other, their amusement at Francesca's eccentricity. Surely Francesca could not have overheard all that? But since then, the woman's manner towards her had changed.

First Fabio had turned against her, now it was Francesca's turn. Matt had never wanted her to come to the castello in the first place. She remembered the scene outside the Palazzo and Matt's insistence she should not go with Fabio. He'd been adamant, something that didn't happen very often with laid-back Matt Grant. At the time she had thought he questioned this stranger's intentions and she had felt quite touched at his brotherly concern. Of course, she'd been pig-headed enough not to go along with his wishes. Yet he already knew Chiesa a Castello and Francesca and had kept that a secret. Fleetingly, she considered he had been jealous of Fabio, but almost immediately she shook her head. There had been no reason for jealousy, at that point Matt had hardly known she existed. She thought of his attitude to her over the past week: friendly concern, free artistic advice, shared involvement in the mural. Only in the confined world of the castello had they been finally drawn to each other, so that Anna had come to believe their destiny lay there all along.

But tragically, the castello had also held Paul's destiny. She felt a surge of affection and overwhelming grief for the little man. He had seen his end, had planned it down to the last detail.

Chance or destiny? Of course she would never know. She had thought Matt and she would discuss it until they were old and grey. At least until they were seventy. Heavens! Now she was thinking like Paul. In this Etruscan place Francesca's forty nine years and Paul's seventy had seen much drama. Every seven years, according to Catarina, there was a life changing step. She thought of her twenty one years. What was her future?

She reached the mausoleum. On such a morning the beehives had their living role. The bees hummed noisily and she gave them a wide berth. The altar looked what it was, a pile of stones; its significance unrecorded. But last night had been no dream. The grass had been dislodged and two large stones marked the votive hiding place where past supplicants had laid their offerings before the gods. Nowadays it was sufficient to offer grapes and wine. Nothing to get excited about. Anna sighed as she sat down on the hot earth and lent against the altar. She closed her eyes, the drone of the bees heavy on the air.

The warm sun and humming sound were hypnotic. She must not succumb. She'd stayed behind to be with Francesca and yet she was nowhere to be seen. Had she already shut herself away? What would she do when they had all gone? Anna imagined an elderly Francesca looking down into the courtyard, no longer descending the steps, her greying hair growing longer and longer until Catarina could use it to haul up her daily needs. Fairy stories were always sad.

She sighed that she could have gone to Pisa for all Francesca cared. Still, the woman knew from Anna's note left by the geraniums where to find her, if that was what she wanted. The image of the flame red geraniums linked with that of the bees, the strident plant chimera tumbling in her muddled thoughts with bronze animal of lion, serpent, goat. The result: chaos.

The serpent had gone, but what of the lion and goat? Did they still fight for supremacy? The question niggled. Who were they? Francesca and herself? In reality they were a mixture of both, timid and aggressive in equal measure.

The castello stood dominant on the skyline. The proof of Francesca's sacrifice, in both time and money. And now there were to be no more folk paying to be part of its fantasy Etruscan world. How on earth was she still going to pay for it all? Anna reflected on Francesca's wild abandoned dance, there beside the beehives. She'd been ecstatic, boasting to the world of her good fortune? Matt had said that bees dance to show the direction of their source of nectar.

Did Francesca have her own source of nectar? Had the gods answered her prayers? Anna got to her feet so quickly she staggered like a drunkard. The hot sun had a lot to answer for. Was it even now giving her delusions? Anna peered from the sacred area and out beyond, through the finger-pointing black cypress into the dark oak wood. What else did it hide beside the tracks of animals? Wild boar, porcupine? She walked towards it. And there ahead of her was Francesca.

The track was narrow. Animal droppings marked their way and porcupine spikes pointed arrow-like in a paper chase into the heart of the wood. Hadn't Matt told her on her first day it was a place of surprises? Francesca walked a known path; Anna followed just feet away, stealthily, silently, and then she stopped. What was she doing? 'Francesca,' she shouted. 'Wait for me.' She shouted again, 'Wait, I'm coming with you.'

Francesca turned, her face like that of a sleep walker, and then, as she realised who was there, her expression softened. 'Oh, Anna, come with me, I want to show you something.' Though the path was narrow, she took hold of Anna's hand.

Hillside and trees merged, rock and stones piled and built. The shape was instantly recognizable. A beehive tomb blocked their way. Anna saw again the crude shape in the middle of the field, built by the hunters. There was nothing new. They followed the stone walls, the curved roof angled above them. The structure had been here a long time, the rocks coloured the green of age. On the hidden side, and almost part of the hillside, the stones had been removed for

310

access.

It was dark and chill. Anna could see nothing. The black was impenetrable. And then suddenly there was light. Momentarily she was dazzled by the yellow beam that Francesca shone into the void. The dankness of the place left nothing to the imagination.

In the moving beam Anna glimpsed Francesca. The mystery of the place was in her eyes. They looked back at her, dark and impenetrable. 'Now you are here, my dear, you can give me your opinion.' Francesca shone the torch on to the side of the tomb, and a painting. The moving figures on the walls danced, Francesca's wild dance depicted there. Unselfconsciously she moved in her soft cream dress. She looked young and innocent. Her partner danced close beside her, hypnotised by the music, his tall body, in Etruscan red, gyrated in perfect rhythm. Instantly, Anna recognised the sketch in Francesca's tower. She could feel Francesca's eyes on her as they moved closer with the torch, to study the mural.

'So this is my hidden place and where I come to paint.' Francesca's tone was difficult to read. It sounded mocking.

Anna could find no words.

'Much easier to paint here than on the baptistery walls. It's damp enough for the plaster to be workable the whole time. No need to add further plaster. I intend to cover the walls. Have you any suggestions for subject matter?' She took the girl's hand and they moved further into the tomb, to stand beside a blank wall. 'How would you like me to depict you?' She did not wait for a reply. 'I'll have no baptistery virgins here. No one is ever as innocent as they appear.'

311

'No,' Anna agreed but she moved back nearer to the entrance and Francesca's fresco painting. Her guide followed obligingly with the light. The figures there were complete except for the features of the male dancer. They were blank.

'You note, as in real life, the absence of a partner for me.'

'Yes,' Anna struggled to make sense of her words.

'All right for you, Anna Miller, no doubt your sketches already feature dear Matteo,'

'Matt, what do you mean?'

'You know very well.' Suddenly Francesca sounded tired. 'I saw you and Matt, together. My tower is not only my refuge but also my informant. The medieval squint is my eyes and ears.'

'Squint? Oh no.' Anna recoiled in dismay.

'Yes, you've intruded into my world, our world.' Francesca caught hold of her arm. 'All of us were there that night in the House of Pan, all except you.'

'House of Pan?' Anna's voice shook. There was that name again.'

'Seeing and hearing you and Matteo brought it all back. Twenty years ago, Sue and Greg making love when it should have been me. Now you and Matteo repeat history whilst I am forced to watch.'

'What has Matt to do with your story—with The House of Pan?' Anna was floundering.

'Matthew was there with the rest of us, all those years ago..' Francesca sighed.

'Matt was there?' Anna couldn't hide her surprise.

'The young son of the owners, left home alone, forced to spy from the shadows on the naked cavorting of Greg and Sue, only feet away from the other watcher—me.' She laughed, 'He was there on the stairs, a fearful young lad, bemused, fascinated, so I caught hold of him and held him like a caring mother should.'

Francesca's ramblings were beginning to make sense.

'Now I see the significance of this week's reunion. By bringing everyone together the gods meant to bring closure for me! But you have opened it up again. You, the interloper, number eight, and uninvited.'

Anna breathed in deeply, clasping her hands together to stop them shaking. 'Fabio might have seen me like that ,but Paul didn't.'

'Paul,' Francesca scoffed.

'How did Paul fit into the House of Pan?' Anna was clutching for any sense. 'He couldn't have been part of your cosy little set up, could he?'

'Oh, but he was. Didn't I tell you? He was the college lecturer leading the student group on the field course?' Francesca voice was distant, fixed in that unhappy past.

Anna could hear the pain. 'So as you can see, my dear, you're the gate-crasher, however much Paul wanted to think otherwise. I find it hard to see why your intrusion was destined by the gods.'

Anna could find no words of reply. She was surrounded by Francesca's past ghosts. And now they included Matt.

Francesca's voice had become petulant. 'Perhaps it could be because this tomb was heaped with hundreds of uterine facsimiles, together with one phallic symbol. So what's new? Man's pleasure was always well catered for.'

Anna could feel her breath inches from her face. Francesca laughed. 'It could be called Greg's tomb.' She sighed, 'But perhaps the Tomb of Hope would be better. I could set up a stall outside a fertility clinic and sell the sacred wombs to would-be clients? They'd probably have the same success rate.' Her words were cynical.

Francesca took hold of Anna's hands and her smile was cunning as she indicated the tomb. 'It's a lucrative business you know, being a tomb robber. Many unexcavated tombs still await discovery, and as they usually clustered together in a necropolis, or city of the dead, finding one here on our doorstep was luck indeed. So now I know Fabio has found another one with the Bucchero Sottile pottery inside.' Excitement was loosening her tongue. 'So no more need for themed-holidays. There will always be buyers for illicit antiques. Up until now, Fabio has had to rely on facsimiles for his Venice establishment.'

Anna was intrigued in spite of herself. 'My chimera with goat, serpent and lion was just a facsimile, surely?'

'Yes, a good copy of the Arezzo Chimera. Of course your second chimera is the genuine article. No serpent; Fabio knew that would appeal to you.'

'Yes, snakes are not my favourite creature.'

Francesca laughed, 'The dead always came back from the underworld in the form of a snake, sent to reveal the future.'

Anna shuddered. 'So somewhere close Paul can see what is

going on then. He can see Matt on his way back to the castello. Perhaps he's here already and looking for me?' The thought startled her back into reality. Matt would never be able to find her there.

She turned and ran from the tomb, into the welcoming light, stumbling over the rough ground until the wood was behind her. The altar loomed and she tripped headlong to the ground. Beyond, the castello stood menacing on its hill. That was no place to run to. Anna felt a searing pain shoot through her ankle.

Francesca crouched down beside her and Anna laughed, 'Francesca, I'm at your mercy, the pliant sacrifice saved for another day?' The woman's eyes were hypnotic, and Anna felt a thrill of trepidation.

Francesca ignored her. 'The supplicants brought their votive wombs here to this temple. Just think, Anna, if your mother had been a supplicant, she would have taken much better care of you.'

Anna could find no reply. She looked up into the sky where the sun was now lower on the horizon; Matt would not be long.

'Life is a lottery.' Francesca sighed. 'Seed planted, new life.' She sounded weary. 'But the soul is built up only to be destroyed. The Etruscans knew the inevitable return into chaos.'

'And with your restoration have come malevolent forces.' Anna struggled to rise.

'Yes. I dreaded a return to Paul's chaos. And now he's conveniently dead.'

Anna's face puckered. 'But it was an accident—wasn't it?'

'Don't fret, my dear, Paul's demise was the wish of the gods. How convenient it was for me.'

315

Anna was speechless.

'All the huntsmen knew it was an accident waiting to happen.' Francesca's laugh was verging on hysteria. 'Paul was leading us back into chaos with his talk of the gods' disfavour. The storm, then the goat,... yes, it was you, Anna, who upset the equilibrium. You with your neediness.' Again the wild, bitter accusation.

'Not anymore.' Anna struggled to rise and winced with pain.

Francesca said calmly, 'Life is a fantasy, a chimera, wouldn't you say? So where is your Chimera now, I wonder?' Anna felt her gilet pocket, seeking the hardness of the bronze. The Etruscan animal figure was no longer there.

Francesca said, 'Don't worry, Matteo has only borrowed it to prove to the powers-that-be that my castello is involved in the illicit traffic of artefacts.'

'Oh!' Anna's heart beat faster. 'I'm sure you're wrong about Matt and his visit to Pisa. He's very loyal to you, Francesca. His intention will be just to register the find. Not to get you and Fabio into any trouble.'

'It is Fabio who is loyal. From the time I made the first offering on the altar of the gods, dear Fabio has been desperate to please. He brings a girl for my yearly birthday procession.' Her voice echoed in the silence. 'And in this special year, it is you. Life is bizarre, is it not, Anna? How it binds us together, you and I.'

'What do you mean?'

'You unwanted by your mother and I desperately wanting a

child.'

Anna looked away from the pained eyes.

'So we both chose to live a fantasy, you with a make-up mother, I with a make-up child.'

'Make up?'

'O, yes, you knew perfectly well Sue was not your real mother. And my child, of course, never existed for a single moment.' Her laugh was brittle.

'But Sue said—'

'Mine was a false pregnancy. How futile, how demeaning! How they would have scorned my fantasy child born only of my desire.'

'H-how sad it has all been.' Anna choked on her words.

'Only the castello with Fabio and Catarina saved me from certain chaos.'

Anna blinked back her tears.

'Never mind, Anna,' Francesca said, noting her distress, 'that was a long time ago. The stone uterus has brought us together now. You are the child I never had.'

Francesca took hold of Anna's hand and she did not protest as the agitated woman groped down into the altar chasm beside them. Anna glimpsed the votive uterus lying deep in the cleft. Their hands united about the Etruscan womb. It was hard and unyielding.

But the body of the serpent was soft. Lazy in the heat, the viper rose, its eyes flashed, and in its fear, it struck. Anna heard Francesca cry out in pain, and then the woman pushed Anna with her uninjured arm, away from the viper's fangs. It was instinctive, as a mother would save her child.

Matt and Fabio carried Francesca to her sanctuary, and laid her on her couch. Catarina administered the antidote, with all necessary speed, hoping it would save her from the viper's deadly venom. Through the long night hours, Catarina watched and prayed.

Anna stood between the two men at the base of Francesca's tower and waited, stunned and saddened by the second horror to hit the castello in a few short hours.

But, in the early morning, the haunting music from Fabio's pipes accompanied Frances Green into that other place; to the feasting and dancing and loving that even as Francesca she had not found in the real world.

Anna was bereft. She went back to Venice. She did not go to the Accademia to stand before the Tempest painting, instead she entered the dark portal of the Palazzo Grassi. The last day of the Etruscan Exhibition had dawned. Soon the relicts of the ancient world that had so haunted them all would be dispersed, consigned to oblivion. The chimera posters had already been torn down.

On a dimly lit mural, deep in the recesses of the exhibition, a man and woman sat on a gilded couch. Francesca and Paul sat close. Francesca was regal, her dark hair piled high, around her neck was the grape-cluster necklace. Her hands were extended towards Paul, and she was smiling at him. Paul looked to be in his element. Brown tanned body, with a loose cloth about his loins, his smile was broad. Before them, a table was laden with a gathered harvest of grapes. Beside them, a small fair-haired girl stood with a large fan in her hand, waving them good-bye.

Anna bought the replica fan at the exhibition desk; delighted to find it was decorated with the tomb painting. She used it on the crowded train to Naples. Matt had gone on ahead and was waiting for her. He was full of the studio he had hired for the two of them. Flooded with northern light, it overlooked the sea. And it was large enough to hold the necessities of life, a large couch beside two waiting easels.

Paul had been right. There was no such thing as chance.

ABOUT THE AUTHOR

ERICA YEOMAN lives in Northumberland with her husband and their cocker spaniel. As an historical geographer she is fascinated by mans influence on the land. For Erica time and place produce their own characters.

Also by Erica:

DEVIL'S DROVE published in 2010 by Room to write – www.roomtowrite .co.uk

SHADES OF INNOCENCE published in 2012

SONG OF THE SELKIE published in 2014

DEATH AT THE CASTELLO published in 2016

53317979R00196

Made in the USA
Charleston, SC
09 March 2016